AZTEC FILE

Dale Dye

"A singular achievement...vivid, terse, exceptionally moving...the tension builds and never lets up."
—The New York Times

"Dye fills this dialogue-driven thriller with plenty of action and lots of military detail—all of which (no surprise) rings completely true."
—Marc Leepson, VVA Books in Review

"Dale Dye has a flair for telling stories and evoking images. His details about Marine life are accurate...Dye has the ability to draw the reader far enough into the story that the reader sees with the author's eyes and feels with his emotions…Dye's ability to tell a story the way it really happens is rare, and one sincerely hopes this book will not be his last.…"
—Orlando Sentinel

"Here, in prose that positively crackles, he takes us along on what has been one great ride."
—Ed Ruggero: Veteran, Writer, Motivational Speaker

AZTEC FILE

DALE DYE

WARRIORS PUBLISHING GROUP
NORTH HILLS, CALIFORNIA

AZTEC FILE

A Warriors Publishing Group book/published by arrangement with the author

PRINTING HISTORY
Warriors Publishing Group edition/May 2017

ISBN: 978-1-944353-13-1

Library of Congress Control Number: 2017905574

PRINTED IN THE UNITED STATES OF AMERICA

10 9 8 7 6 5 4 3 2 1

To Julia Dewey Dye, the real Chan, who pulls it all together and pushes us forward. And to Bear who is very happy to be the hero in print that he is in our lives.

Rio Grande Valley

From the outside, it looked like any number of sun-baked south Texas homesteads gamely resisting urban encroachment throughout Hidalgo County. The ranch house sat on the western quarter of a 90-acre spread that once fed a small herd of Charolais cattle. That was before the owners decided ranching just five miles north of the Mexican border was a whole hell of a lot more dangerous than profitable. Now the tortilla-flatland around the faux-adobe walls of the old house lay lonely and fallow. The prairies and pastures on either side of a winding gravel road that ran off Highway 281 southeast of McAllen, Texas was overgrown with jimson weed and wind-warped Manzanita trees. But if he squinted against the glare and let his imagination run, the visitor approaching in his new Ford F-250 pick-up could see the attraction of living in a rambling old barn of a house like this one. It could be soul-satisfying, a throwback to the days when a man planted his roots deep and lived off the land.

On the inside, as the visitor followed his host through a long dark hall and into a high-ceilinged room, the house looked like an old hunting lodge. The furniture was rough-hewn of unfinished native wood with not a hint of plastic in sight. The walls were spotted with game trophies bearing huge antler racks. Deer, elk, and antelope shared wall space with fat largemouth bass. There was a full-figure stuffed mountain lion in one corner of the room that seemed to be snarling at the porcine javelina that glowered back from the opposite corner. And everywhere he looked, as the visitor accepted a cut crystal glass his host offered from a wet bar built into an alcove just off the big central room, there were locked cases containing lovingly maintained rifles or racks of gleaming handguns.

Shake Davis couldn't help feeling like a sweet-toothed kid in a candy shop. Reluctantly pulling his gaze away from the guns and game on display, he sipped at the dark liquid in his glass and nodded approvingly at his host.

"This is really good stuff. Am I impolite if I ask what it is?"

"Not a bit of it," said the lanky man who lured him down to the Rio Grande Valley with a disturbing revelation about threatening events in northern Mexico. "It's a special blend of bourbon made by a friend of mine in Paducah, Kentucky." Joaquin Sutler folded himself into a padded chair and pointed at a matching seat on the other side of a big field-stone fireplace. "In these parts, we call it bourbon and branch. Branch water makes it right tasty. Comes from a lit-tle creek that runs through here." Sutler pronounced the word "crick" in a slow, slightly nasal drawl that Shake had learned was the mark of a true native rather than transplanted Texans like himself and his wife. A lot of the country vocabulary was similar to what he grew up hearing in rural Southeast Missouri, but the tone and tenor was unique to born Texans.

"Well, I damn sure appreciate the hospitality, Joaquin, but you didn't call me down here just to drink whiskey." From the time Shake had met the man the day before at their new Lockhart homestead, just south of Austin in the Texas hill country, Shake had found the lanky Marine Corps vet-eran and retired Texas Ranger prone to talk around topics, taking a roundabout route to get at what he wanted to say. Probably a hold-over from a long career in law enforcement, Shake had long since decided. Joaquin Sutler defined the word taciturn, not the kind of guy who liked to be rushed.

Shake would eventually get the responses he wanted, usually after long silences when Joaquin seemed to be either drifting or dreaming. Attempts to speed up conversation on any topic just set the man off on a tangent. He waited quietly, silently identifying the firearms he could see around the room while Sutler shifted in his chair and sipped whiskey.

"It's like I said when I dropped by your place, Shake. We got a situation down here—specifically just across the border in north Mexico—that myself and some others consider a genuine threat to national security. Now I don't use terms like that lightly. What we want is some experienced eyes on that situation, you know? We're needin' someone who knows the right people and has some decent credibility to take a look. Some old pals of mine from the Marine Corps said if there was a man like that available outside official circles, it would be Gunner Shake Davis."

"I'm a little unclear about the 'outside official circles' thing, Joaquin." Shake handed over his glass as his host brought a bottle and pitcher of water from the bar and set it down on a table inlaid with colorful tiles. "If you folks have seen what you described, why not just turn it all over to the Feds?"

"We tried that, Shake." Sutler poured fresh bourbon and water for them both and then retrieved a manila file folder that he tossed on the table. "Take a look at those."

Shake studied a series of a dozen or so color photos obviously taken with a sophisticated camera and a good long lens. He could see a small cadre of men dressed in jeans and nondescript shirts. Some of them were sporting camel-back hydration packs, and one guy had a distinctive high-vis orange backpack that looked like something a medic might carry. Some were armed and some weren't. The guns he could see were mostly AKs or clones from the Kalashnikov stable. They were doing what he'd often done in his own military career. Several views showed an instructor—or what might be a range-master—demonstrating field stripping in front of the assembly. There were other shots of different activities. It was hard to determine what was happening but if Shake had to guess from the gear he could see, it was some kind of explosives or demolition class centered on a rusty old GMC delivery van. He counted four men, all of them swarthy, stringy, and tough. They could be Middle Eastern, or Mexican, or just Anglos with deep tans. And there were no identifiable landmarks to indicate the training was being conducted in Mexico. It could be a bunch of survivalist yahoos playing soldier in Arizona or some other arid location north of the border.

"Those are all prints from the digital camera we used. There's plenty more on the disc, but it ain't enough to get the right people off their dead asses, Shake. Hell, son, I pulled out every contact I ever made in the Marine Corps, in the Rangers, everything I could think of, told them about what we saw and where it was, showed them the pictures. We went to Homeland Security but they mostly shrugged us off like we were a bunch of right wing loonies—except for one fella. At least he said they'd put a drone up over the site."

"Did he do that?"

"Got a call from him just last week…he's an old Aggie or we'd probably have never heard anything at all…and he claimed they took a look where we told them to but they couldn't see nothing but cactus and sand. We sent a couple of our Tex-Mex guys down to take another look and sure enough, the people we saw were gone—probably crossed the border and headed north. God knows what they've got in mind, but from what we saw, you know it can't be good."

"Day late and a dollar short, I guess." Shake had been up against parts of the national security bureaucracy often enough to know the drill. There was a lot of lip service paid to the see-something-say-something trope, but the guys flying the government-issue desks thought everyone outside the system was a de facto unreliable source. Regardless, if the people Joaquin and his group spotted in Mexico were now on this side of the U.S. border, it was a law enforcement problem. "Even if the authorities aren't willing to go down into Mexico and investigate, you probably put them on alert to be watching for something coming from south."

"I ain't so sure. They just don't seem to think the southern border area represents a real terrorist infiltration threat like those of us who live down here know it is. You know, if it ain't a hijacked airliner or a truck full of dynamite they just shrug it off, and it's gonna bite us all in the ass sooner rather than later. You've got to understand, the people who live down here have pretty reliable contacts with the Mexicans in the little towns and cities on the other side of the Rio Grande. Those folks tell us there's a regular group of Middle Eastern types who show up and do some training out there in the desert and then just disappear. Those Mexicans may be poor, but they sure ain't stupid. They don't want any part of that kind of thing."

"I'm guessing you reported all this to the Border Patrol guys down here?"

"One bright spot there, Shake. We got real good relations with those poor overworked bastards. They seemed to take what we reported seriously. Trouble is, the Border Patrol has got its hands full just handling the flood of illegals that cross the Rio Grande every day. Under the current system, they can't even do much about that. It's like a damn old fishing tournament with the Border Patrol, you know? Catch and release. On top of all that, there's a powerful stretch of border for them to patrol and they ain't got near enough money or manpower. I'm told by my Ranger contacts that the Border Patrol has reported what we found to the Mexican authorities, but that's pissin' in the wind."

"Why? Won't the Mexican authorities do something about it?"

"Not hardly, Shake. The Mexican cops and military just ain't sophisticated enough to find these guys and the few that might be prone to pursue the situation are either tied up with chasing druggies or they get paid off to look the other way."

"Paid off by whom, Joaquin?"

"Well, now we get to the nut of the problem. Whoever these bastards are—whatever they've got in mind—they are apparently in bed with the Mexican drug cartels. Them bastards will do anything to turn a dollar, and if the terrorists pay them enough, they provide cover. Any law enforcement that starts sniffing around down there either gets whacked in ambush or the druggies let the bad guys know and they just move—break camp and head for another stretch of Mexican desert. There's a lot of it down there, and it ain't hard for experienced men to hide in it."

"So you want me to find these guys—then what? If you're looking for someone to whack people down in Mexico, you've got the wrong man."

"I know that, Shake. Hell, if we wanted to hire some bad-asses to find these people and blow them away, that's doable with the right amount of money. I believe it's bigger than just the one bunch of hombres we saw down in Tamaulipas State. We got terrorists training for cross-border missions just south of us, for Christ's sake, and we can't get anything done about it. That might change with you as an eye-witness. You know the right folks and they'll listen when you speak."

Shake sipped whiskey and stared into the mesquite fire Sutler had laid and lit in the fireplace. He wasn't at all sure he did know the right people in the shady zone between military, intelligence, and law enforcement anymore. His most reliable high-level contact in those dark circles—the man who calls himself Bayer—had been forcibly retired after the Cuban rescue mission, but he might still have the ear and the trust of influential people. Bayer didn't need official status with his record of reliability and a new conservative administration in Washington that had an avowed agenda of taking it to outfits like ISIS and Al Qaeda worldwide. Maybe there was something he could do, but Shake wanted to be sure he was consorting with reliable people.

"Tell me more about these folks we're supposed to meet, Joaquin."

"All good and true Americans, Shake. And I ain't talking about a bunch of bubbas or paranoid minutemen either. Most of them coming by tonight to meet you are veterans—a goodly number of Marines and some serious ex-soldiers, a couple of retired Rangers like me. What we all got in common is that we love this country and we'll do whatever we can to defend it. There's an old boy named Chavez —Army vet—did a couple of tours with Special Ops teams over in the Sandbox. He's got family down in Tamaulipas State, and they tipped him off to this stuff happening damn near in their backyard. That's what got us interested, and then we started getting reports from Nuevo Leon and some other places close to the border. We put together a couple of teams driving around like *touristas* on a tear, and that's when we got those pictures."

Shake took another look at the photos. It was hard to believe that what looked to him like a rehearsal for a raid or guerilla-style tactical training could be pulled off so blatantly without drawing some serious official interest or surveillance, even if diplomatic issues or Mexican corruption made action difficult. He needed more information and perspective. "Look, Joaquin—I don't know why the right people aren't taking this more seriously, but I'm down here with you for the next couple of days anyway. Let me make a few calls and talk to some people I know."

"That's all we're asking, Shake. You talk to these folks coming by tonight, maybe you'll want to go on down there and see for yourself."

Shake was toweling dry after a shower in a well-appointed guest room in a loft on the second deck of the big house when his phone chirped. Caller ID indicated the man called Bayer had gotten his message and was returning the contact.

"Davis—send your traffic."

He got the laugh he intended from his old friend in the Virginia suburbs. "They can take the Marine out of the Corps, but they can't take the Corps out of the Marine. Where the hell are you, Shake?"

"South Texas—way south—damn near in Mexico. You at home?"

"I'm rambling around the same shack in the shadow of the flagpole. That's about as close as they let me get these days. Guess I don't have to tell you retirement sucks."

"You still in contact with any big dogs in the FBI? Still got your oar in the water at CIA or Homeland Security?"

"A few of them will still talk to me—just not about anything important." Shake could hear a change in the pitch of the voice on the other end of the call. The man called Bayer had picked up on the question. A guy like him with long years of experience running clandestine operations for various overt and covert agencies around the world wouldn't miss the overture. "You got something down there?"

"Not sure just yet. Maybe. Probably not something to discuss on the phone—especially your phone. Check your email. I sent you some photos. We'll talk after you take a look. Call me on this number in the morning."

"You sure you want me in on this, Shake? It might be bad medicine. I'm not exactly sunshine and lollipops with the establishment these days."

"There's a new administration, Bob. I'm thinking attitudes will change. If you want back in, I don't see how they can ignore your record."

"Yeah, maybe. I'll take a look and we'll talk tomorrow. Chan OK?"

"She's teaching at U-T and loving the new place. We're fine." Shake could hear loud voices and a general hubbub from the room below the loft. "Meeting some people. Gotta go. More later."

It was all pressed jeans; boots and big belt buckles among the ten or so people gathered in the big room, but Shake didn't get any warning signals as he moved around and shook a lot of strong hands. There were three females in attendance, all of them middle-aged and attractive, in similar western attire. They looked like the kind of independent women that socialized easily and on a solid par with the men.

Whoever these people were and whatever they did for a living in the Rio Grande Valley area, they didn't seem like a gaggle of ultra-right wing conspiracy nuts. There was money and influence here. Shake could almost smell it. Their small talk was calm and about innocuous topics like business, local politics, hunting, or fishing. Most of them seemed to know a little about Shake's military background, and all were polite and respectful.

After he made initial rounds, Shake settled on a stool near the bar. Joaquin Sutler approached with a stocky Hispanic man in tow. "This is the guy I was telling you about. Gunner Shake Davis, meet Manny Chavez." Shake shook the proffered hand and smiled at the stocky man smiling back at him. From the haircut and deep tan, Chavez hadn't been long out of uniform. Like most recent combat veterans, he moved like a cat with no wasted motion and eyes that swept his environment regularly looking for potential threats. If he had to guess without any further information, Shake would peg the man as some kind of operator beyond regular combat-arms experience. There was a subtle vibe about the man that Shake recognized. Sutler indicated the guy had done a couple of tours in the Sandbox, which was a modern military term applied to any number of Middle Eastern battlefields like Iraq, Afghanistan or Syria, so Shake decided Manny Chavez was likely former Special Forces—maybe even a Delta guy.

"I saw you down at Bragg one time," Chavez said. "You were out on a range at Smoke Bomb Hill when my unit was doing kinetic entry drills." Definitely SF and probably an officer, Shake decided as he nodded over a sip of whiskey. Only a Green Beret officer would use a term like *kinetic entry*. If Chavez had been an enlisted Marine Raider or SEAL, he'd have referred to the exercise as "blowing shit up" or something similar.

"I had an old buddy in the outfit," Shake admitted. "He wanted me to see some of your new toys for explosive breaching. It was impressive stuff."

"That would have been Chief Hillman?" The man's grin got wider. "He told us some stories about you and him in Beirut. That was before my time. If half of it was true—well, you guys are legends in the community."

"Half would be about right," Shake said, leading Chavez over to a seat near the fireplace as Joaquin Sutler walked away to circulate among his guests. "Joaquin tells me it was your family down south that spotted whoever these guys are out in the desert." Chavez nodded and leaned forward in his chair with elbows on his knees. He glanced around the room and took a deep breath.

"I got an aunt and uncle run a little cactus farm down in Tamaulipas. They live way the hell out in the desert due south of a little Mexican burg called Providencia. They harvest agave for the tequila makers. I used to go down all the time and help out before I went into the Army. My uncle's a pretty savvy guy and he started looking around when he heard explosions south of his property. He spots these guys with guns and it doesn't look right to him. He called mc and I went down to take a look."

"Did you take the pictures?"

"Not that first time—didn't have any camera gear with me. I went back down there two days later with a buddy who was an Army photographer. We brought them up here and showed them to Joaquin. Figured him being a Texas Ranger and all, he'd know what to do and how to get to the right people."

"How come you didn't take them to the people you know at Fort Bragg?"

"Well, the truth of it is that me and the Army didn't exactly part on good terms. There was some trouble with a raid my team made in Afghanistan. Lawyers claimed we blew away an innocent civilian. There's more to it than that, but bottom line is I was in command, so I took the heat. Nobody got court-martialed in the end, but I decided to get out when my EOS came around. I would have stayed, I guess, but you know how it goes. Zero defects and all that happy horseshit."

"I know how it goes." Shake nodded. "We're either gonna get over that kind of stuff or we won't have an Army worth putting in the field. Combat—especially combat of the SpeOps nature—is messy business."

"There it is…" Manny Chavez raised his glass and polished off its contents. "Anyway, I'm doing OK down here in the Valley. This group of vets…" He waved his hand generally toward the assembled crowd. "We take care of each other when and where we can. Good people—and we all want what's best for the country."

"You fairly sure the guys you saw down south were Arabs? It was hard for me to be sure looking at the pictures."

"You mean were they Muslims? Yeah, no beards—we noticed that right away. But you gotta figure they'd shave to keep from being profiled if they were headed north across the border, right? We got close enough to hear them at one point. It sounded like some kind of language class, you know, Arabic to English. I heard enough Arabic on deployment to know it when I hear it."

Shake was about to probe further, but he was distracted by a woman striding across the room in their direction. He'd met her during the first round of introductions. Carlotta something…he couldn't remember the last name. She owned a bakery or tortilla factory or some such enterprise in McAllen. She had a long fall of jet-black hair, lively brown eyes, and a complexion that proclaimed a Hispanic lineage. She was short and curvy with fulsome breasts that strained a pale blue western-cut shirt worn over form-fitting Wrangler jeans. Shake stood as she approached, thinking idly that she'd be a good model for a Rubens paining. She shifted a drink in her hand and pointed at Manny Chavez.

"Manny, you cain't hog our guest all night. Let somebody else get a word in edgewise." She offered a hand to Shake and smiled showing a bright array of well-kept teeth. "I know you won't remember, darlin', but I'm Carlotta Valdez and I just wanted to say how proud we are that you'd make the trip down here to give us a hand with our little situation."

"I'm not sure how much help I can be."

"Oh, Lordy, darlin', we damn sure got hold of the right man. Ah told Joaquin we need a man that had some solid cred for the job. Ah was an Intel weenie for six years in a U.S. Army uniform and there were a number of files I read that featured your name right prominently. Your reputation precedes you, Gunner Shake Davis."

"More like my reputation exceeds me—but I'm intrigued by what you all are saying." The crowd had gathered around the fireplace in the big room and guests were maneuvering for seats as Joaquin Sutler moved center stage, sipping his drink and waiting for the murmur of conversation to die down.

"Thanks for comin' by tonight and helpin' me dispose of some excess whiskey." There was a ripple of polite laughter and Sutler waited for it to ebb before he continued. "For the past six months, we've been tryin' to get the right folks to

listen to us about what we know is goin' on south of the border. We got no way of knowin' if any of the people we con-
tacted took us very seriously—but I've got to believe they
didn't. There's been no follow-up beyond that one drone
flight our Aggie buddy from Homeland Security ran. That
turned up a dry hole as y'all know and I believe what we
reported has by now been stuck in some file and won't see
the light of day again until some bad-ass hombre comes
north and kills a bunch of Americans. We ain't about to let
that kind of thing happen."

Sutler scanned the crowd with the same look of solid de-
termination and purpose that he'd displayed when Shake
first met him at the new house in Lockhart. Retired Texas
Ranger Joaquin Sutler likely turned criminal guts to water
just by showing up with a big hat and a bigger pistol. Shake
didn't peg him as the kind of guy who chased conspiracy
theories or suffered from paranoid delusions. No doubt he
was a real patriot in the founding fathers sense of the term.
And that seemed to fit the kindred spirits in the room who
had all expressed frustration with bureaucratic indifference
to what they perceived as a real threat to the nation, the kind
of threat most of them had enlisted to fight one way or another at some point in their lives.

"We need us someone who can get some official attention beyond lip service," the retired Ranger continued.
"Now, all y'all have had a chance to meet our distinguished
guest," he said with a nod at Shake who stood next to Carlotta Valdez at the back of the assembly. "And I invited him
down here to meet y'all, get our perspective on the situation
and maybe use his influence to get something done about
what's happening south of the border." As the group turned
to acknowledge him with smiles, Shake just lifted his glass
and nodded. It was still a little too early for him to commit

to what they wanted him to do. He needed more information. Joaquin Sutler seemed to sense that.

"Shake, I know we're askin' a lot of you. Is there anything else we can say? Any questions you have that we can answer?"

"Well, most of you are veterans, I guess, so it won't surprise you to know I need to think this thing over before I launch across the line of departure." He got the smiles and nods he expected from that. "What was it George Patton said? Make plans to fit the circumstances but do not try to create circumstances that fit the plan?"

Manny Chavez pointed a finger at Shake and winked. "I also believe General Patton said a good plan violently executed now is better than a perfect plan next week." That drew some shouts and whistles from the crowd and Shake distinctly heard a couple of loud Marine Corps "ooo-rahs" in the din.

"I made a call earlier this evening," he said when the noise subsided. "I'm trying to determine if my contacts are still solid anymore. You can probably understand from your own experience with this thing that the key is to convince someone who has the clout—and the balls—to take effective action. Given all we hear from various law enforcement and security agencies and the stuff that's happened lately in Paris and Berlin, I'm a little shocked that they aren't paying more attention."

"Let me give you some thoughts on that…" Carlotta Valdez hooked an arm around Shake's elbow and led him up to the front of the crowd next to Sutler. "If y'all don't mind, I'm gonna hold a little school here. Shake's new to Texas so he likely don't know what we do about the border and such."

Manny Chavez stood and handed Shake a full glass of whiskey. "Better have this at hand, Gunner. When she gets on a roll about this, it takes a while before you see daylight."

"I was briefin' generals while you were out chasin' camels in the Sandbox, Manny." She pointed a stiff finger at Chavez like she was aiming a handgun. "When it comes to intelligence more is better." Carlotta gently pushed Shake down onto a seat on the hearth and then sat beside him. There was some comfortable heat from the mesquite fire at his back and some slightly less comfortable heat from Carlotta's thigh that was pressed tightly against his. Shake just crossed his legs, sipped his whiskey, and tried to pay attention as she started to speak.

"There's a complicated situation down here." She held up her left hand which was adorned with big silver and turquoise rings, none of which suggested it might be a wedding band, and began to make her pitch. "Number one is a fixation on what they're callin' domestic terrorism. Y'all know what that means. Homegrown, radicalized Muslims who set off an IED like the Boston Marathon bombers, or shoot up some gathering of folks like what happened in Orlando or San Bernardino, right?" When she got the nods of understanding she expected, Carlotta rattled the ice in her glass and continued.

"The powers that be tend to look at that stuff as the new—or most immediate—threat which takes the focus off the long land border with Mexico. In a way, that's understandable. You deal with today's problem today and worry about next week next week. That said, I believe there's a fairly steady flow of trained jihadis comin' into the country from Mexico while ICE and Homeland Security and everyone else is solid focused on the airports and seaports that handle international traffic. And I'm bettin' those people who just walk across the border down here are the stick-stirrers, the facilitators for the so-called homegrown or lone-wolf stuff we've been seein' lately. ISIS or AQ gets their folks into northern Mexico, slides them across the border into some friendly mosque, and then they got free rein to teach local recruits all the necessary tactics, techniques, and procedures." Carlotta pointed at Chavez again. "You ought to recognize that drill, Manny. It's what our Special Forces do all over the world, right?"

She got a sober nod from the ex-SF trooper and continued. "That's one thing. And it wouldn't be so damn scary if we had any kind of effective control of our border with Mexico, but y'all know how that goes." She drew an affirmative rumble from the crowd. "The border is leaky as hell every place you look—California, Arizona, New Mexico—but the longest and leakiest stretch is right here in south Texas. The previous administration made all kinds of promises and didn't do a damn thing down here, mainly because they just believed in open borders and all the folks comin' across illegally were just poor Mexicans lookin' for a better life or refugees runnin' from one tyrant or another and claimin' political asylum. No news in all that, especially for us who live down here. You can't swing a cat anywhere in the Rio Grande Valley without hittin' an illegal. Hell, we hire them for damn near everything because they're mostly cheap, reliable labor. But that ain't all they are. They're also a diversion, a smokescreen for the jihadis who join the crowd and slip into the U.S."

"Let me break it down for you, Gunner." Manny Chavez leaned forward in his chair and set his glass on the floor between his hand-tooled boots. "We know how come FBI and Homeland Security and all the rest ain't taking us seriously. It's pretty simple when you live down here near the border.

Somebody from these parts complains about terrorist threats from south of the Mexican border and everyone immediately thinks we're bitching about illegals taking away jobs or gang-banging or running drugs, which is something we've seen for decades. And we know how to deal with that stuff. That ain't what we're talking about here, but everyone seems to believe it's just us south Texans blowing smoke. I've even heard that there are people who think we're just crying wolf, you know? Maybe we're just using the terrorist threat to get some action on the border situation in general."

"That's about the size of it, Shake." Joaquin Sutler held out his glass for a toast. "I know I'm speakin' for everyone here when I say we'll give you all the support you need. And the folks here pull a lot of weight all across the valley, believe me. If we can just get you to go take a look for yourself and get this situation some attention with the proper people, we'll be grateful, Hell, the entire nation will be grateful."

Shake was working on a huge platter of chicken-fried steak and eggs the next morning with Joaquin Sutler, Manny Chavez, and Carlotta Valdez all gathered around a big table in downtown McAllen's Longhorn Café. Sutler drove him down for breakfast shortly after Shake called home to check with Chan. She was OK but a little leery about what was being proposed by the Texans he'd come to meet. It wasn't that she pitched a bitch or tried to guilt him into coming home. They were mostly past that kind of stuff. And Chan had enough time on the inside of the national security establishment to know that if her husband was considering some sort of cross-border reconnaissance trip, he most likely had sufficient reason to take the risk involved. Shake knew that didn't mean she wouldn't worry, but Chan wouldn't make a full-blown domestic crisis out of it—at least not yet.

They were in the middle of discussing what sort of equipment might be needed for an excursion into northern Mexico, talking about things like cameras, night-vision gear, and vehicles. Manny Chavez insisted he could safely get what was needed into Mexico indicating the border in some areas was as leaky going south as it was coming north. Joaquin Sutler seemed sure that he could get all the navigation and surveillance gear that might be required. Shake was about to ask about weapons when his phone chirped. It was the man who calls himself Bayer.

"I need to take this," he said, standing and eyeing the noisy crowd in the diner. "I'll be out in the parking lot for a little bit." He connected the call on the move and asked Bayer to hold while he maneuvered his way outside.

"Think he'll do it?" Manny Chavez buttered toast and watched Shake head out the door.

"Hard telling." Joaquin Sutler poured coffee from the plastic jug in the middle of the table. "He ain't one to go off half-cocked."

"I believe I can talk him into it—given a little time with that boy." Carlotta Valdez grinned and ran a hand through her hair. She'd hoisted most of it up into an attractive pile and went a little heavier than usual on the make-up for the morning session.

"Jesus, Carlotta. He's a married man," Joaquin grumbled.

"Ain't they all?" Carlotta smiled and attacked a large pile of pancakes.

Shake pulled open the passenger side door of Sutler's pick-up and sat inside to get out of a drizzling rain that was cur-rently wetting the Rio Grande Valley area. Bayer apologized for interrupting Shake's breakfast. He'd been pouring over the photos and needed some more information before he be-gan working his contacts.

"So, you think we're looking at jihadis training south of the border?"

"We might be—or we might not be. How did you come by the photos?"

Shake explained what he'd been told about the origin of the photos and added some information about what the little group of south Texans was trying to do about it. "They seem to think if I go down there and see this kind of thing person-ally—assuming I do and assuming I can find something sim-ilar going on—that I can make the case with the right people who will do something about it."

"And I would be the happy sap that gets you in front of the right people so you can plead the case. Is that about right?"

"Affirmative on your last, and frankly I don't think these people are flakes or a bunch of paranoids. They live down here and that means a lot. You know, I tend to believe they saw what they saw and that it's an ongoing problem. This guy Chavez I told you about says he heard them speaking Arabic, for Christ's sake." Shake shifted the phone to his other ear and watched a couple of trucks splash through the parking lot.

"Listen, Shake, there's no doubt in my mind about the problem. What's missing is a focus on it. It could be a trusted operator—or two of them if you're willing to count me in the mix—might get something done to stop this stuff before it detonates somewhere in our country. Or maybe we could get the FBI to gin up a task force with the Mexican national police, something like that. But it's gonna take more than the photos you sent me. I mean, they could be photo-shopped or taken during a session with survivalists out in the Sonora or somewhere like that, you know?"

"I know. The thought occurred to me. It's what's pushing me toward taking this on."

"Well, if you do, try to get some sort of reference into any photos you take. You know, like when they put a ruler or something into a photograph to give perspective, right? You can't ask the bad guys to pose in front of a road sign or anything like that, but we'll need something that definitely says they are in Mexico."

"And something that indicates that they are definitely jihadis, right? Maybe I could take some long-range sound recording gear and pick up some of the conversation or instruction."

"Anything that will help build a case, Shake. You get that kind of stuff and I think I can get us into the executive suites at FBI or Homeland Security. I'm gonna start making some feeler calls this morning."

"Good deal. I'll let you know what I decide. Anyway, I've got to go back home before I do anything definitive. Maybe I'll call Mike in on it if I decide to head south and check it out."

"You damn sure don't want to try something like this on your own. I'd also try to recruit that Chavez guy you told me about. He knows people down there and he's gotta look more like a native than you or Mike."

"OK. Thanks for the call. I'm here tonight and then back to Lockhart in the morning. I'll be in touch."

Shake wandered back into the café and found his seat. The waitress had removed what was left of his steak and eggs. He reached for the fresh coffee Sutler was pouring into his cup. "That was my guy in Washington," he told the group. "Retired now but still well-connected at some very high levels. He's seen the photos."

"What's he got to say?" Manny Chavez wanted to know.

"He says he'll front me with serious people, but…"

"Do we like the sound of that?" Carlotta Valdez picked up a fork and moved home fries around on her plate. "But what?"

"But we're gonna need more than we've got. We need to get some better photographic evidence; something that definitively shows these guys are in Mexico and that they are definitely jihadis and not just some drug cartel hitters on a training exercise."

"Figured as much," Joaquin nodded patting his big mustache dry with a paper napkin. "I've seen enough circumstantial evidence to know the drill. Photos need context."

"Look…" Shake sipped coffee and decided he'd try to help but there was no sense or value in just heading for Mexico without better intelligence. "We need to do this thing short and smart. I can't go down across the border and spend all my time wandering around hoping to find something. So here's what I propose. Manny, you be the S-2 and get hold of your family down south. We need to know when the next batch of these guys shows up—when and where, what they're doing, how many—all the intel you can get. We'll move when we get that information. And you better plan on coming along when we go. Can you get some short-notice time off?"

"He can." Carlotta Valdez said. "Manny works for me, darlin'. He runs the production line at my plant down here."

"Copy that—and good news. We'll need his local contacts and my Spanish is a little rusty. While we wait for word from Mexico, I'll make up a list of things we might need that I don't have. Joaquin, you be the S-4 and try to get everything on that list."

"That I can do," the former Ranger said. He looked over at Carlotta. "But it might get pricey."

"Let me worry about that." Carlotta waved a dismissive hand in the air. "I've got access to a pretty hefty slush fund from my husband's assets. If you don't run me broke, I'll stand for what we need."

"That helps," Shake said polishing off his coffee. "We've got some sort of sketchy plan anyway. I'll head back up to Lockhart tomorrow morning and inventory my gear—and I want to see if an old buddy of mine wouldn't like to absorb a little Mexican sunshine."

"Speaking of which…" Carlotta said. "There's a band and dancin' over at the Sunshine tonight."

"What's that?"

What's dancing or what's the Sunshine?"

"I know about dancing. It's something I don't do worth a damn."

"Well, the Sunshine is a little local honk that attracts good country bands and serves top-shelf tequila alongside cold Lone Star. They got a particularly good band tonight—friend of mine plays pedal steel with them. I thought we might all drop by and relax a bit."

The Sunshine Saloon on the western outskirts of McAllen was a big, tin-roofed joint that was stylishly ramshackle like any good-time Texas roadhouse. The main structure was brightly lit by neon beer signs in vibrant pastels and surrounded by patios where locals perched on a split-rail fence smoking and hitting on long-neck beer bottles. It looked like a big Saturday night for what a sign swaying in the breeze across the gravel parking lot advertised as a live show featuring Gary P. Nunn and The Bunkhouse Band. The gravel parking lot that wrapped around the Sunshine was crowded with pick-ups, Jeeps and muscular SUVs. If there was a Prius or SmartCar dealer anywhere in the Rio Grande Valley, Shake thought as he cruised for a parking spot, the poor bastard was starving to death.

As he keyed the fob to lock his truck, Shake saw Manny Chavez wheel into a nearby spot and walked over to meet the former soldier who was behind the wheel of a maroon Chevy Tahoe kitted out with fog lights and a winch on the front bumper. Chavez wheeled around his vehicle and opened the passenger door for a nicely constructed brunette woman.

"Shake Davis, meet my wife. Vicky, this is the guy I was telling you about." She grinned widely enough to make little crow's feet appear on either side of her blue eyes and offered a hand. "It's really nice to meet you, Mr. Davis." Shake started to protest the formality, but Vicky Chavez help up a warning hand. "I just refuse to call you Shake until you tell me how you got that name."

"Short story and not very interesting," Shake said as they headed for the entrance. "My Mom named me Sheldon. My Dad didn't like it much and protested by refusing to give me a middle name so I couldn't just switch to that. It was Sheldon Davis or nothing right up until I joined the Marine Corps. That presented a problem or two."

"I bet it did," Manny Chavez laughed. "We had a guy in my basic platoon actually named Ignatz! The poor bastard barely survived."

"No mercy for the weak or those with funny-sounding names, I guess. Anyway, I was desperate for a nickname or something—anything besides Sheldon—and so when some guy suggested Shake might be cool, I just went with it."

"Well, Sheldon's pretty cool these days."

"It is?"

"Sheldon Cooper? Big Bang Theory on TV?"

Victoria had more to say, but Shake didn't catch it as they stepped into the Sunshine and hit a high-decibel wall of sound. George Strait was complaining that all his exes lived in Texas while a crowd of dancers swirled around a big space fronting a low stage that was set up with amps and instruments but empty of musicians just then. Out on the floor, the males were doing the driving and the females mostly just backing up with them in what Shake had come to recognize as the Texas Two-Step. As Manny and Victoria Chavez searched the crowd for Joaquin and Carlotta Valdez, Shake stood watching the action through a cloud of tobacco and beer fumes. Apparently, you could still smoke in a place like this in south Texas. On a few tables he saw paper bags containing hard liquor of one brand or another that got sloshed by serious drinkers into plastic cups full of ice.

Cowboy hats, everything from pricey and lovingly creased Stetsons to mangy old sweat-stained straws, were everywhere he looked. Honky-tonkin' in the Rio Grande Valley apparently required a big hat as much as it did money for the drinks three or four hard-looking waitresses were distributing to the tables scattered aimlessly between the long bar and the dance floor. Nice place, good crowd, Shake thought as he followed Manny Chavez toward a table in the corner of the joint. There was a high-spirited happiness in the muggy air. A guy could have fun here. A guy could also get killed. He'd seen some serious blood spilled in similar places when broken long-neck beer bottles suddenly turned into improvised weapons.

Joaquin Sutler was hovering over a bottle of Lone Star with his ubiquitous cream-colored Stetson pushed back off his brow. He grinned and pointed at the empty chairs leaning against the table to keep them from being pilfered by partiers crowded nearby. Carlotta scooted one around next to her and motioned for Shake to sit. "C'mon right here, darlin'. We're gonna Texas you up some tonight."

A waitress who looked like she could double as the bouncer swivel-hipped through the crowd in response to Joaquin's signal, and Carlotta ordered a round of beers with Patron tequila shooters. When the drinks arrived, she peeled off bills from a sizeable roll and added a generous tip to in-sure steady refills as required. "I've been needin' this," she said lifting her shot-glass and licking at the salt on the rim. "You boys can keep your money in your pocket. Tonight it's on me." Carlotta was clearly out to party, and she was cer-tainly dressed for it. Her jeans had been swapped for a short denim skirt with fringe that barely tickled her knees. She had stout but nicely shaped legs stuffed into a pair of boots that looked like they cost more than Shake's truck, and her bosom was just barely contained by a halter-top bearing the Texas state flag outlined in sequins.

She scooted closer to Shake and grabbed at his elbow. "Now as soon as Gary P. gets up there to play, Gunner Shake Davis, we're gonna do us some dancin'."

"No use tryin' to fight it, Shake." Joaquin said around the neck of his beer. "Carlotta gets into one of her dancin' moods—and you will dance. It's either that or fight."

"My Mom did teach me not to fight with girls, but she never got around to teaching me to dance."

"It ain't so much dancing as it is bulling through the crowd in a place like this," Vicky Chavez laughed. "And the two-step is just a waltz. Guys push and girls pull."

"Don't worry about it, darlin'." Carlotta helped the waitress unload another round of tequila shots. "I'll teach you everything you need to know."

"So, you run a business down here?" Shake felt Carlotta's foot searching for his ankle under the table and tried to change the subject.

"Yeah. Food packaging and processing mostly. We lost a big government contract a couple of years ago and it sorta looked bleak for a while. Then my no-good husband up and died which freed up enough money for us to re-tool and now we're hummin' right along again."

"You probably ate some of what we made, Shake." Manny Chavez pushed shot-glasses around the table and grinned. "We used to be the biggest source for MRE's in the country. Then the damn Yankees who owned the company moved the operation to Cincinnati. Carlotta refused to fold and worked her ass off trying to keep it all afloat. About that time, I was out of the Army and looking for work. She hired me and we converted to retail food prep and packaging. I run the floor and help manage the business."

Carlotta checked her watch and glanced up at the bandstand where a few musicians were fiddling with the instruments on stage. "There's old Roy," she said pointing at a lanky man sliding in behind a pedal steel guitar and fiddling with the tuning keys. "I'm just gonna go up and say howdy."

As she pushed through the crowd, Shake watched and wondered if she was a woman bound to seduce him or just a natural flirt. He had some acquaintance with flirtatious females over years of hanging out in bars around the world, but it was beginning to look like Carlotta Valdez was a different breed of cat: an energetic force used to getting what she wanted one way or another.

"What's the story on her?" Shake turned around and reached for his beer. "I caught that comment about a no-good husband."

"Carlotta was married to an old boy named Leonard Warnick," Joaquin said. "They hitched up shortly after she got out of the Army but they never were a very happy couple. She refused to take his last name and he fooled around with every gal they had working in the factory. That said, they made a pot full of money…"

"Which is why they never got divorced," Vicky Chavez added. "She wanted out a couple of times, but old Leonard knew he'd lose everything in court, so he just fed her cash and refused to split."

"Then the cancer got him about three years ago," Joaquin continued. "He died and left Carlotta everything that he hadn't already pissed away. When they lost the MRE contract, she could have sold out and never turned another lick, but she just ain't the kind to quit."

Shake tossed off a second tequila and chased it with beer. He knew from hard experience that imbibing like this for long would make for a very bad head, and he had a long drive north in the morning. Plus he needed to stay sober enough to fend off Carlotta Valdez, who clearly was not the kind to quit.

By the time Carlotta got back to the table, the crowd was roaring over the appearance of singer-songwriter Gary P. Nunn who was a statewide favorite performer, a talented guy who turned out a bunch of country hits mostly with a Texas theme. He opened with a number called "London Homesick

Blues" which Carlotta announced was her hands-down favorite dance tune. She hauled Shake up by a hand and led him protesting all the way to the dance floor.

"It's just one-two-three, one-two-three," she said molding herself into his body and swaying a bit to help him pick up the rhythm. "You just steer the bus, darlin', and I'll do the rest." In a turn or two past more experienced couples, Shake sort of had the knack. It wasn't too hard if you let yourself feel the music rather than strictly listen for cues. And Carlotta Valdez was plastered so tightly to his body that any mistake he made with his feet was quickly corrected by her ample body English. By the time they'd made a single circuit of the floor, Shake was beyond concern with his feet. He was feeling nothing but Carlotta's hips and boobs.

They cruised more easily through two more numbers as Gary P. Nunn and his Bunkhouse Band segued from one of their hit tunes to another. Shake could feel the heat and sexual tension all around him as they passed dancing couples, some swaying gracefully and others grinding hard against each other. It was almost palpable, a sort of vertical preparation for horizontal invasion, as he thought of it in military terms. He was a married man very much in love with his wife, but he was also human and the feeling in his crotch just then was too familiar for him to risk anymore close contact with Carlotta on the dance floor of the Sunshine Saloon. When they passed near the perimeter of the dancing area, Shake broke contact and dragged Carlotta toward a cold beer which he hoped might damp the heat down to controllable levels.

Joaquin was at the bar talking to an older gent with a similar mustache and an identical Stetson. Manny and Vicky Chavez were still out on the dance floor when they reached the table. Shake held Carlotta's chair for her, placing it a discreet distance from his own, but she scooted it closer and reached for a tequila shot with one hand. Her other hand wound up on his thigh and the beer he was chugging didn't do much to help him ignore it.

"Carlotta, you seem like a straight-up kind of person. Can I ask you a question?"

"That's me, darlin'. Ask away." She patted his thigh and moved her hand a little closer to his crotch.

"Are you aiming to wind up in bed with me?"

"I'll admit the thought crossed my mind." She smiled and her hand came out from under the table. She reached for a nearby beer bottle and picked at the label. "What do you think of the concept?"

"You make it hard to say no—but I'm gonna have to pass. I'm old-fashioned about some things. Marriage is one of them."

"Oh, hell, Shake…" She hit the beer hard and reached for a glass of tequila. "I'm just a horny old gal, I guess." Carlotta grinned and downed the drink. "You know how it goes—tequila makes my clothes fall off. I don't mean any harm and I respect a good marriage. Mine damn sure wasn't."

"I've been there, done that, believe me. The t-shirt's hanging in the closet. My first wife had a drinking problem. You know, her problem was where to get the next drink. It got nasty and we had a daughter to think about. I was gone too much with the Marine Corps, all the usual horse-crap that causes way too much long-term pain in a short-term life. When I met Chan, my wife now, and decided to give marriage another shot, I promised myself that I'd make it work—and that means I've got to say no, even to an exciting woman like you."

"Well, I believe that's the kindest way I've ever heard to tell a woman she's sniffin' around the wrong dog. What is it they always say in the movies? Can we still be friends?"

"We damn sure can." Shake extended his Lone Star for a toast. "In fact, I'm hoping you'll be my advisor and Intel source on this Mexico thing."

Mike Stokey was sitting at the bar in a little strip mall joint playing video poker. He was 18 dollars into the last of the three twenties he allowed himself to piss away gambling every week and looking at four cards of a royal straight flush. All he needed from the mindless machine was the ten of clubs and he'd walk away with a grand in his pocket. The little light in the lower right corner of the screen blinked incessantly urging him to hit the draw button and play the final card of the hand.

"I'll get around to it," he mumbled and reached for the glass of scotch near his elbow. Like most Vegas venues, this place served free drinks to players and late on this Sunday morning with the bar almost empty, Mike was taking full advantage. There's not much to do when you're unemployed in a place like Las Vegas, Stokey thought, and what little there is to do just bored the shit out of him. He'd grown up in Vegas and had some fond childhood memories of desert excursions that always fired his imagination. The place kept sucking him back from all the other exciting places he'd lived or worked over the years. He could live anywhere in the world—yet here he was.

He pondered that with mixed emotions and rattled the ice in his empty glass to call for a refill. Money wasn't the issue. He and Linda did fairly well on the pension payments that appeared in their bank account each month. But when you'd spent most of your life walking on a very shaky tightrope in the clandestine intelligence game, plodding along aimlessly as a disconnected entity in a place like Las Vegas could get depressing.

Mike let his finger hover over the game screen, staring at the four cards lined up neatly, patiently waiting for him to call up a fifth to match. Little moments like this were what he craved. The odds against a big hit were astronomical, but he wasn't doing it to make money. The attraction was an element of risk—low risk compared to most of things he'd done before that bastard Bayer had forced him into retirement—but at least it was some kind of action, something to raise his pulse rate above a dull throb.

Stokey took a big hit from his fresh drink and mashed the button to draw a card. Eight of diamonds. Shit! He was thinking about feeding the monster another twenty or maybe moving to a different machine when his phone danced on the bar. The name that popped up on caller ID brought a smile and a better mood immediately.

"I've been wondering when you'd get around to checking in, Shake. You been on radio silence or what?"

"Traveling," Shake replied. "I'm headed home to Lockhart. You still in Vegas?"

"Affirmative, for what that's worth." Mike noted that his best friend and frequent partner on some serious misadventures around the world sounded a bit more chipper than he did on his regular health and welfare calls. "You caught me at a bar playing video poker. Had four cards to a royal just a minute ago—and drew a turd. Story of my life."

"A thing like that can drive a man to drink."

"Which is precisely what I've been doing—that and pissing away my fun money on poker machines. How you doing, Shake? Chan OK?"

"Yeah, she's good. You know, living the dream, puttering around that big house when she's not teaching up in Austin. I'm OK—staying in shape, running a little bit, working on bushcraft out in the shop. It's all good, just a little…routine, you know?"

"I know. Retirement sucks like a Hoover vacuum cleaner. Dudes like you and me, Shake, we just aren't—I don't know—we just aren't designed to putter. I hate that fucking word."

"So you'd be OK to travel? Linda wouldn't pitch a bitch if you disappeared for a week or two?"

"She's got the interior decorator thing up and running. Takes a lot of her time, you know. She probably wouldn't notice I'm gone." Mike could feel his pulse accelerating. "When do you need me, and where?"

"Down in south Texas. Probably fly into McAllen. I checked and there's a direct flight from Las Vegas, but don't buy a ticket just yet. I'm waiting for word on when to go. Soon as I get that, I'll call and you'll fly."

"Not that I give a shit, but are you gonna tell me what's up?"

"Not on the phone, Mike. I'm sending you a brief by email. Take a look at that and just pack what you need for a civilian-style camping trip. Leave the high-speed moto gear. We'll be going low-profile."

"Copy all." Mike broke the connection, finished his drink, and swiveled off the barstool headed for the door.

"No luck?" The bored bartender asked as Mike Stokey breezed past her. "Lots of luck," he said with a big smile, "just not on your damn machines."

Wafic Aziz had trouble rousing from an exhausted slumber when the phone he'd been given by a brother in the faith began to warble. The ratty quilt that covered him against the stale air in the little basement room felt like his mother's arms, and he didn't want to heave it aside to deal with the call. *Duty drives the warrior and denies him comfort.* Wafic groaned, reaching for the instrument flashing on a fruit crate that served as a nightstand next to the lumpy cot where he'd spent his first night in America. He tried to sound aware and alert, but he couldn't manage much more than a grunt.

"You are awake…" The caller wasn't asking a question. He was a hard man, a tough taskmaster and the ISIS mission commander that Wafic was duty bound to obey absolutely during the time he was on this mission in America.

"Yes, Hasim, I am awake." Wafic had to concentrate hard to keep from responding in his native language. The rules were very strict: Only English, no matter how crudely spoken. Americans were instantly suspicious of anyone speaking Arabic he'd been told on the long trip north from Mexico. Wafic's English was still a little crude and spoken with a distinct accent despite much practice. He'd never be taken for a native English speaker, but that didn't matter much. He was here as a technician and not a social butterfly. The less he had to do with American *kafirs* the better. The English-only restriction was mainly for phone conversations that might be monitored, or for times when infidels might overhear a conversation.

"A brother from the mosque will come to see you shortly with food and drink. When you are ready, he will bring you to me."

"His name?"

"Ibrahim."

"The chosen one?"

"Yes, but he doesn't know that yet. Keep it that way."

The phone in Wafic's hand began to beep. The call was ended. Good, he thought, glancing at his watch, less than one minute. He'd been trained to keep any and all calls on the American cellular networks short and vague. Hasim was abiding by the same strict rules he'd outlined during the training in Mexico. He washed at the cold-water tap in a corner of the room next to a toilet bowl and then spread a small rug for morning prayers. It was hard to focus. He kept thinking about the time in Mexico.

The training was not difficult, but the border crossing, following a well-paid Mexican criminal, was miserable and terrifying. At least in Mexico he'd been in familiar surroundings, an area much like his home in Syria. Wafic rose and stretched his achy body. Northern Mexico was much more reassuring and familiar than this concrete sprawl on the outskirts of the American city of Dallas, a place he thought of as the cowboy city. He'd seen some cows during his trip north from the border. There were some sheep and even a deer or two glimpsed during rides in a series of different vehicles including cars, trucks, and vans. But there had been no cowboys on horseback like the ones he'd seen in American films. The driver-escorts, all American Muslims, all faithful subjects of the Islamic State and covert soldiers of the Fourth Caliphate, had just laughed and made references to a sports team when Wafic asked about cowboys.

A voice hailed him by name and Wafic opened the door to admit a lanky young man with pale skin and green eyes. His hair was a reddish brown reflected in the wisps of an immature beard on his cheeks and chin. Ibrahim, the chosen one, and Wafic quickly realized why that was. Due to some quirk in the family gene pool, Ibrahim did not look Middle Eastern at all. He was a True Believer from a devout Iranian family who came to the U.S. after the father was killed by Crusader forces in Iraq, but Ibrahim could easily pass for an American teenager. He was perfect for the mission.

After a furtive glance over his shoulder at a dark, empty hallway, Ibrahim whispered a greeting in Arabic wishing Allah's blessing of peace on a newly arrived compatriot. "English only…" Wafic grunted and motioned for Ibrahim to enter.

"It ain't much, is it? We were hoping to do a little better for you." The young ISIL adherent in stylish jeans and a colorful windbreaker jacket strolled into the dark little room and held up a paper sack. Wafic listened for tell-tales in the young man's voice, but his English was unaccented. Ibrahim sounded just like many of the frivolous Americans on internet productions. He'd brought a paper cup of tea, bread, and some sort of spread in a plastic container. As Wafic investigated the food, Ibrahim took another look at the surroundings barely lit by a single overhead bulb shining through a pasteboard shade mottled with dead insects. "We wanted to put you up at *Noori Masjid* but Hasim said that probably wasn't cool."

Wafic spread some of the stuff in the plastic container on bread—it smelled like some sort of couscous—and nodded. He'd seen the mosque—one of three in Plano, Texas he'd been told—on the way to this place. It looked prosperous and well-tended, which likely meant the American authorities had it under surveillance. A basement room in a mostly abandoned building that once housed a men's clothing store was a better choice. And Wafic didn't plan to spend much time in the little room. It would serve until he finished his part of this mission and moved on to the next.

"You want to shave?" Ibrahim asked when Wafic was finished with his meal. "I can get a razor and stuff for you. There's a little stop-and-rob near here." Wafic massaged his chin and felt the bristles. His beard was normally dark and heavy but he'd shaved just before leaving the training site to follow the Mexican guide across the Rio Grande. He was bristly but not unkempt or properly bearded yet which might keep him from unwanted stereotyping. It could wait. "You can buy me some things when we return. I'm anxious to see Hasim. We should go." Wafic shouldered the bright orange backpack containing his formulas and reference materials and headed for the door.

As they walked up to ground level and across a nearly empty parking lot, Ibrahim punched a key fob. A small boxy car parked nearby beeped and flashed its headlights. It was a beat-up machine with a chrome strip above a fender that identified it as a PT Cruiser. It was a mustard yellow color with a badly cracked windshield, but the interior was luxurious and the dashboard console was ablaze with LED displays that blinked, beeped, and glowed. Wafic, a former student in electronics and chemical engineering, was fascinated. He ran his hands across the dash, trying to determine what each instrument signaled regarding the vehicle's status. "Is this yours?"

"I wish—but I can't afford a car yet. I borrowed the wheels from a brother at the mosque. He's cool with it. We can use it as long as we need it."

They headed out of the parking lot, driving due east of Plano and north of Dallas according to the GPS built into the little car's console. On the highway, they passed several police cars, and when Wafic reflexively slid lower in the passenger seat, Ibrahim opened the center console and pulled out an American baseball cap. It was blue and grey with a star on the front and lettering that spelled Dallas Cowboys. "Wear this," he said to his passenger. "You will look just like another fan. The police around here love the Cowboys."

It took most of an hour to reach their destination, much of it driven on bumpy side roads that ran south of the main highway between Dallas and its sister city Fort Worth. When Ibrahim wheeled into a parking lot behind a chain-link fence that surrounded an aging brick warehouse, he pointed through the windshield. "A brother from the mosque owns this spread. I think they used it to store farm machines and all like that before the trains quit running out here."

The building was isolated, spotted by itself on a vast tract of open land. There were rusted train tracks running close to one side of the structure and a series of wide doors that Wafic assumed must have been used to load or unload cargo from freight trains. It didn't look as if there had been a train or much of anything else working in the area for a long time. It was just a windblown, abandoned building miles from anything else, a sensible site to work undetected and unmolested. As Ibrahim parked the car, the ISIL commander responsible for this mission in America stepped out of the building and motioned for them to enter.

The interior of the building was cavernous with weeds growing up through a cracked concrete floor. Wafic began to explore with his eyes as soon as Hasim released him from a welcoming embrace. He immediately saw pallets stacked in a corner. Each was piled with what looked like 50-kilo sacks. He followed Hasim toward the pile and as he read the labels, his eyebrows arched in surprise.

"We were told the Americans restrict sale of ammonium nitrate." In an isolated place like this one, Wafic felt safe to speak in their native language. And he needed that if they were to discuss technical details.

"They do," Hasim responded in Arabic as he patted one of the plump bags. "They have all sorts of rules and regulations in place ever since the bombing of one of their Federal buildings back in 1995."

"Then how do we come to this supply?"

"By the grace of Allah," Hasim said. "The brother who owns this place found this cache of fertilizer just sitting here when he bought the property. He's an educated man and, well, he mentioned it to some others—and the word spread to us. It's a gift from Heaven, is it not? It's been here for nearly twenty years, but I'm told that makes no difference if the material is properly stored."

"That's true," Wafic said as he walked around the musty pallets, stooping to feel if any of the fertilizer bags had been damaged by water or weather. They all seemed pristine, but he'd know more when he did a few experiments.

"It's a good start," Wafic said. "And it's much better than the plan for using potassium chlorate. If this material remains suitable, we have most of what we need to make ANFO."

"What's that?" Ibrahim was poking a finger at one of the bags as if he expected it to react in some way to his prodding. Wafic looked at Ibrahim who nodded. It couldn't hurt to tell the young designated martyr what was planned for the mission to strike at the *kafirs*. Where, when, and who were questions that Hasim would address when the time was right.

"ANFO stands for Ammonium Nitrate and Fuel Oil," Wafic said. "When properly mixed and accelerated, it makes a powerful explosive."

"Very cool," Ibrahim said with a gleeful smile. "Like that dude McVeigh used in Oklahoma City."

"Yes," Wafic said. "Precisely like that. We simply need a supply of drums or barrels and a quantity of kerosene or fuel oil."

"It's all being arranged," Hasim said checking his phone. "Sources have been found and we have brothers who will make the necessary purchases at widely dispersed locations." He pointed at a glassed-in space toward the rear of the main warehouse. "Back there is running water and what you will need to concoct the proper mixture."

Hasim sent Ibrahim for lunch and then led Wafic toward the rear of the building. "What do you think?"

"I think we are lucky that you found this material. Can we rely on the brother who owns the property to remain silent?"

"He is a rich man," Hasim said. "He travels a lot to oil refineries around the world. He is also a True Believer—and he has family in Iraq. We have him under control."

"There remains much work to be done even if the ANFO turns out to be a reliable option. How long do I have?"

"Not as much as you want, but likely as much as you need if I understand the chemistry, my brother. The event in Fort Worth commences in two weeks."

"That's really all I know right now," Shake said as he wrapped an arm around his wife and muted the game show they'd been mostly ignoring on TV. "What I can't figure is why the various outfits that are supposed to be so damn concerned with this kind of stuff aren't listening—or reacting for that matter."

"You know they probably get hundreds of tips like this, right?" Chan picked up a thick folder of student essays from her International Relations seminar at U-T and began to page through the stack. "Most of them come from paranoids and racist yahoos, so they don't get their panties in a bunch over everything or they'd start to miss the real threats."

"I think this is a real threat—which is why I want to go take a look for myself. Unless you've got some strong and reasonable objections."

"What if I did, Shake? Would it make any difference?" Chan Dwyer Davis tossed the papers back on the coffee table and turned to face her husband. They'd been married for nearly ten years at this point, both veterans of some serious—often dangerous—missions and incidents while she was working for the Defense Intelligence Agency and Shake was freelancing mainly to avoid terminal boredom.

"If you really didn't want me to do this thing, I wouldn't do it." Shake was fairly certain he was serious about that. Chan meant the world to him, and that world was a pleasant and rewarding place with her in his life. The security of his country was important to Shake Davis, always had been in and out of uniform, but someone else would have to look

into the situation in Mexico if it meant risking his relation-
ship with his wife.

"You know, I did some research while you were down
south with your Texas Ranger pal." Chan reached for her
phone and scrolled for a while until she found what she
wanted. "A friend of mine from DIA pointed me to this."
She handed Shake her phone with the screen showing an ex-
cerpt from a story that ran in The Washington Times earlier
in the year.

> *According to sources high in the National Security in-
> frastructure, a smuggling network has managed to
> sneak illegal immigrants from Middle Eastern terror-
> ism hotbeds straight to the doorstep of the U.S., in-
> cluding some connected to the Islamic State in Iraq
> and Syria (ISIS), also known as ISIL for Islamic State
> in Iraq and the Levant. Those same sources also indi-
> cate that at least one immigrant who was apprehended
> in Arizona revealed plans to conduct attacks in North
> America. Unconfirmed reports indicate that Mexican
> members of several infamous crime cartels use their
> expertise to assist these Middle Eastern men getting
> clandestinely into the country using tracks and cross-
> ing points that they know well from drug smuggling
> operations. Agents of Homeland Security and the FBI
> are supposedly investigating the situation, but spokes-
> men for both organizations refused comment for this
> story.*

"So they know about all this stuff already?" Shake
handed back the phone and pondered what he'd heard from
the people down in the Rio Grande Valley. If what they said
about bureaucratic intransigence was true, and if Homeland
Security et al knew there were seriously bad actors crossing

the southern borders, why would they blow off the reports and pictures Joaquin Sutler and the other South Texans showed them? "This doesn't add up…"

"Or maybe it does," Chan said. "Could be Homeland and the FBI don't want something like this publicized any more than it already is. You know there's a lot of stuff that goes on outside public knowledge. Maybe they were paying attention to your pals but just didn't want them to know it."

"You mean because they might start waving the flag and beating their chests and get a lot of bad-ass Texans all stirred up while there's an official investigation being conducted?"

"Could be—maybe something like that. I mean the last thing they'd want is a bunch of heavily armed Texas patriots patrolling the border and shooting at anything they see headed north, right? God knows our relations with Mexico are at low ebb with the new President claiming he's gonna get Mexico to pay for a wall on the border."

"I need to talk to Bayer and see what he's hearing."

"Good idea." Chan walked out on their screened back porch and sniffed the air. Hickory smoke from Lockhart's famous barbecue joints blew in on a gentle spring breeze. "And if you really feel like you and Mike need to go to Mexico and see for yourself, I guess I'm OK with it."

Shake joined her on the porch and suggested they drop by Black's BBQ which was only about a block from their new home. "I'll make a call and get Bayer's take on this," he said as they headed for the front door. "And if we go south of the border, it will be strictly reconnaissance, I promise."

Early the next morning while Shake was busy chipping away at some pecan limbs he'd about half decided to make into legs for a stand-alone bar he promised to make for the house, Chan called him to the phone. It was the man who calls himself Bayer.

"Did you get the *Washington Times* thing I sent?"

"Yeah. Nothing new there. I saw it when it came out in the papers."

"What do you think? Are the Feds already all over this thing?"

"Hard telling, Shake. I'm having a hard time getting any of my old sources to talk about it, but I've still got some calls out. At this point, all I would say with any degree of confidence is that Homeland is basically aware that some goons of Middle East extraction have before and can now come into the country across our southern border."

"So what are they doing about it? How come the folks down along the border in South Texas keep getting the official brush-off?"

"I can't get completely straight answers from the folks who will still talk to me but there's a little high-level hubris involved. Some bureaucrats who think way too much of themselves really don't like the idea of being scooped by civilians in jeans and cowboy hats. That's my take on it."

"OK. Regardless, they won't be ignoring it, right?"

"Word I get is they caught one guy in Arizona, an Afghan who claimed ISIS ties just like the Times story said. Since then no more—and so I guess they've turned their attention to other matters that they consider more pressing."

"Like what for Christ's sake?"

"Like trying to keep decent relations with Mexico, which the current administration is making a little difficult, and stopping the drug traffic coming into the country. Those are just a couple of things. Homeland and the FBI might be watching it, but they're playing it close to the vest, you know? And every time we get some homegrown incident like San Bernardino, Orlando, or that whack-job who just shot up the airport in Fort Lauderdale, priorities get scrambled. They've only got so many assets to cover all the bases."

"What's the bottom line?"

"I think this is a case of the hierarchy in National Security not being able to see the forest for the trees. And I think if what your pals down south in Texas say is true, then we're gonna get bit on our collective American asses sooner rather than later."

"So, maybe we get a little professional recon, some reliable stuff that can't be ignored and then see if we can rearrange some National Security priorities?"

"I have always been a firm believer in good reconnaissance, Shake. You win the recon battle and you win the war."

Shake was rummaging around in the kitchen looking for edible leftovers. Chan was teaching and wouldn't be home for supper. Bear, their big Golden Pyrenees, was parked on a couch, pawing the air in one of his squirrel-chasing dreams. The house seemed like a big, lonely cave. Shake was contemplating wiring in a new set of lights in his woodworking shop so he could work out there at night. Often he did some valuable thinking about difficult problems when he was showered in sawdust. He'd just about decided to warm some cold beef ribs and potato salad when the phone rang. It was daughter Stacey calling from Boston where she was working on some project for her employers at the Woods Hole Oceanographic Institute. He was glad to hear her voice. They hadn't been in touch very often since the big move to Texas.

Stacey was about to embark with her Navy Reserve unit for her annual active-duty stint, and Shake knew she was worried about leaving her research to deploy with the unit to the turbulent Middle East. The big news was that she'd gotten a kind of reprieve. The Navy offered her a temporary slot at the Navy Diving and Salvage Command in Panama City, Florida. She was full of questions about the assignment. They talked for 20 minutes, and then Shake went to feed Bear and himself.

He was gnawing on rib bones, barely focused on the TV when the phone rang again and he picked up the handset hoping it was Chan with updates about when she'd get back from Austin. It was Manny Chavez down in McAllen.

"I just heard from my uncle. He says there's another bunch camped out south of his place. They showed up yesterday."

"Same drill?"

"Pretty much. He heard a few booms and snuck out there to take a look."

"Did he say how many?"

"He counted five—two of them locals for sure. My uncle said he recognized one of the Mexicans. They're probably security or Coyotes to get them across the border."

"OK, Manny. You cobble together a full brief, everything your uncle knows. Treat it like mission planning. You know the kind of things we need to know."

"I'm on it now."

"Good deal. I'm gonna get my buddy spooled up and on an airplane. Did you all get the stuff I asked for?"

"We got almost everything on your list, Shake. Joaquin and Carlotta have it all stashed down at the plant."

"See you as soon as I can get there. I'll call you from the truck when I've got the word on my buddy's flight. Name is Mike Stokey, and he'll be inbound from Las Vegas. You guys will probably have to put him up until I get there."

Shake broke the connection and called Mike to get moving. Then he called Chan to find out when she'd be home. He needed to let her know he'd be gone for a while, but that was the kind of thing he needed to do in person.

"So what do we know at this point?" Shake walked into the big room fresh from a two-hour nap he'd managed after arriving at Joaquin Sutler's spread late in the day. Stokey, Manny Chavez, and Carlotta Valdez were all gathered around a large-scale map of northern Mexico that was pinned to a wall.

"It's like I told you on the phone, Shake. My uncle heard some explosions south of his place and went to take a look. He says there are five guys playing with dynamite or something, most of them armed and all of them look just like the first batch he spotted. They're doing about the same kind of thing, he says."

"And he thinks two of the five are Mexicans?" Shake poured coffee from a jug on the bar and joined the crowd around the map. Someone had drawn a circle around a little pueblo called Providencia which looked to be about 30 miles south and a little east of the border crossing at Reynosa.

"Check—and both of them are strapped to the max. *Tio Manuel* says he recognized one of them, a guy named Miguel Sandoval-Ortega."

"Did they spot him?"

"Nah. *Tio Manuel* knows how to stay out of sight when he wants to, and he's working on his home turf. I told him to play it cool and not take any chances."

"This Sandoval-Ortega hombre…" Joaquin continued. "He's a bad dude, Shake. This ain't the first time I've heard his name. Rangers and the Border Patrol have had him on their shit lists for a while. He's a major player in runnin' dope or little girls across the border from either Tamaulipas or Nuevo Leon. He's also been known to hire out as muscle for anybody that wants to get something illegal done down south."

"I've heard about him." Carlotta added. "Used to run drugs for the Sinaloa bunch. He's a ballsy bastard. Friend of mind swears she saw him one time at a Starbucks in downtown McAllen. I did some checking with business contacts down there, and they say the dude is Teflon—very well connected with heavy-hitters in Mexico City."

"Well, that kind of confirms what Joaquin said about Mexicans being involved in this, right?" Mike Stokey was rapidly bringing himself up to speed on the situation. "It's gotta be that the ISIS or AQ people are hiring protection and escorts across the border just like you figured. So how good are guys like this Ortega? They gonna be a serious problem?"

"They ain't trained troops or anything like that," Joaquin said. "On the other hand, they're all vicious bastards. They got no problem with killing people, if that's what you're askin'."

"It's a hitch, Shake. Whatever we do, we're gonna have to avoid the security. If we can't manage that, it's gonna get ugly. You OK with going down there unarmed?"

"Hell no, I'm not." Shake glanced around at all the weapons stored in the cabinets lining Joaquin Sutler's hacienda walls. "But the Mexican authorities frown on gringos running around their country packing heat. And the last thing we want to do is get into a gunfight."

Mike Stokey shrugged. "It ain't always about what we want, Shake. There are times when a gunfight is unavoidable—like when the other guy shoots first."

"If you're plannin' on taking weapons," Joaquin said, "and it might be a good idea with them two hombres workin' security down there, you're gonna have to do it the hard way, on foot and away from any of the standard crossing points. They're pretty tough and plenty savvy about that kind of thing at the border down here ever since that Fast and Furious bullshit. If the Border Patrol don't search your vehicle, the Mexican police on the other side damn sure will. Anyway, I wouldn't go with anything much more than handguns. Easier to ditch them in a hurry."

"I've been thinking about that." Manny Chavez swept a finger across the blue line of the Rio Grande from Reynosa toward a body of water marked as the Falcon Reservoir. "There are a bunch of places all along in this area where we can cross at night with damn little chance of being observed. Suppose I take you and Mike across on foot. We carry anything we don't want to advertise with us. Then we have Joaquin and Carlotta drive across at Reynosa and swing north to meet us. When we're all hooked up south of the border, we drive down to my uncle's place and get started from there."

Shake nodded and took a closer look at the map. "It would make it easier and quicker, I guess. Joaquin, would they pitch a bitch if they found the cameras and recording gear in your truck?"

"Probably not," the retired Texas Ranger said. "It's gonna look legit if we tell them we're nature photographers or somethin' like that. Lots of Texans go down there to do stuff like nature studies or painting. And Carlotta could maybe take some ready cash to buy us out of any trouble with the Mexicans."

"I'll do that, and I've got a big four-wheel drive Jimmy with a camper on the back," Carlotta volunteered. "They see that kind of expedition all the time at the Reynosa crossing. We'll look just like another couple of rednecks crossin' over for a little cultural exchange."

"Manny, are you sure about those crossing points?"

"Well, I've never actually done it myself, but a guy works for me at the plant used to be a Coyote before he went straight. He'll point us where we need to go and then we just wade across the river like wetbacks in reverse."

The next morning, Shake and Mike Stokey stood in the big room sipping coffee and admiring a rack of semi-auto pistols. Joaquin Sutler, the former Marine, was clearly a firearms connoisseur. Not unusual for a guy who spent most of his working life in Texas law enforcement, Shake thought. He identified pristine Colts, Smith & Wessons, Glocks, Sig Sauers, and pistols from Springfield Armory. It was all high-end stuff. And all of it in .45 ACP.

"Man after your heart," Mike said, pointing at a custom Kimber 1911, the same kind of pistol Shake generally carried. "Not a nine in sight. Joaquin seems to prefer the big bore when it comes to handguns."

"Smart man," Shake said as he poured from the coffee pot. "Texas Rangers don't usually have much use for mouse guns. And you know how I feel about it. A 230-grain slug is a reliable fight-stopper no matter where it hits."

"You made up your mind about taking some weapons south with us?"

"I'm thinking about it." Shake wandered toward the wall map which showed the states of Tamaulipas and Nuevo Leon. He was preoccupied with spotting something that they could use in photographs that would definitely show that the men training down there were in Mexico and not in some desert north of the border. Coupled with his own expert observations of what they were up to and any sound they could record, they might have evidence solid enough to prompt some action.

"Where is our host this morning?" Mike was in an upbeat mood. They had spent most of the evening packing their rucksacks and this morning both were dressed in comfortable, well-worn boots and soft khaki, almost like a quasi-military uniform. It felt like they were back in harness, prepping for an active-duty mission. As they hashed out what they thought they might need, Stokey was laughing and relating every little piece of equipment to some half-true war story. Whatever this deal turned out to be, Shake thought, Mike was happy to be involved. And if he told himself the naked truth, he was just as happy about it. It just felt good to be doing something a little chancy, off on a mission again where there was an opportunity to use his war dog senses and skills. If that made him an adrenaline junkie—well, there were worse things.

"He went downtown to get Carlotta and our surveillance gear. Manny Chavez is due to report in shortly. I had him call his uncle to see of anything's changed since last report."

"So, we go tonight?"

"We go tonight—unless something has radically changed."

They heard tires on gravel and looked out a front window to see Carlotta pulling up to the house in a mud-specked dark-green GMC pick-up with a big camper fitted into the bed. Right behind her was Joaquin in his vehicle. Joaquin had a cardboard box in his arms when they walked into the house. Carlotta was back in her jeans and swinging a set of keys.

"Did y'all get a look at my camper? That's a nice piece of gear that I damn sure wish I'd had back in my Army days." She winked at Shake. "Sleeps three—or four if somebody wants to cuddle. The camera gear and all the other stuff is in the back. You boys can help me fetch it if you want to check it over."

Shake sent Mike to help Carlotta retrieve the gear. He wanted to check it all for fit and function and maybe run a little training exercise before they headed for the border. Joaquin plopped his burden on the bar and pulled out two black plastic containers. Shake immediately recognized them as pistol cases. "Take a look at that," Joaquin said and handed one to Shake.

Inside was a new Para Ordnance Range Master in .45 caliber and two eight-round magazines. "Got another one just like it," Joaquin tapped the other case. "And there's fifty rounds of 230-grain ball ammo. One of the guys you met last time you were here owns a gun-shop downtown. These two forty-fives are off the books—lost in transit or some such crap. Point is, they can't be traced to him, so he was happy to have them go to a good cause."

"Fairly nice pistol," Shake said as he press-checked the chamber and aimed at the map on the wall through a set of de-horned Novak combat sights. "You thinking we ought to take these with us down south?"

"Well, Shake, I damn sure would. You know an old Texas Ranger and former Marine just don't feel properly dressed without a handgun on his hip."

"And if we have to shit-can these things, nobody's the wiser."

"That's about the size of it, pard. I figure one for you and y'all carry mine across with you on foot. I'll pick it up when we meet up later."

"OK. Everybody will probably feel better if we've got something to defend ourselves. But I'm gonna get sticky about who is directly involved here, Joaquin. Once we get across the Rio Grande, you, Carlotta, and Manny are gonna be strictly support. Mike and I do the close recon." Shake looked at the old Ranger's hang-dog expression. "I get it that you want in on the action if there is any—but that ain't gonna happen. You run the rear-echelon support deal, Joaquin. That's in the form of an order. The proper Marine Corps response is *Aye-aye, Sir.*"

"Aye-aye, Sir."

"Very well. Now let's go over the cameras and sound gear."

Carlotta and Joaquin had done nicely with the equipment required. The basic set-up was a brand-new Canon Power Shot digital body in a rugged carrying case containing a variety of lenses. The basic camera was fitted with 50-175mm zoom lens, but they also had fast wide-angle glass and a big 300mm zoom. The sound recording equipment was also top-shelf, an Orbiter long-range electronic listening device that plugged into an eight-gigabyte digital recorder. It was all compact, lightweight, and quiet: the kind of gear that's suited for clandestine surveillance. Of course, it would only be as good as the people handling it. Shake intended that be restricted to himself and Mike Stokey, but they ran some tests and everyone got the basic gist of using the camera and sound gear.

They were padding, repacking, and adjusting the carrying cases when Manny Chavez arrived with his old Army rucksack slung over a shoulder. He was wearing dark jeans, a black windbreaker, and an old knit watch-cap. He looked like a throwback to the old World War II OSS images. "This is just for the crossing," he said dropping his gear. "Dark is best for night work. I've got some khaki stuff for crawling around in the sand."

"Good tip," Mike said. "I'm gonna go dig out my jeans and adjust." He pointed at his ratty old jungle boots and at the similarly worn pair of Danner RAT boots on Shake's feet. "These gonna be OK, or do we need to find something else?"

Chavez held up a foot to show his own desert combat boots. "You'll be fine," he said. "Supposedly we can wade across so you want something that dries in a hurry and has some traction. The guy who told me about the crossing point said he used to do it barefoot, but I don't want to try that."

"Did you get hold of your uncle?"

"Yeah, just before I left the plant. He says our targets are still playing grab-ass in the desert. Only thing changed is that somebody towed a little camping trailer out there. *Tio Manuel* says the guy who brought it stayed on—so that makes six at the site.

"Three unknowns and three security guys?"

"That's what it looks like to him."

"No factor," Shake said. It was just one more sentry to be avoided, and he doubted that local thugs would be overly motivated on watch at a remote location in their own backyard. He retrieved the map from the wall and spread it on the bar for everyone to see.

Manny penciled in an X at the crossing point selected. "Water's low right here, and the river makes a hook just this side of the reservoir. We cross there and then head for this point." He drew another mark at a road intersection just south of the Reynosa border checkpoint. "It's about five miles, and the walk will give us some time to dry out. Once we meet up with Carlotta and Joaquin, we drive some country roads to here." He drew another circle farther south. "That's my uncle's place."

"What about border patrols?" It all seemed way too easy to Shake who knew from hard experience that few simple plans failed to become seriously complicated once you got rolling.

"Joaquin helped some with that…"

"Yep," Joaquin pulled a notebook out of his shirt pocket and squinted at a page. "Old law enforcement grapevine paid off for once. I got the latest Border Patrol schedule for the area south of the reservoir." He tore out the page and handed it to Shake. "Y'all just have to stay low and watch for their vehicles. You're pretty safe to cross anytime between patrols, and there ain't that many in the area."

Shake showed the schedule to Mike and pointed at the line that read 0130. "We'll try this," he said. "I've done enough sentry duty to know that will be close to end of shift. Hopefully they'll be tired and a little less alert."

"How about patrols on the other side?" Mike asked. "The Mexicans patrol on their side, right?"

"Yes—and no," Carlotta said. "They've got some cops that drive around a bit, but they ain't very anxious to catch anyone. A lot of them are on Coyote payrolls anyway. I don't think you'll have any problems with them."

"Copy," Shake said. "So we're good to go. Joaquin, you and Carlotta cross late this afternoon. Park near the intersection marked on the map and break out the cameras. If anyone asks, just tell them you're waiting for a beautiful sunset or something. Stick around until we join up. We'll cross sometime around 0130 or shortly thereafter. Then we hoof it to the rendezvous, and you drive everyone to Uncle Manuel's place which will be our FOB or Forward Operating Base. Manny, is your uncle OK with all this?"

"No problem. He knows we're coming, and he's got no complaints. Maybe we could float him and my aunt some money for the cover and hospitality." He looked across the table at Carlotta who nodded and patted the pocket of her jeans.

"Good. How about comm?"

"Service on American phones can be a little spotty," Carlotta said. "You boys got your phones set up for roaming?"

Shake nodded. He considered the roaming feature a necessity with all the travel he did. Mike just shrugged. "Didn't even bring mine," he said. "Damn thing just gets me in trouble. I figured if I needed to call home, I'd use Shake's phone."

"Don't worry about it, sugar." Carlotta winked and patted Mike's hand. "Joaquin and me are gonna stop at a place I know in Reynosa and buy four burners set up to work on the Mexican networks. And we got the radios." She pointed at a canvas carryall next to the camera bag. "You said top-end stuff, so we got Motorolas just like the military uses. There's one for each of us wetback commandos, and I got headsets to keep the noise down."

"Manny, how far is it from your uncle's place to the objective area?"

"Not sure about that. I'll call and ask, but you gotta figure it's a mile or two."

"Those radios are mainly line of sight," Shake said. "So they might not work all the time. Everybody carries one of the Mexican phones. If the radios don't work, we use them. Carlotta and Joaquin, you two program all the numbers into the phones as soon as you get them so we can call each other by just hitting a button. You know, set them up for a speed dial kind of thing. And we keep any and all transmission, either phone or radio, to a minimum. No happy chat on either device." Shade checked his watch. "We've got time for lunch and then we'll roll."

Late in the afternoon Carlotta drove Shake, Mike, and Manny Chavez out along Texas Highway 83 northwest of McAllen until they reached a big sweeping curve in the road where it started to bend around Falcon Reservoir. Their selected cross-spot was about a kilometer back in the other direction, but Shake wanted to hang out until dark at some place further from the regular Border Patrol routes. They found a little cantina and pulled off the road.

"We'll hang out here for a while and then walk to the site," Shake told the pair slated to cross by vehicle. "You guys go ahead and cross when it feels right. We'll see you on the other side. If anything weird happens on either end, we call using the U.S. phones. They should work this close."

They lingered over tacos and a couple of beers until it got dark. When Joaquin called Shake to report they'd crossed into Mexico with no problems and were headed for the rendezvous site, they paid the tab and left the cantina. They walked back in the direction of town, staying south of the highway and trying to look like a trio of hikers or backpackers headed for home. Close to an hour later, Manny Chavez checked the map and pointed them further south. They threaded through cactus and sage brush until he spotted the river meandering parallel to a dirt track. "That's the trail the Border Patrol uses," he said. "We can lay up here and wait."

They nestled in a stand of tall Carrizo cane and watched the Rio Grande for a while, listening to sparse traffic along Highway 83 to the rear of their position. The river was just a darker ribbon on the moonless horizon. Shake could barely make out some scrub trees on the other bank less than 100 meters from their hide site. No telling how deep it is until we give it a try, he thought. And then, as he'd done in so many remote sites around the world waiting for action to start, Gunner Shake Davis rolled over and went to sleep.

Wafic Aziz had been experimenting in the back of the warehouse for three days now. He worked all day every day and returned to his basement hovel late at night when Hasim brought his dinner and they read passages from the holy Quran together or further dissected the plans for the upcoming attack.

He was a meticulous man with solid training and experience in manufacturing and employing explosives. Rushing the process of producing ANFO from ammonium nitrate and fuel oil was foolish. If he did not kill or immolate himself, the rushed product might possibly be of low-order, resulting in an ineffective detonation and less than the planned damage. So Wafic had plenty of time to think as he worked mixing the chemicals, testing the old fertilizer, and going over the details necessary for maximum effect from his bomb.

Wafic's experience with what the enemy called Improvised Explosive Devices or IEDs had begun in Iraq when local forces battling the Crusader Infidels recruited him from university. They recruited a lot of his fellow students in electronics or chemical engineering, but none proved as promising as Wafic Aziz. The bomb-makers from Iran who supported the faithful fighting in Iraq found him a quick study with a knack for improvisation. Later, his name and contact had been passed to fighters of the *daesh* and he went to Syria to support the faithful of the Fourth Caliphate. And then, after a spectacular success with a chemical bomb he'd designed and detonated near Aleppo, he was selected for the assignment that took him on a long, difficult route from

Syria, through Hungary, into western Europe, and finally into Mexico for a special mission.

Wafic Aziz considered himself a very successful soldier of Allah. For this mission in Texas, he would design a bomb to go off in the Infidel's back yard and do massive damage. And then he would move on to the next assignment in California. Wafic hoped it would be a target in Los Angeles. He was anxious to see Hollywood. At this early stage, only Hasim had the details and Wafic knew only that it involved a bomb—and he would not die in employing it. An expert technician like Wafic was too valuable in the struggle to die as a martyr. That little sliver of eternal glory would go to younger, less educated men like Ibrahim, an American citizen whose sacrifice would drive the police mad trying to understand why one of their own citizens would do such a thing.

This latest batch of slurry felt about right to his touch on the broomstick he was using to stir the sludge in a large steel pot. It was time for another test. He cut a quarter-stick from the industrial dynamite Hasim had brought and selected one of the electrical blasting caps from his backpack. They were good caps, of reliable Russian manufacture, that he'd been issued in Mexico. Next, he carried the big pot outside the warehouse where Hasim waited to see if they'd managed to get it right this time. Wafic watched him run 50 meters of electrical wire to a place around the corner of the building, where they'd be safe from the effects of the blast he hoped for with this batch of ANFO. Using his teeth as he'd been taught by his instructors, he crimped the wire to a blasting cap, inserted the cap into the quarter-stick of dynamite that would provide the necessary accelerant, and lowered it into the solution in the big pot. Then he followed the wire to the observation site. He pulled a nine-volt battery from his pocket and glanced at Wafic.

"Are you ready?"

"Will it be very loud?"

"Not so bad," Wafic responded. "The ANFO is not compressed or compacted. I think there will be more flash than noise." He carefully split the wires and used his teeth once again to strip insulation. "Now we see if the mixture in this slurry is correct," he said with the detached air of a scientist conducting an experiment in some pristine lab. And then he touched the bare wires to the battery terminals.

The resulting flash and bang rolled over the flat Texas plains like a bolt of lightning. Wafic merely smiled and shrugged, but Hasim was shocked by the violence of the detonation. "That power from so little of the solution!"

"ANFO is powerful stuff," Wafic said, "and much more destructive when it is compacted in sealed containers." Wafic rounded the corner of the building headed for the detonation site marked by a circular patch of scorched earth. "That was barely two liters. The slurry is correct. It will work as planned."

"We will need a great deal of it," Wafic said, walking around and searching vainly for any sign of the pot that held the explosive.

"Measured in gallons, we will need about three hundred or six fifty-five-gallon drums."

"They are being cleaned and properly painted. A brother in Dallas has bought ten of them from a junkyard."

"When they are delivered here, I will begin to mix and prepare."

They walked back into the little laboratory Wafic had established at the rear of the big warehouse. Hasim opened his briefcase and cleared some space on a counter. He spread two maps that had been marked with yellow highlighters. "This one," he said, pointing at a large-scale street map of Fort Worth, "indicates the route you will take to reach the coliseum."

Wafic studied for a while, tracing the indicated path, and then tapped a location less than a block from the perimeter of the Will Rogers Coliseum. "This parking area will suffice," he said. "You should be waiting for me here. I will arm the bomb and send Ibrahim on his way."

"Very good. And how is the bomb detonated?"

Wafic poked through a pile of electronic refuse on the counter and held up something that looked like a garage-door opener. "This will be the trigger. It will be wired to a blasting cap inside a stick of dynamite that I will insert in one of the ANFO containers. When Ibrahim is in the proper position with the truck, he simply presses this switch."

"That's all there is to it?"

"That's all Ibrahim is required to do," Wafic said. "I am thinking about a back-up system should the initial detonator fail for some reason."

"Good. I am working on the truck. We have made the measurements in the target area and determined the kind of truck required. There are several rental firms that have what we need."

"Most important is the paperwork, Hasim. Ibrahim will need something to get through the initial security check."

"We have that in hand." Hasim pulled a clipboard from his briefcase. "There will be a manifest like this one indicating an order for liquid supplements to cattle feed." Wafic glanced at the clipboard and noted delivery manifest sheets bearing the logo of a company called Livengood Feed and Seed. "It is a well-known firm. Ibrahim will get through to the loading docks with no problems."

Wafic turned his attention to the second map which displayed the layout of the Will Rogers Coliseum. "The loading docks are not the target. Attacking them would be a waste of my efforts."

"Yes—and not the effect we desire. Ibrahim will make a right turn here." Hasim indicated a spot where an interior pathway led away from the docks. "Then a left turn to get through this gate. At that point, he drives directly into the mezzanine area." He waved his hand over the stadium diagram. "There will be huge crowds there."

"You should obtain the truck, brother. Ibrahim will need practice time."

Banks of the Rio Grande

Shake was shouldered tight on Manny Chavez, peeking through the cane stalks closer to the track that ran parallel to the river. It was 0140 and they were watching a Border Patrol vehicle that was shining a spotlight across the Rio Grande and onto the brush-covered banks on the Mexican side. Mike Stokey was behind them, rechecking the waterproofing of the gear in their rucksacks.

"Good to go when you're ready," he whispered and crawled through the cane to get his own view of the vehicle passing their front. There were two agents—a man and a woman—in a white Humvee with green markings. The male was driving while the female handled the spotlight. Both of them were gazing intently at the river as they rolled past the cane field in low gear.

"Let them pass," Shake whispered. "When they get further down the track, we'll make our move."

They watched the vehicle trundle along probing the dark with the spotlight until it suddenly made an abrupt left turn and bounced over the scrub heading in the direction of Texas 83. That was unexpected. "How come they turned off?" Shake glanced at Manny for an explanation. "Think they spotted us?"

"Not a chance," Manny said shrugging into his rucksack. "They never even looked in our direction. It's probably like you figured, you know?" He pointed at the luminous dial of his watch. "Almost 0200. Probably end of their shift and they're headed back for relief."

"Probably right." Shake had figured the patrols for about a four-hour stint. Anything longer than that tends to degrade a sentry's attention. Much longer staring into the dark and guards, policemen, and soldiers lose their edge. Then they start missing important details or spooking at shadows. "Let's go. Ten-meter interval. Manny leads, I'll take slack and Mike walks drag."

Following Manny Chavez, they scrambled across the perimeter road down to the water and slowly stepped into the Rio Grande. The water was cold but without much noticeable current which likely had to do with dams and regulators to their west around the Falcon Reservoir. They moved slowly in single file, carefully searching the rocky bottom for firm footing. About halfway across they were up to their chests, but Shake could sense that they were starting to encounter rising ground. As they were nearing the Mexican banks, several spears of intense white light suddenly split the darkness off to their right. Shake ducked automatically until just his head was above water. He saw Manny and Mike in a similar frozen position staring wide-eyed at the bright light reflecting off the water. They heard an amplified, authoritarian voice booming over the river. Someone was identifying himself as a U.S. Agent and ordering someone else to halt in place with hands in the air.

It was frightening. It was also not intended for the three men who were trying to sneak into Mexico. The action was about 50 meters upstream to the west of them, where Shake could see the beams of intense light focused on a line of four people standing in the river with water up to their chests. Three of them had their hands raised. The last man in line was moving slowly away from his companions. There was some additional shouting in Spanish, more urgent this time. One of the spotlights shifted to follow the moving man.

There was an amplified order for him to halt and raise his hands. They could hear several of the men trapped with their hands in the air begging the agents on the U.S. side not to shoot.

"It's a bust," Manny whispered to Shake who had drawn up closer to him. "They caught some mules crossing. Probably drug smugglers."

"OK," Shake said, motioning Mike forward closer to the bank. "Good distraction and not our problem. Let's get across while they're focused on that."

They were slithering up onto Mexican soil when the shooting started. Shake understood the shouted Spanish command for someone to drop a weapon. That was followed by a ripping series of pops that he instantly recognized as coming from an AK or clone. He'd heard that sound way too many times to mistake it. They bulled further into the scrub brush and looked upstream into a series of muzzle flashes that were raising gouts of muddy water on the surface of the Rio Grande. Over the crackle of gunfire, they heard some of the people in the river screaming for a cease fire. And then it got quiet.

"One of those assholes opened up with an AK," Mike whispered. "Bad idea."

"It looks like they've had enough," Manny said. In the cone of light to the west of their position, they could see agents on the riverbank hauling three men out of the water. "We better beat feet before the Mexican cops get in on the action."

"Take it slow and head southeast." Shake checked the compass on his watchband and pointed. Then he fell in at the back of the line lagging well behind Manny and Mike, thinking hard about the incident they observed. Something wasn't right. It all took place in bright lights focused on the smugglers, and he had a combat-honed eye for detail. There were four men frozen in the middle of the river when the lights hit the water. Three guys surrendered immediately and it looked like the last one in line was trying to make a break. Last time he looked, there were only three men pulled out of the water and arrested. So where was the fourth man?

He came out of a stand of cactus and mesquite near the road that paralleled the banks of the river on the Mexican side. A short, wiry man dripping Rio Grande water onto the sand was pointing a folding-stock AK at Manny Chavez and Mike. Shake was far enough behind them to duck behind a stand of prickly pear cacti without being noticed. He watched closely, fairly sure he hadn't been seen by the man with the gun who was now conversing in Spanish through clenched jaws. Manny was trying his best to assure the smuggler that they were just tourists out on a nighttime stroll. That was a little weak considering they were drenched with Rio Grande river water. The gunman looked like a desperate high-school kid in ratty jeans and sweatshirt with a big soccer ball pictured on the front. Shake could see hanks of long dark hair streaming from under a green mesh baseball cap jammed backwards on the kid's head.

He was high on adrenaline from the close encounter with the law and not buying Manny's story at all. Shake could see his eyes: white, wide, and almost glowing in the dark. Clearly this was the guy who had enough balls to shoot his way out of a dead-drop ambush. He wouldn't dick around much longer with a couple of gringos. Shake wished he could reach the pistol in his rucksack, but that would take too much time and make too much noise. He needed to improvise.

He reached down onto the ground and felt around for a good-sized rock. When he found what he wanted, something about the size of a softball that would make some noise when it hit the sandy soil, he reared back and tossed it into the dark, aiming to the right of the gunman so that when the guy spun, he wouldn't sweep his muzzle across Manny and Mike. The rock hit with a satisfying thud and when the gunman whirled to look Shake made his move.

Vaulting the prickly pears, he hit the guy hard in the back with a cross-body block that would have gotten him fined and suspended in the NFL. "Get the gun!" He yelled at Mike and covered the Mexican's body with his own. It was 200 pounds against half that, and the smuggler didn't have a chance to move much before Mike kicked the AK away into the dark.

The man was struggling hard to get out from underneath Shake when Manny knelt down and spoke to him in Spanish. "Relax, amigo. If you don't quit, we might have to shoot you."

"Who the hell are you guys?"

"We're not cops. That's all you need to know."

"Anybody bring any rope or wire?" Shake asked as he cautiously levered himself up off the smuggler.

"Wasn't on the mount-out list," Mike said as he emerged from the dark carrying the AK and training it on the smuggler who was sitting up with his eyes locked on the muzzle of what had once been his gun. Stokey dropped the magazine and checked the ammo supply. "What do we do with this broke-dick?"

Shake pondered that as he stripped the man's backpack and opened the flap. Inside under some smelly old clothes were two plastic-wrapped bricks of what he presumed were drugs of some sort. There was a lot of whatever it was, probably worth millions once it was cut and distributed to avid dealers and junkies in the States. "I guess we know what that bust upriver was all about."

"You fuck with that stuff," the little man said in passable English, "and there are people who will hunt you down and kill you."

"Either that or they'll hunt you down and kill you for ripping them off," Shake said. "Amigo, you got about one minute to disappear. If we see you after that…" He tapped the man's forehead between the eyes. "You get a bullet right there."

The man backed away toward the coast road until he was nearly lost in shadow, and then he took off running into the dark. They listened to the water squishing in the man's cheap sneakers until they couldn't hear anymore. Shake flipped open the Kershaw pocket knife he carried everywhere and cut a slit in the plastic wrapped around one of the bundles. He didn't know much about drugs but it was some sort of powder, probably heroin. Manny Chavez snapped a little flashlight onto the stash and whistled softly. "That's raw opium, Shake, I saw a pot full of that stuff in Afghanistan." He hefted the bundle. "That's maybe three or four kilos—worth a lot of money. See what's in the other one."

Shake slit the wrapping on the second bundle. It looked rock salt when Manny hit it with his light. "And that's cocaine. Man! That little turd was carrying about a zillion dollars on his back."

"Yeah, well somebody just lost a zillion dollars. None of this shit is gonna wind up on the street." Shake hacked at the bundles to widen the cuts he'd made and nodded at Mike who had the AK propped on a hip. "Mike, field strip that thing. We dump everything in the Rio Grande and then Char-lie Mike."

When they had the dope and the beat-up weapon deep-sixed in the Rio Grande, Mike checked his watch. "We're running late. Let's move out before that asshole comes back with some buddies looking for his dope."

They walked quickly south, shivering as a night wind blew against their wet clothes, and headed for the intersection where they were scheduled to meet Joaquin Sutler and Carlotta Valdez. Shake's phone was stashed in an exterior pocket of his pack, and he reached for it to call and report progress. What he retrieved when he swung the pack off his back was a zip-loc bag half full of water with his iPhone floating in it. Either he'd somehow jarred the bag open or it had simply leaked during the crossing. Whatever the cause, his phone was useless.

"Manny," he called to the shadow walking ahead of him in the dark. "My phone's screwed. Give Joaquin a call and let them know we're inbound."

The man who calls himself Bayer looked away from the Washington Nationals game he was watching and checked the phone that was dancing on the coffee table next to the TV remote. It was the call he'd been expecting for the past two days. It was also about the last shot he had at finding out what—if anything—was happening at serious governmental levels concerning terrorist activities south of the U.S. border in Mexico. Bayer grabbed his phone, muted the TV, and made the connection with Joe Carr, an old and trusted friend who now worked as a Supervisory Special Agent in the FBI counter-terrorism section.

"Hey, Joe. I really appreciate the call-back."

"Sorry I took so long to get back to you." Bayer could hear tension in the voice over the sound of helicopter rotors in the background. "I'm on the road—down at Lackland Air Force Base—and I've been pretty busy."

"Did you get a chance to look at the photos I sent?"

"Yeah, I saw them. Did Shake take those?"

"No, he just passed them along to me. Some friend of his in south Texas took the pictures. Shake and Mike Stokey are heading down to see for themselves—maybe get some better stuff that definitely shows bad guys are training in Mexico."

"You need stop them. Right now."

"How come, Joe? You know those two—anybody can get some credible proof of what's going on down there they can."

There was an extended silence on the other end of the call. Bayer heard vehicle engines and some muted voices.

"Listen…" Joe Carr was nearly whispering. "This is deep background, right? You don't know anything about it—and if you do you didn't get it from me."

"I know the drill, Joe. What's up?"

"We're ginning up a surveillance op in north Mexico. It's a joint task force: FBI and some *Federales* from the GOPES, their SWAT guys. That's what I'm doing down here at Lackland."

The man who calls himself Bayer nodded and smiled. He figured if the Feds were onto this thing, that was the way it might be handled.

"That's good news, Joe. Well done."

"Listen to me. What you saw in those pictures is the real deal. Our response is in a delicate stage right now. If Shake is headed down there, he's way off the reservation. You need to call him off in a hurry."

"OK, Joe. I really appreciate the tip. I'll call Shake and tell him hands off. And thanks again."

The man who calls himself Bayer punched off the call and thought for a few moments while the Nationals batters went down in order on TV. If the Feds were getting spooled up, it meant someone with clout was acting on the situation in Mexico—which would explain why they turned off the south Texas civilians. Neither confirm nor deny, keep the thing under wraps, don't let well-meaning civilians compromise security. It figures. He scrolled through his contact list until he found Shake's mobile number. After six rings, the call went to voice mail.

"Shake, it's me. Call back right away. I've got some important stuff for you. I'll tell you about it when you call. And whatever you do, don't go to Mexico or if you're already down there, freeze in place. Don't go near the thing we talked about, OK? Call back—right away."

He felt as if there was more he should do. Leaving messages was frustrating and he never trusted voice mail—not his or anyone else's. Maybe it was just an old spook's suspicions, but he was getting an eerie feeling about this deal, like the familiar bad vibe he got when a major case was about to be blown by circumstances beyond his control. Shake needed to know it was time to hit the brakes and let the Feds handle the situation in Mexico. He glanced at the TV and thought for a few minutes. Maybe Chan could help pass the word. He reached her between classes.

"Hi, Chan. You doing OK? Yeah, I'm fine—trying to reach Shake. I called his cell but it went to voice mail. It's pretty important that I get hold of him."

Chan Dwyer told the man who calls himself Bayer that the last thing she heard Shake and Mike were in McAllen, Texas and planning to go to Mexico. "And you ought to know what that's all about," she said with a little heat in her voice.

"OK. Well, nothing for you to worry about, but I've got some important information for him. Can you call and get him to call me back right away?" Chan promised to do that. And that was the end of his immediate options for updating Shake Davis and Mike Stokey, either in Mexico or headed in that direction.

The man who calls himself Bayer switched off the TV and walked to the bar where he poured himself a stiff slug of scotch. Then he retrieved his phone and checked the time in Mexico City. It was just coming up on dawn down there. Shake probably had his phone switched off while he was sleeping He'd check his messages before too long and call back. He'd get the message, Bayer reassured himself, and he'd be glad to hear someone serious was on the case.

On the drive south along Mexican Route 40, the trio that crossed on foot filled Joaquin and Carlotta in on their close call crossing the river. "You got lucky," Joaquin said as Manny Chavez directed him east off the main road onto an unmarked desert track. "It was probably the local DEA guys on a bust. They move on tips they get from the Border Patrol that's turned some mule. They do a lot of shootin' when things get sticky but they don't do much killin', and most often they ain't aimin' to anyway."

"You should have seen the load of dope that guy was carrying," Manny said. "I'm no expert, but that stuff had to be worth a couple of million on the street."

"No wonder the guy decided to try and shoot his way out of it," Mike said from the back of the camper where he sat wrapped in a blanket trying to dry his clothes. "Whoever sent him north is gonna be pissed about losing a load worth that much."

"Damn glad it got short-stopped," Joaquin said. "Last thing we need in the Valley is more dope on the street. Unfortunately, that dude will likely be back swimmin' across the river tomorrow night."

"Guess you had to let the little shit-ass go," Carlotta said. "I'd like as not have shot him dead right there. Druggies down around here play rough on both sides of the border."

"Chief cause of homicides in the Rio Grande Valley," Joaquin added, "is squabbles over drugs. Them cartel boys get ripped off or shorted and they send shooters to settle the score. Happens all the time."

"Just some kid," Shake shrugged watching the sliver of bright orange sun beginning to show on the eastern horizon. "He looked like he should have been in high school—bad-ass when he's got a gun and a punk otherwise."

When they stopped about a mile from their destination to stretch and relieve bladders bruised by barely passable country roads, Carlotta called a huddle under the dome light in the camper and showed them the phones she'd purchased in Reynosa. All had sim-cards that worked on the local Mexican network, and she had them programmed for one-touch calling. "They ain't fancy by a long-shot," she said as she handed out what looked like old flip-phones. "No camera or internet connection, but they'll do for what we need."

"How's it work?" Mike Stokey, the technophobe of the group, powered his phone and stared dubiously at the green glow from the instrument's tiny screen.

"Easy as one, two, three, sugar. If you can count, you can call. Press one and you get me or Joaquin. Two is Shake, three is you and four is Manny."

Uncle Manuel was standing in a patch of barrel cactus that covered his front yard when they arrived. It was barely dawn, but he looked like he'd been up and active for hours. He was a little man, about as tall as his wife was wide. The couple proved to be gracious hosts. Aunt Carmelita hustled them inside a small adobe and clapboard hacienda lit by oil lamps that gave the comfortable interior a smoky warm glow. Between Manny's fluent Spanish and Shake's basic familiarity with the language, they managed to communicate adequately through some small talk that led to a meal of coffee with rice and beans wrapped in fresh tortillas. When they finished eating, Shake and Manny went outside to unload equipment from the truck. In the glow of early sunlight that promised a hot day, Shake glanced around the horizon. It was an isolated area, and he could see no other structures anywhere in sight. An old Chevy pick-up was parked beside the house under an overhang, and there were a few goats bleating for food in a small corral. Otherwise it was nothing but open spaces as far as he could see. Closer to the house, what might be considered a front yard was just a leveled patch of hard-scrabble dirt, sand and cactus. Dotting the horizon at irregular intervals was a series of poles that supported a pair of wires swaying in a gentle breeze.

"They get power from Providencia," Manny said, pointing at the wires, "but it's not very reliable. Last year I bought them a generator and they mostly use that because the power out here causes their lights to flicker. Carmelita prefers the oil lamps anyway. They got a radio that runs on batteries. Uncle Manuel says he don't want a TV, but I think Carmelita's gonna talk him into it soon. Good people, you know? They don't have much, but they don't want or need much either. "

"How do you call them?"

"They've got a cell phone. Carmelita loves it and she keeps it charged so she can talk to her *amigas* in Providencia. *Tio* Manuel gets on it when she tells him to."

Back in the little central room of the house, Manny, Shake and Uncle Manuel sat examining the map. Manny pointed out landmarks he thought his relative would recognize and tried to determine where the old man thought the activities he reported were taking place. Uncle Manuel studied for a bit, turning his head left and then right. He knew the land intimately but he was having trouble connecting what he knew with lines and numbers on paper.

"It's about three clicks from here, Shake." Manny tapped a spot on the map due south of their position. "He's not sure about where it is on the map. He wants to take us out there and show us."

"Manny, we can't risk that. What if something goes wrong? Just ask him to give us a little walk around so we can get oriented. We'll figure it out from there."

They walked for a half-hour in the direction Uncle Manuel indicated. There were a few stunted trees, a patchy carpet of thorny plant life, and lots of cactus. Not much else, and Shake wondered how the old man would approach their objective without being seen.

Uncle Manuel pointed at a spot on the southern horizon where they could see a rocky mound topped by two boulders leaning against each other to keep from toppling. "There's a long stretch of low ground on the other side of those rocks," he said in a raspy voice while he squinted at the distance and rolled a cigarette. "It's maybe this deep…" He drew a hand across his chest. "I get in there and walk right up to where they are. There's plenty mesquite, chaparral, maybe a few little trees all along the ditch. It crosses a little trail and then runs up to a small hill—*la colina*, you know? If I want to see them, I just follow the ditch and watch from the high place."

"We need to take a look at that approach, Manny. Let's get back to the house and pack up the gear."

"You still dead set on just you and Mike for the close recon?"

Shake thought about it for a while, considering Manny Chavez and his Special Forces background as they walked north toward the house. He didn't like to risk anyone else, but Chavez was a trained soldier with good field skills and

he was familiar with spoken Arabic. That and another
weapon might be handy. "This trip will be mostly to get the
lay of the land. We'll get serious when we know how to do
it. You go with us and we take the pistols."

"Who the hell are those dudes?"

Air Force Technical Sergeant Cynthia "Sid" Atwood, on her second day of detached duty with the new CT Task Force, straightened up in her seat and leaned toward the wide screen she was assigned to monitor. The high-resolution imagery streaming into her console from the optical suite in an RQ-4B Global Hawk circling high over northern Mexico showed three individuals moving toward her surveillance objective area. It looked like the people she'd been assigned to watch were about to have company.

"You seeing what I'm seeing?" She turned to the mission specialist seated next to the officer flying the UAV and adjusted her view, slewing the cameras toward a long dark shadow that marked what she assumed was a wadi or meandering ditch that ran toward the area they were monitoring.

"I've got them," the mission specialist said. "Three guys in that long cut—first time we've seen anyone but the original six."

"Way they're moving, I'd say they probably weren't invited to the party, right?"

"Looks that way—and they're carrying some kind of gear. I'll see if I can get some better detail. You better call the Watch Officer."

Sergeant Atwood lifted a receiver next to her screen and punched a number. The FBI Watch Officer simply growled his name, and Atwood glanced back at her screen. "It's Sergeant Atwood over in the tank, sir. We just spotted three individuals approaching the site. We're trying to get a better look now."

Three minutes later, FBI Supervisory Special Agent Joe Carr swept into the little air conditioned box that housed the Air Force UAV crew and technicians borrowed to support his new counter-terrorism task force. He leaned over Atwood's shoulder, staring intently at the screen.

"How close are they?" Carr had a sinking feeling that he knew what—and who—he was seeing.

"I'd guess about three hundred meters, sir." Atwood adjusted the view and judged the scale with her fingers. "We picked them up when they entered frame down here." She pointed to the bottom of the screen. "We've been keeping the cameras on the objective per the watch order, but we periodically scan a little wider."

"OK. Can we get a closer look at those guys?"

The pilot and mission specialist made some changes in the Global Hawk's flight path while Atwood zoomed the cameras, trying to pick up all the detail on the men in the ditch the optics would allow. They were moving slowly through the wadi with the morning sun at a difficult angle that kept them mostly hidden in dark shadow.

"Hard to get much better than this," Atwood said when she had the best view available. "We'll do better when the sun's a little higher."

"You're the trained observer, Sid. What do you think?" Agent Carr was willing to ponder some forlorn hope that there were other possibilities.

"Have you got any people doing ground surveillance down there?"

Carr just shook his head and Atwood turned back to study her screen. "Well, I'd say from the way they're moving that these guys don't want to be seen by our subjects on the ground." Atwood had some experience analyzing UAV imagery of Taliban and other insurgents sneaking up on targets in Afghanistan. "And I'd say whoever these guys are, they move like pros—like trained soldiers." Atwood guessed the men approaching through the wadi were probably a reconnaissance element or a raid force, but she didn't say that. She was still not too clear from her skimpy mission brief just what was happening down in Mexico. The FBI guys said they were operating on a need-to-know basis and the Air Force folks didn't need to know much about why they were watching six people milling around a cheesy little camping trailer in the Mexican desert.

"No weapons visible, sir," the mission support specialist said from his console. "They're all wearing rucksacks and one of them has some kind of case. Maybe a camera case?"

Joe Carr just nodded. He was sure by now that he knew exactly who at least two of the three men approaching the objective area were. What he didn't know was exactly what to do about it.

"Stay with this as briefed," he said. "If those people do anything weird or make contact with the subjects, notify me immediately."

Back in his office on the other side of the hangar, Joe Carr felt like he was staring into a very dark hole. If Gunner Shake Davis and former CIA field agent Mike Stokey and whoever the hell else they had with them did anything more stupid than they were already doing down in Mexico, an important mission that was already way behind the power curve might be blown all to hell. Carr walked to a window that looked out over the base perimeter and thought about his conversation with Bayer. So Shake and Mike were trying to get proof that terrorists were training and staging in Mexico for missions in the U.S. It was good initiative, poor judgment. Joe Carr had argued mightily to get something serious done about that situation ever since they'd busted that ISIS puke in Arizona. It had taken months for the overly cautious bureaucrats, lawyers, and diplomats in both countries to authorize action by an international task force. Now it was finally up and running with suspects under surveillance and the Mexican authorities finally cooperating. What he really—*really*—didn't need at this early stage of the game was rogue elements compromising his mission.

He snatched open a desk drawer, grabbed his personal phone, and hit redial to get hold of the man who calls himself Bayer.

"Didn't you talk to Shake?"

"Got his voice mail. I left a message for him to call me."

"He didn't get the message, or maybe he decided to ignore it. I just saw him and Mike Stokey and they're down in Mexico about to screw up an important operation."

"You saw them? I thought you said you were at Lackland."

"Never mind that. If he calls, you tell him to cease and desist. I mean it—seriously, you tell them to get the hell out of Mexico right now."

His desk phone rang. It was Sergeant Atwood who reported that the three individuals were lying up on a piece of high ground near the objective area. They were taking pictures and using some other piece of gear that had yet to be identified. Atwood added that whatever the equipment was, it didn't look like any weapon she'd ever seen.

"Thanks, Sid," Carr said. "Stay with it and let me know if anything else happens. Pass the word to your relief crew. I want to know everything those three guys do."

"Are we authorized to shift away from the primary objective to stay with them, sir?"

"No. Primary surveillance targets remain the same. Just let me know if or when those three others move."

Carr hung up and dialed another number for the cell phone carried by his counterpart in Mexico City. "We've got a little problem at the objective site," he said. "Are you ready to move on short notice if necessary?"

"I'd like twenty-four hours if possible to get the Mexicans and the helicopters ready. It's like herding cats down here."

"I'll give you all the lead time I can, but figure we're gonna have to go sooner than we expected."

Supervisory Special Agent Joe Carr hung up and closed his eyes to think. They were probably safe. He knew from experience that old hands like Shake Davis and Mike Stokey could do close reconnaissance without getting spotted. He knew from classified reports he'd read that they'd both done plenty of that kind of thing in the past. And Gunner Davis had been the most revered instructor on staff when Corporal Joe Carr had gone through the Marine Corps' Reconnaissance Training Battalion. Old sweats like Davis and Stokey knew how to avoid compromise. But the third man was the unknown factor. Likely someone Shake or Mike hired, but you never knew. What if it was some vigilante or a local yahoo with no field experience? And what if he went nuts or something? Things could get dicey in a hurry and the bad guys might scatter and disappear if they knew they were being watched.

Tamaulipan Mattoral

Shake was shooting pictures while Mike Stokey aimed the long-range microphone toward the three men clustered below their perch. They were about 50 meters distant and 20 meters above the camping trailer which was parked near a stand of Manzanita trees. The little patch of high ground at the rear of the clearing was just as Uncle Manuel said, and it had enough large rocks and stumpy vegetation to hide observers who were used to hiding and understood the principles of concealment. The fact that the morning sun was at their backs also helped, and Shake had decided that mid-morning was their best bet for seeing without being seen.

So far, in the space of two hours and using one of the longer lenses in the camera bag, Shake had gotten good shots of most of the faces, and he was now training the camera on the rusted old pick-up parked near the trailer. There was a security guard leaning on it, smoking and fiddling with the sights on what looked like a well-kept Ruger Mini-14 rifle. The truck bore Mexican license plates and tracing the tags might prove valuable, so Shake framed the guard but focused on the plates. He was still trying to figure a way to get the people gathered in this remote patch of desert near something which definitely said Mexico. What he wanted was some kind of road sign or location marker with the bad guys clustered around it, but that was probably wishful thinking unless they shifted locations for some reason.

Mike Stokey tapped Shake's leg and pointed at his headset. "Must be some kind of language training," he whispered.

"One guy is pointing to stuff and saying the word in English. The others are repeating it."

Shake just nodded. Nothing incriminating in that, but maybe they'd start working with weapons or demo before dark. That would be the money shot. He caught movement to his right and swept his lens toward a blocky man wearing sunglasses who stepped out of the trailer. He looked around the horizon and then strolled toward a campfire where another man was poking at a smoke-blackened coffee pot. The man at the fire had a stubby sub-gun—maybe a mini-Uzi or an old MAC-10—strapped across his back. He stood as the man from the camper approached, and Shake redirected Mike to point his sound gear toward them. Sunglasses walked with a sort of swagger, like a man in charge. Shake figured he was likely the man identified as Miguel Sandoval-Ortega. He was cradling a short double-barrel shotgun on his hip, and there was what looked like a Beretta M-9 tucked in his belt. None of the men sitting around on rocks in the language class showed any weapons. Just as advertised: Three strapped bad-asses for security and the others were the ones who would eventually cross the border. Shake wanted to get some action out of the authorities before that happened.

The security guard near the truck said something to Ortega and then walked directly toward the base of the hill where Shake and Mike were perched. Shake reached to his side and tugged on a length of clothesline borrowed from Aunt Carmelita which served as a silent signal device. On the other end was Manny Chavez who was down lower in the rocks as rear security with the second pistol. Chavez tugged back to let Shake know he'd seen the approaching man. Fortunately, it was only a piss call. The security man emptied his bladder, looked around the site, and then walked back toward the campfire. These guys were complacent, just standing around not much interested in doing any roving patrols, which was just fine with Shake. The 45s they were carrying would come up significantly short against the firepower below if they were busted and got into a gunfight.

"Well, that was certainly boring." Mike Stokey swabbed his plate with a hunk of tortilla and reached for his coffee cup. "Three hours of kindergarten language classes, followed by watching them eat canned sardines and do their afternoon prayers."

"Did you see the three goons when the prayer rugs came out?" Manny pulled off the headset he was using to listen to the conversation between the security guards. "They stood around staring like they were watching some kind of voodoo ritual."

"At least we finally got them rigging demo charges before we had to take off." Shake pushed his plate aside and picked up the camera body. "It ain't much—and it won't mean much more than the first photos you guys took. Maybe we'll do better tomorrow." He flashed through the photos on the disc until he got to the series he wanted. "This dude looks to be the honcho," he said, showing the frame to Carlotta. "There's one in there where he's got his shades off. Take a look and see if that's this guy Ortega."

Joaquin leaned in to look over her shoulder. "That's him," he said. "See that tat on his neck? That's an old-time Sinaloa tag. I remember it from the BOLOs we used to get at D Company Headquarters over in Weslaco."

"Well, he's a greasy bastard, ain't he?" Carlotta flipped through the photos on the camera screen and made a face. "And them other two critters look like they been whipped with an ugly stick." Joaquin pulled up a chair next to her and they looked at the rest of the photos shot earlier in the day. "Don't need no beards or turbans to tell them others are Arabs," Carlotta said. "And look here, that's their holy book one of them's holding. See all the Arabic writing?"

"Doesn't help much," Stokey said. "That could be any American Muslim out communing with nature anywhere in the world. We gotta do better than that, or we're just wasting time down here." Stokey grabbed a light jacket against the desert wind and headed for the door. "I'm gonna go walk off some of Carmelita's chow. Anybody up for terrain appreciation?"

"Love to, sugar." Carlotta plugged the camera into her laptop and began to load the photos from the training site. "But I'm gonna be a while gettin' all these happy-snaps into my computer."

Manny Chavez was over in a corner of the sitting room with his relatives huddled around an old radio that was broadcasting a Texas Rangers baseball game in Spanish. The signal came through the desert air clear and crisp. Shake walked over to listen for a while but he couldn't follow the rapid-fire commentary very well.

"Carlotta's got you set up to sleep right next to her out in the camper," Joaquin said with a lewd grin. "I reckon she's got her sights set." He began to dig around in a backpack and fished out one of the pistols.

"We had the talk last week in the Sunshine," Shake said, wandering around the dimly lit room and staring at some of the old photos Carmelita had framed and hung on the walls. "It ain't gonna happen."

"You take a gal like old Carlotta…" Joaquin said as he carried the pistol over to the dining table. "No don't always mean no."

Shake just shrugged. "You planning on doing some shooting, Joaquin?"

"Not unless I have to. Just an old gun-nut that's curious is all. I never seen the insides of one of these Para Ordnance 45s. Thought I'd strip her down and explore."

Shake walked past some aging photos of the Chavez family until he spied a print hanging over one of Carmelita's smoky oil lamps. It looked like something she'd torn out of a magazine. It was familiar, a semi-circle of six tall marble pillars emblazoned with the imperial eagle. At the center was a statue depicting three young Mexican men—teenagers really. They looked toward the horizon with wide eyes and a firm set to their jaws. He remembered it was called *Monumento a los Ninos Heroes.* He'd seen it in person many years earlier at the urging of an old Marine buddy. Shake smiled, remembering the day when he walked into a tailor shop to have the red stripes worn by all Marine officers and NCOs sewn on the seams of his dress blue uniform trousers.

From the Halls of Montezuma – 1966

"T hem are called blood stripes," the salty old Master Gunnery Sergeant said as Shake watched a seamstress tack the red stripes on his trousers. "You know what they stand for, right?"

I had heard the story of fighting in the Mexican-American War just like every other Marine in regular history classes. According to a firmly entrenched legend, the red stripe worn by all Marine officers and NCOs was in commemoration of the blood spilled by Marines in the 1847 assault on Chapultepec. I'd also heard it was mostly myth, a Marine Corps folk-tale, and I said so. That didn't sit well with the Master Guns.

"Young agent, I'm thinking you need a little Professional Military Education." He poked me in the chest with a stubby finger. "Look here—I got a buddy on embassy duty down in Mexico City knows every detail. Why don't you go visit the Halls of Montezuma?"

Yeah—why not?

It wasn't hard to come by ten days' leave. I didn't take any delay *en route* from Lejeune to Camp Pendleton when my orders came through, so there was plenty of time on the books. And the story of my escapades down in Castro's Cuba got to the West Coast before I did, so I was pretty much on everybody's good-guy list. The Company Commander approved the time off, but when word got around that I was planning to spend my leave in Mexico, I got a call to report to the Sergeant Major of the 1st Reconnaissance Battalion. Way too many young Marines from Southern California commands crossed the nearby border into rowdy spots like Tijuana and wound up bloody or in trouble with the law. The Sergeant Major wanted reassurance that I wasn't about to embark on a monumental binge through bars and whorehouses—which he seemed to think was the only reason a Marine would go to Mexico.

The old Master Gunny helped with that. He explained that he was sending me down to stay with the Embassy Marines in Mexico City for some PME. The Sergeant Major was dubious, but he wound up approving the leave once he felt confident that I had enough money to buy my way out of a jam and would return on time and undamaged. I swung by the mainside PX to pick up some civilian clothes which turned out to be harder than it should have been. I've never had to worry much about what I wore. It was either some variety of uniform or my one pair of jeans and an old polo shirt. But the Sergeant Major said I would need to be in "appropriate civilian attire" down in Mexico City. It was regulations for off-duty Marines visiting foreign countries, so I wandered around the PX clueless until some nice lady finally took pity on me and selected a couple pairs of conservative trousers and a shirt or two to match. My spit-shined dress shoes would work, so I didn't have to shell out for footwear and I still had my old boot camp AWOL bag so luggage was handled. I was good to go and looking forward to it.

A bus ride got me to LAX where I lucked out and got a cheap military stand-by seat on a direct flight from LA to Mexico City. The Master Gunny arranged for his buddy to meet the flight, and I had a number for Gunnery Sergeant Jack Paxton at the U.S. Embassy in case our wires got crossed. The stewardesses were attentive and pleasant. They seemed to know I was military despite the civilian clothes. It

was probably the high-and-tight haircut or the Marine emblem on the windbreaker I sometimes wore for PT. Anyway,
I got a couple of free beers to drink while studying the history book Master Guns gave me. By the time we landed, I
was pretty well versed on the Mexican-American War circa
1846-1848. Marines serving with General Winfield Scott
were mentioned in passing, but there had to be much more
to it than that. Marine Corps history made a huge enough
deal out of it to include a reference in the Marines' Hymn. I
wanted details.

The brand-new passport I'd been advised to get while
based at Camp Lejeune with the globe-trotting 2nd Marine
Division prompted barely a glance from the Mexican Immigration guy and no one seemed overly interested in digging
through my AWOL bag, so I wandered down to baggage
claim looking for another Marine. Gunny Paxton was easy
to spot in undress blues with a blazing white barracks cover.
He was a handsome stocky man with dark eyes and a hard
set to his jaw, just the kind of look the Marine Corps loved
to showcase in foreign embassies around the world. He spotted me immediately and waved. We shook hands and I did
what Marines the world over do when they meet another Marine in uniform. I examined the rack of ribbons on his left
chest. He had been in Korea during that war and a few other
places. He was wearing a short-sleeve uniform shirt so I
couldn't see any hashmarks, but counting the stars on his
Good Conduct ribbon told me he had about 16 years in the
Corps.

"Welcome to Mexico City," he said in a gravelly voice
that told me he'd likely been a Drill Instructor for a couple
of those years. "We've got you set up to stay at the Martine
House on the Embassy compound. I'll have some of the off-

duty people take you out for tacos and beer tonight, and then we can do a walk-around at Chapultepec Park tomorrow."

"Master Gunny says you're pretty much an expert on that stuff." I threw my AWOL bag into the back seat of a white government-issue Chevy while he crawled behind the wheel. "Always been a big Marine Corps history buff," he said. "I figured since I'm gonna be stationed right here where it happened, I got a chance to make it come alive a little bit. You'll see what I mean tomorrow."

Dinner with some of Gunny Paxton's off-duty Marines was in one of their favorite haunts along the city's *Paseo de Reforma*, a main drag not far from the embassy. The place featured a bevy of beautiful waitresses with raven black hair and curvaceous figures wrapped in classical Mexican dresses. I did my unsuccessful best to keep from staring at her ample cleavage when one of them brought us pitchers of *Modelo Especial*. The chow was decent, I think, but I drank too much beer. By the time a fourth pitcher was delivered, I decided I most definitely liked the dark exotic look of Mexican females. Fantasizing about finding one to spend a little of my leave time with caused me to lose track of what was being said around the table. I'd get distracted and the guy telling a story or bitching about something would have to repeat it. They probably thought I was an idiot—or an asshole.

Gunny Paxton showed up the next morning in civilian clothes carrying a book of notes and maps he'd compiled during his time in Mexico City. We walked a couple of blocks along the main drag through throngs of tourists and locals either sightseeing or going about their business in the bustling city. The air was thin and full of what Californians call smog. The Gunny said it was a result of the altitude at better than 7,000 feet above sea level and the hordes of trucks, taxis and jalopies that coughed clouds of exhaust fumes into the air. We turned toward Chapultepec Park and stopped at a little cantina for coffee.

"So how much do you know about the Mexican-American War?" He began to page through his notebook as he sipped coffee. I just shrugged and tried to remember what I read on the plane.

"Well, I know it lasted a couple of years—1846 to 1848. Mexico was fairly pissed over losing Texas, and President Polk had his eyes on more Mexican land which at the time included what are now California, Arizona, and New Mexico. So we spooled up General Zachary Taylor and went to war with them in 1846. "

"OK…" Paxton turned to an old map in his notebook and spun it around so I could see. "Show me what we did when that happened." I examined the map which looked like a copy of something from a history museum. All the borders were different, but I recognized the routes American forces took when they moved on Mexico with a mixed bag of regulars and volunteers that included a detachment of Marines from the U.S. fleet standing offshore.

"So, we attack into Mexico from north and east heading for Mexico City." I ran my hand in those directions across the old map. "General Winfield Scott lands on the east coast and fights some big battles here, here, and here." I jabbed my finger at spots marked Veracruz, Cerro Gordo and Contreras. "The Mexicans got beat up pretty badly, so they asked for an armistice—in August 1847, I think."

"Good enough so far," Paxton nodded. "The armistice went into effect 20 August 1847, but it only lasted until early September. Then the shooting started again and that led right here to Chapultepec." The Gunny tossed a handful of pesos on the table and stood. "That's where it gets really interesting. Let's go."

We walked toward a sprawling park and saw a huge monument at the gate. It was all white marble and looked a little like someone had misplaced the candles on a birthday cake. There were six tall marble columns with spread-winged Imperial Mexican eagles on the face of each one. In the middle of it all was a statue of three young men who looked like they were either dying or ready to from the anguish on their sculpted faces. Inscribed on the base of the monument was *A Los Defensores La Patria* 1846-1847.

"That's what they call *Monumento a los Ninos Heroes* and it's a big deal to the Mexicans. The columns represent military school cadets who refused to surrender during the assault on Chapultepec Castle and died in place as big-time heroes."

"I read about that."

"Yeah, well don't believe everything you read, Davis. There's a lot of argument among historian about what really happened. The Mexican version is that six kids from the military school that used to be up there," he said, pointing at a huge ornate castle-like structure on a nearby hill, "refused to be evacuated with the other kids when the Americans attacked. The boys were from thirteen to seventeen years old and all studying to be officers in Santa Ana's Mexican Army. Supposedly one of them, a young guy by the name of Juan Escutia, wraps himself in a Mexican flag and jumps to his death rather than surrender."

"That must have taken a huge pair of balls."

"It doesn't take balls to commit suicide, Corporal Davis." Gunny Paxton shook his head and grinned. "If you're a good soldier, you die fighting the enemy. You don't voluntarily give the enemy your life no matter how shitty the situation might be."

We walked away from the monument and climbed the road leading to the top of Chapultepec Hill where Gunny Paxton said we'd get a better idea of how the fighting progressed. The ornate structure stood about 200 feet above a surrounding park and we reached it after a steep climb that left us both panting. Our destination used to be an Imperial palace, but now it housed the Mexican Natural History Museum. "You can come back some other day and take a look at that," the Gunny said steering me toward a long balcony that overlooked the entire sprawl of Mexico City to the east of the castle mount. "For today, we focus on the battle of Chapultepec."

"So the armistice is in the crapper," I said.

"Yeah," he confirmed, "and on 8 September, General Winfield Scott moves on Mexico City. Assault troops are under command of Army General William Worth…"

"Worth—as in Fort Worth in Texas?"

"Check, and he is ordered to attack the city through the Belen and San Cosme gates. Those were over in that direction." He pointed at the city sprawl, but I couldn't see anything that looked like a gate through a dingy cloud of smog. "Now, in order to get troops to those gates, Worth needs to get past two strong points: a fortified old mill they called Molino del Rey…" He pointed to the west of the castle toward lower ground. "And you're standing on the other one. This place was the highest ground, which made for excellent defense. It housed the Mexican Military Academy among other things, and it was a kind of symbol to the Mexican people who knew they were getting their asses handed to them in the war with the gringos."

"I read something on the plane that said the fight at Molino del Rey was a bitch."

"It was that, Davis. Fortunately it didn't last too long. See, the Mexican defenders at one stage fought off an American attack and then they snuck out at night and bayoneted all the wounded. That pissed off the American troops and they decided that there was gonna be no mercy. The next day they overran the mill and slaughtered everybody they could find."

"So now they've gotta get up here and take the castle. How many Mexicans were holding this place?"

"There were about a thousand soldiers under Mexican General Nicolas Bravo, who was one of the good ones in a generally bad bunch, plus some cadets from the military academy. There might have been about two hundred of them. Most were either killed or evacuated after the assault got started—except for those six who decided to stay. And Bravo's got thirteen cannons up here positioned to fire downhill."

"Now our arty comes into play, right?" I pointed at the American cannon and field artillery batteries marked on the Gunny's map.

"Affirmative. General Scott orders his artillery to pound the crap out of the fortifications up here so he can go for the high ground. The next day on 13 September at 0800, two assault elements began charging up here and trying to scale the walls. Things got intense—lots of bayonet and hand-to-hand stuff—and the Americans were still pissed about Molino del Rey, so they didn't take many prisoners. An hour and a half later, General Bravo is a POW and our flag is flying over Chapultepec. But the action ain't over by a long shot."

"I'm missing the whole Marine Corps connection, Gunny."

"There were Marines in the initial assault attached to Army Brigadier General John Quitman's 4th Division. They got ate up a bit crossing the open ground below the castle from the south, but they recovered after the castle fell and took off running east and chasing the Mexicans who were retreating toward Mexico City. This is where it gets interesting. There were about thirty-six Leathernecks under three Marine officers. Senior man was Captain George Terret and he had two lieutenants: First Lieutenant John Simms and one Second Lieutenant Charles Henderson, who just happened to be the son of Colonel Archibald Henderson, Commandant of the Marine Corps at the time."

"The grand old man of the Marine Corps—longest serving Commandant we ever had. He was boss for forty years, right?"

"Thirty-nine to be exact. Anyway, his son is with the Marines at Chapultepec, and they're chasing retreating Mexican soldiers down a long causeway that leads to the San Cosme Gate to the capital. They're under heavy fire all the way but going balls to the wall. And that charge prompts about twenty soldiers under a lieutenant by the name of Ulysses S. Grant—the future American President—to join the party. Lieutenants Simms and Henderson make it to the end of the causeway with about eighty-five men and they try to storm the gate. No dice; too much fire from the defenders. So Simms takes seven Marines around to the left while Henderson goes right up the middle with the rest and they manage to take the San Cosme Gate. Mexico City is now up for grabs. General Quitman rushes in reinforcements and they blow right through to the Grand Plaza. Quitman puts Marines in place to guard the National Plaza which is…" Gunny Paxton raised his eyebrows and pointed at me.

"Which is the place once known as the Halls of Montezuma."

"Bingo, Corporal Davis—hence the line of a song we both know and love. When the surviving Marines get back Stateside, they present Commandant Archibald Henderson with a sword. On the blade are inscribed the words 'From the Halls of Montezuma to the Shores of Tripoli'."

"And 90 percent of the Marines who fought here were KIA? That's what we heard in boot camp. That's what started the blood stripe tradition?"

"Remember I told you not to believe everything you read?" Gunny Paxton shut his notebook and smiled. "Truth is out of about four hundred Marines who fought here, only seven of them were killed."

"That's disappointing…"

"Never let the facts get in the way of a good war story, Corporal Davis. And Marines had started to wear a red stripe on their trousers in 1840 before this war even started. We copied it from the Doggies."

Gunny Paxton had the watch the next day, and I spent it shopping for a souvenir which was mostly boring and unproductive. I had no idea what I might do with a straw sombrero back at Camp Pendleton, so I tossed the one I bought into a handy gutter where it was immediately policed up by a gaggle of kids who were following me and offering various relatives for sexual pleasures beyond my wildest imagination. I ate a bowl of delicious meatball soup called *albondigas* for a late lunch and then wandered aimlessly around downtown Mexico City wondering what to do with myself for the next eight days. Around dusk, I found myself in a quiet part of the big city, an area that looked like it catered to families rather than tourists. There were kids playing in well-kept yards and none of them wanted candy or offered their sisters for sale. The people sitting on shaded porches waved and smiled as I passed. It was pleasant in a non-touristy, comfortable way and it made me forget that I was in a foreign country.

At the corner of this shaded street was a little cantina with a neatly-lettered sign in the window announcing it was called *La Fiesta*. No neon glitz or hustle, it looked just like a corner bar, a neighborhood watering hole. Inside I was the only white face, but that didn't seem to be a problem. I got nods and smiles from the locals as I walked up to the bar.

The barkeep had oil-slicked hair and a pencil-thin mustache. He reminded me of Leo Carrillo playing the Cisco Kid on my favorite TV show when I was little, the only fictional character that held my interest beyond Sgt. Rock and the Combat Happy Joes of Easy Company. I glanced up at the beer signs hanging behind the bar and decided what I really needed was a taste of the local busthead. You know, when in Rome—and all that happy horseshit.

"Tequila, por favor." I pulled out a big wad of pesos that I'd gotten for my U.S. dollars at a local kiosk and watched the barkeep's eyebrows lift. This was not a place where gringo high-rollers usually visited. I peeled off some bills, pocketed the roll, and waited for my drink. It came in a smudged glass that was somewhere between a quick snort and highball size. The barman policed up some money and left me alone. Looking around the place in the dim light, I could see the locals were over me and back to their own concerns. They were mostly laughing or listening to a clunky old jukebox in a corner that blared songs full of wheezy accordion music backing voices that seemed to be moaning or crying as much as singing.

There were just two or three other solos at the bar, and most of them were sucking beer through big mustaches. I sniffed the drink and looked around, smiling politely whenever someone returned my glance. At the back of the joint was a stunning woman who seemed to be circulating happily among the customers. She was voluptuous. Short and buxom with sturdy legs showing beneath a knee-length skirt that hugged her hips, she had a brilliant smile full of white teeth that glowed in the candlelight when she smiled. Unlike the waitresses at the only other local place I'd visited, the long hair cascading down her back was maybe a dark brown, or some other color between jet black and tawny maple. And she didn't act like a wage slave. She seemed more like a greeter or an emissary of good will. Everyone wanted to talk to her. She was gorgeous, a sexual fantasy, laughing with people in a familiar way, giving equal time and attention to both men and women.

It was hard for me to turn away, but there was a smoky old mirror behind the bar that let me keep an eye on her, so I spun on my stool and hit the tequila. It went down like a mouthful of paint thinner. This was clearly stuff for the hardy Mexican drinker brought up on hot sauce. My eyes watered and I fought to keep from gagging. The barman heard my gasps and came over showing a big smile. *"Ten ciuadado,"* he said and swept the glass off the bar. He was back in a couple of minutes with another drink in a better-looking glass with salt crusted around the rim. *"Prueba esto, amigo,"* he said, then plucked a few more bills from the bar and walked away chuckling. I was sure the concoction sitting before me was a margarita as I'd had one or two of those in Mexican restaurants on the other side of the border.

The initial hit of tequila was still threatening to leave my belly for some fresh air. My eyes were watering and I was trying to catch my breath as I tried to decide if I should give the new drink a chance. That's when the woman I'd been watching slithered onto the barstool at my side. She smiled and offered me a napkin. I just stared like a clueless dip-shit, so she began to dab at my watering eyes. "Tequila will Te-kill-ya," she said in a whispery voice and flashed those snow-white teeth in a friendly smile. "Sorry if it didn't go down so well." She spoke good English with a distinctive accent that I recognized from some of the Chicanos I knew in the Marine Corps. There was a non-native lilt and pronunciation peculiar to Latinos that spoke English as a second language.

"Thanks," I said trying to sound cool. "I'm new at this."

"Is it your first time in Mexico City?"

"First time…"

"You like it here?"

"Little early to tell—but the girls are beautiful."

Dumb-ass thing to say, but she just raised an eyebrow. I decided to go for broke and stuck out my hand. "My name is Shake."

She pondered that, smiling and staring at my hand. "As in shake hands?"

"As in short for a name I hate," I said. "Everybody just calls me Shake even if they don't shake my hand."

She laughed and it was like hearing the bass throb from a bandstand. The sound came from deep in her throat, a mixture of giggle and gargle. She looked at me curiously as if she was deciding whether it was a joke. And then she took my hand. She had soft skin but not what I expected. She shook like a man, firm and dry with a pleasant pressure.

"What's your name?" I asked, feeling the heat of her presence and hoping she wouldn't just hop up and leave after the introductions. She pointed at the glass sitting on the bar and it took me a minute.

"What? Your name is Tequila?"

She wet her finger and rubbed some salt from the rim of my glass. I swear I could see little gold flecks dancing in her dark eyes. She pointed again at my glass and then it dawned on me.

"Margarita. Your name is Margarita?"

"*Si*, my name is Margarita—Margarita Estella Chavez. My family owns this cantina. How do you come to be in Mexico City?"

I rambled on through a couple more drinks about coming down to visit Chapultepec and a bunch of other stuff. She wandered away occasionally to visit with customers at the tables but she always seemed to wind up back next to me. By the time the barkeep announced they were about to close, I'd told her my whole life story. There wasn't much to it except for a couple of Marine Corps sea stories. I resisted the temptation to tell her too many personal things as that just didn't feel right—or very interesting—but she probed and seemed genuinely interested in all the details about my hometown and my folks. Maybe she was just being polite, doing what a good hostess does to keep paying customers happy, but if that was all it was, she was a damn fine actor.

"Listen," I said when she returned to the bar after shuttling some over-indulged customers toward the door. "You've really been very kind. I mean—I think you're terrific. Is there a way I might see you again? You know, maybe take you to dinner or something?"

She thought about that for a bit, leaning on the bar and staring into my eyes like she was searching for something to help her make up her mind about me. "Maybe," she said with a smile. "Everyone has to eat, and I know some places that you might enjoy."

"Just let me know where and when."

She talked for a while with the bartender who just smiled and shrugged. "*Bueno*," she said. "Tomorrow night we will meet at this place." She pulled a pen out of her pocket, scribbled on a paper napkin, and handed it to me. "I will be there at seven. Will you?"

I pocketed the napkin and stuck out my hand. "I promise. Shake on it?"

"Shake with Shake…" She laughed again, that wonderful chuckle that seemed so genuine and enticing. Then she took my hand and led me to the door.

Dinner the next night was an event. We met at a huge outdoor restaurant surrounding a plaza where Mexican singers, musicians, and dancers kept up a continuous show. She was wearing a long pleated skirt and a low-cut blouse that pulled my eyes to her chest like a magnet. I'm sure she noticed, but Margarita didn't seem to mind. Or maybe she was used to it. She had an earthy, open aspect to her beauty that attracted attention, and I wasn't the only guy there that was staring in her direction.

The menu was all in Spanish but I recognized *albondigas* and ordered it. Margarita was delighted with my choice and told me that her mother made the best meatball soup in the country. She'd been born right here in Mexico City and was studying off and on at a big university with hopes of working overseas as a diplomat. She had the personality for it, no question. Despite my clumsy attempts to be suave and attractive—two of many things which I definitely am not—she laughed a lot and made me comfortable. She pulled me up for an audience-participation folk dance, but I just watched from the sidelines as she lifted her long skirt and stole the show. She inspired the mariachi quartet providing the music, moving with a fluid grace, alternating between snappy little steps and long swooping swirls. And she got a standing ovation when the music finally stopped.

It was a wonderful evening that ended with a sweet kiss when she left to go home. I offered to take her, hoping to build on the brief body contact that left me breathless and sweating in the cool night air. She said she could make it fine on her own which was disappointing, but my spirits improved when she made a date for the next day when she would take me to the Mexican National History Museum.

When she chugged away in a cab, I stood for a while staring at the departing tail lights. There was a full moon over Mexico City that night, and I smiled up at it as I began to walk in a direction I thought would lead to the embassy. My heart was pounding like I'd just finished a hard PT session. All I could think about was seeing Margarita again. By the time I'd covered a block or two, I was fantasizing about seeing her naked. It was clear at that point that sleep was out of the question. It had been a good night, a very good night, and I didn't want it to end. What this night called for was a celebration.

Looking around at an intersection where I had to wait for traffic, I noticed I had wandered very near the monument that marked the entrance to Chapultepec Park. There was a string of touristy joints along the street ahead, but none of them seemed right. I wanted something more ethnic, some place that would remind me of her. I turned down a little side street and immediately found a noisy cantina about half a block from the main drag. It was fairly crowded and I had to shoulder my way through a clutch of men smoking and joking outside the entrance. Inside it was smoky and muggy with a distinct sleaze factor. There were clutches of whip-thin angry-looking guys sucking on beer bottles and a bevy of chubby girls wearing too much make-up and not enough clothes. It should have been a warning. I should have turned around and found another bar, but I was lost in a romantic cloud. That was my first mistake.

A couple of overweight guys split to make room for me at the crowded bar. The one on my right was wearing red bandana around his sweaty forehead. The one on the left had a cascade of greasy hair trapped by a sweat-stained John Deere cap. I clocked the evil-eye they flashed, but I was in too good a mood to pay serious attention—or exercise any sober judgment about what I did next—which was buy them a beer. When the barkeep showed up with three bottles, I pulled the wad of cash out of my pocket and held it out so he could take what he needed. That was my second mistake.

I had two more beers and bought two more for my new *amigos* who didn't speak much English. They seemed to squeeze closer to me with each drink and they needed a bath more than the beer I was buying them. After an hour or so, I decided it was time to leave. It was *adios* and *gracias* a couple of times and then I was back out on the nearly deserted streets. Trying to get my bearings, I decided to walk toward the park. From there I could probably remember the way back to the embassy.

They were waiting for me near a stand of nicely trimmed hedges just on the other side of the park entrance. Good place for what they had in mind. It was well away from the spill of light from the monument, an easy spot to drag somebody off the street and into the trees along the park perimeter. The guy in the John Deere hat shuffled around trying to get behind me. His buddy in the red bandana held out a hand, pointed at my trousers and said something about *dinero*. There was no *por favor* to it. These clowns wanted to take my money. In a better state of mind, I probably wouldn't have said *fuck you guys* but that's what I said and that's when I saw the knife. It was long and thin like something you'd use to slice grapefruit or gut a fish.

I was focused on that blade, but I felt the second man make his move behind me. He looped a fat forearm around my neck but I grabbed an elbow with one hand and a hunk of hair with the other, thrust back hard to upset his balance, and rolled him over my shoulder. He hit the pavement hard and I stomped down on his solar plexus. The air blew out of him with a groan, and I figured he was down for a while. I turned to run back toward the monument where there might be a cop or watchman on duty. The guy with the blade blocked that route and dropped into a combat crouch. He looked like he'd been in a knife-fight or two prior to this encounter. I was flashing on my close-combat instruction. *You are never completely unarmed. There's always something you can use.*

Grabbing the John Deere cap off his buddy's head, I danced around to the right side of red bandana and swatted at the knife blade hoping he'd lunge. I needed him to commit and throw himself off balance. He was too smart or experienced for that. He whipped the knife under the hat and cut a long gash in my right forearm. Ignoring that as best I could, I managed to hit him hard with an overhand left that crunched into his head just below his right ear. That set him back a step and I tried to slip past but he grabbed my arm and stabbed at my mid-section. I saw the flash of the blade and contorted away from it but he slashed right through my shirt and opened a long wound along my ribcage. I doubled over, feeling blood running down my side, and he got cocky. He took a long, wild swipe at my face which turned him around and that gave me a shot at his legs. I kicked hard and heard a crack when my foot impacted the side of his knee. He went down and I stomped on his hand until he let go of the knife. Kicking the blade away into the dark, I turned and ran back toward the monument and the light.

I was sitting at the base of the *Monumento a los Ninos Heroes* dripping blood on the white marble when a security guard spotted me. In minutes I was surrounded by Mexico City cops. A couple of them took off to look for the guys who attacked me, but I have no idea if they ever found them. Before they got back, I was in an ambulance and headed for a hospital. A very nice doctor put 12 stitches in my right forearm and 23 more in the flesh over my ribcage while an English-speaking cop took my statement. He seemed sort of bored with the whole thing after it became clear that I hadn't committed any kind of crime. The doctor whacked me with a tetanus shot and decided I needed to stay in the hospital overnight, so I called the Marine House at the embassy and got Gunny Paxton out of bed. He was not happy.

He showed up at the hospital the next morning with an officer in civilian clothes. The officer went over events with me and said he'd have to file a report, but there was nothing much to worry about as I was the victim and not the culprit. Gunny Paxton had my AWOL bag with him and he'd packed all my gear. His considered opinion was that I should leave Mexico City and do my recuperating back at Camp Pendleton. And his considered opinion came in the form of an order.

I wrote a long, stupid mash note for Margarita, put it in a hospital envelope and asked the Gunny to deliver it to *La Fiesta* when he had the chance. I don't know if he did that or not. I never heard from her again, and I had enough trouble explaining to the Sergeant Major why I returned damaged from my short leave in Mexico. The old Master Gunny thought it was hilarious that a modern Marine wound up spilling blood at the Halls of Montezuma.

The baseball game was over. Rangers won by two runs in extra innings. Manny and Mike were drowsing over Uncle Manuel's checker board. Aunt Carmelita was making up a cot for Joaquin. Carlotta was outside in the camper, hopefully asleep. Shake outlined some vague plans to head out for further reconnaissance at mid-morning and decided to get some rest.

The dome light was on when he pulled open the door of the camper. Carlotta was propped up on an elbow reading a Louis L'Amour western. She was wearing an oversized sweatshirt and not much else as she closed the book and rolled over in the little berth along one wall of the camper shell. "That's you right over there," she said pointing at a similar berth along the opposite wall. There was very little space between the two beds, but Shake decided to trust that she'd stay put for the night and peeled off his shirt.

"Looks like you've been punctured a time or two." She pointed at two keloid dimples on his upper right chest.

"Vietnam—I caught a couple of AK rounds—nothing too serious." He plumped at the flimsy mattress and decided to keep his khakis on that night. There were more scars from war wounds below the belt that didn't merit display or discussion.

"Did you get him?"

"Get who?"

"The guy who shot you—must have been a guy, right? Or was it one of them female VC guerillas we heard about?"

"I have no idea, Carlotta. Never saw the guy. I was shooting at muzzle flashes. Apparently, he had a little better view of the action."

She just lay there staring as he tried to get settled for the night. When he stretched for a pillow, Carlotta reached across to trace the scar on his ribcage. "How about that one? That ain't no bullet wound."

"Knife—different kind of combat—couple of idiots tried to rob me down in Mexico City. It was a long time ago."

"You are a man with a colorful past, Gunner Shake Davis. I'm gonna get you to tell me about some of that."

"Not tonight, Carlotta." He snapped off the dome light and rolled into the bunk. Sleep was a long time coming. He spent a couple of hazy hours thinking about Margarita Estella Chavez. Was she still alive? Did she ever become a diplomat? What might have happened if those two assholes in Mexico City hadn't ended his leave so quickly? There were more questions with no answers when he felt Carlotta's hand on his thigh. It was warm and still. She didn't move it toward his crotch. Maybe it was an accident. Maybe it was just Carlotta doing some wishful thinking as she slept. Shake ignored it and finally fell asleep.

H asim, the ISIS representative, was pacing and shouting into a cell phone at his ear when Wafic Aziz arrived at the warehouse to begin filling the 55-gallon drums that would constitute the explosive heart of his bomb. Wafic noted with some surprise that the conversation was in Arabic. He set Ibrahim to moving the containers to a little sluice they'd built to make filling them with the ANFO slurry easier and safer. Then he prepared tea on a little hotplate and tried to make some sense of the one-sided phone conversation.

Hasim was angry and arguing with someone. He would listen for a while, pacing like a caged beast, and then start shouting that he was the command representative and his orders would be obeyed. At one point, Wafic heard him say that a schedule must be advanced, that there was bound to be increased security. That worried him regarding the mission at hand, and he vowed to ask some questions when the phone call ended.

"That's odd," he said when Hasim finally jammed the cell phone in a pocket.

"What's odd?" Hasim accepted a cup of tea and sipped at it.

"You were speaking our language on the phone. Isn't that dangerous?"

"A chance I had to take," Hasim sighed trying to get his temper under control. "I was talking to a brother in Mexico. There is only so much I can manage when talking to a stupid man who refuses to do as he's ordered."

"Is there anything you need to tell me?"

"It's nothing to worry about," Hasim waved a hand dismissively. "I have heard from our sources down in Mexico that there is a special unit forming, specifically designed to hunt for our people crossing the border."

"Is this information reliable?"

"It comes from the same people we employed to get you and the others across the American border. They are well-paid and well-connected."

"Yes. Well, that is Mexico. We are here with a vital mission at hand."

"There are other missions planned, Wafic. And they will be harder to accomplish once we make the attack in Fort Worth. I want to get things moving before that happens."

Wafic was putting what he'd heard in context. "You want the brothers in Mexico to make their crossing earlier than planned."

"Yes, we need to get started, get them into the U.S. and hidden before something happens to make crossing the border too risky."

"And you are getting an argument about that?"

"The man leading the follow-on team is an idiot! He's an Iranian who once served in the Revolutionary Guards Quds Force. He resents taking orders, and he's too stupid to grasp what I'm telling him."

"So what will you do?"

"He will be receiving a call soon from our superiors in Raqqa. He will listen and obey—or the security force we've hired will eliminate him."

Wafic nodded and finished his tea. He had other things to worry about and experience had long ago taught him to focus clearly on the task at hand. A man who dealt with explosives did not live long any other way.

"The situation does not affect our schedule?"

"No—as long as the *kafir* cowboys do not change the date for their big event."

Tech Sergeant Sid Atwood was on duty at the monitors when her civilian boss walked into the task force tech-support tank. She was sipping morning coffee, and her brown eyes were glued to the monitor as she motioned for the watch commander to take a look.

"A little action this morning," she said as Carr gazed over her shoulder. "I don't know what it means, but this guy…" She pointed at one of the figures that she knew by now was supposedly some kind of Middle Eastern terrorist in training, "…has been doing a lot of talking on a cell phone. He doesn't look too happy. We've seen him take at least two calls, and he's calling someone right now. Saw him punching numbers. Wish we had the ability to monitor that."

"We do," FBI Supervisory Special Agent Joe Carr said. "You guys ain't the only game in town, you know?"

"You've got some spooks that can hack his phone calls?"

"That's need to know, Sid—strictly need to know. Have our watchers showed up this morning?"

"Not yet. I'll let you know if and when we see them."

Carr's cell phone chirped and he pulled it out to look at the caller ID. "I gotta take this. Let me know what develops." He walked out away from the little metal cube packed with electronics where his cell reception would be better and clicked on to the call.

"We got some interesting traffic from down south." The CT Task Force rep at the National Security Agency in Fort

Meade, Maryland sounded anxious. "It was between two Arabic speakers. We got it translated and I'm sending you a transcript."

"Give me the quick and dirty."

"No names as usual, but the guy who placed the call is somewhere near Dallas, Texas. We're working to refine that. You know where the other guy is."

"Yeah, we're doing facial comparisons in the data base. We'll have a name before long if he's in there. So what did they have to say?"

"Mostly they were yelling at each other about a change to some schedule. I got the impression the guy in Texas was telling the guy in Mexico to pack it up ASAP and get moving. Given what we already know, I'd guess that means head north, right?"

"OK, I'll get back to you after I've read the transcript. Let me know right away if you can do any better on the Dallas location." Carr ended the call and made another.

"How close are you to ready?"

"A lot closer than we were yesterday down in Mexico City. I've got two helos and most of the bodies moved to the jump-off area."

"We got some new information so it might go in a hurry. How quick can you get in on the site?"

"Probably need a half-hour to get loaded and airborne. We're sitting about thirty-five miles southwest of the objective and the Blackhawks will cruise at around one-fifty knots—so call it twenty minutes from here to there."

"Work on cutting down the launch time. I'll get back to you."

Tamaulipan Mattoral

Shake and Mike lay prone on the hill watching the training site at mid-morning. According to their reconnaissance SOP, Manny Chavez was down below them on rear security and connected by the signal rope. It was a little more promising today. There had been a phone call to one of the guys in training and that had thrown some crap in his game—whatever it was. There was some florid discussion accompanied by plenty of arm waving, and Mike got a good recording of some angry outbursts in Arabic. It looked and sounded like an argument or at least a very heated discussion. The point was that it was in Arabic rather than the fractured English they'd picked up previously, and Shake was hoping it might reveal something incriminating.

Before the call, they'd gotten some good shots of two men working with what looked like dynamite and what appeared to be either Semtex or something like C-4. The detonations had been spectacular and this was clearly not the kind of thing your bog-standard survivalist could do for kicks out in some American wasteland. He still didn't have anything on camera that definitely said Mexico, but what they had plus sworn statements about where it was observed should be enough to instigate some official action. Shake was thinking about calling it off and heading home when Mike tapped his shoulder and pointed.

He reoriented his long-range microphone and tapped his headset. "He's on the phone again—more Arabic." Shake eyed the little compound. All three security men were idling around the campfire eating something out of tin plates. It didn't look ominous and security was definitely not concerned with any change in routine, but the phone calls were unusual and they instantly put a halt to activities. Shake had a feeling that he was watching something develop down below, something different than what they'd been observing for the past two days.

Through a long lens, he watched the man on the phone end the call. He stuffed the phone in a jacket pocket and spoke to the others sitting nearby in the shade. They rose wordlessly and walked toward a small pop-up shelter tent that appeared to be their field accommodation. Senior man with the phone approached the campfire and spoke to the security team. Shake nudged Mike and told him to point the microphone in that direction. Mike listened intently and then whispered, "Hard to hear it all, but at least they're speaking English." Mike pressed the phones to his ears and concentrated. "He's telling Ortega they've gotta move. Ortega is arguing about that—talking about money or something. Shit. I'm losing them."

Ortega and the phone man had turned their backs to the hill and were walking around to the other side of the trailer, both in a serious discussion that involved gestures at the northern horizon. And in that direction is the border, Shake thought as he began to piece together the clues. Over by the little pop-up tent, he saw a man tossing bedding and clothing to his buddy who began to stuff it into a backpack. The two security guys around the campfire were on their feet and seemed to be waiting for orders.

He jerked on the line to Manny Chavez and scooted back to where he could be heard. "It looks like they may be gonna move out of here," he whispered. "Head on back and tell Joaquin to pack up and be ready to roll. It's gonna take some time to pack all their shit and sanitize the site. We're gonna hang out here for a little while and then we'll be right behind you."

"We gonna try and follow them?"

"If we can. I'll call you with updates."

Manny Chavez took off running down the ditch headed north in a crouch. Shake crawled back next to Mike. He set the camera aside and pulled out his little Mexican burner phone to check the charge. It showed a full green bar. Activity at the site left no doubt there was a move in progress. Two security men were hooking the trailer to the truck. Two other men were digging a hole and burying something Shake couldn't see clearly. Ortega was pacing around the clearing talking on a cell phone. "See what you can get on that," he told Mike. "He's probably calling his highers for instructions."

"We gonna hang around?"

"Just a little bit longer," Shake said. "And then we split."

S pecial Agent Joe Carr stood watching the monitor in the UAV tank with his phone in his hand. He'd read the transcript sent by his man at NSA, and it was clear to him that the yahoos training south of the border were pushing up their schedule for moving north. He didn't intend to let them get any closer to the United States than they already were.

He backed away from the monitor and addressed everyone else in the tank, UAV pilot, observer and analyst. "If I was to ask for a consensus here, what would you folks say is happening at the site?"

"Somebody got orders to hit the road," the pilot said.

"They're packing up to beat feet," his observer added.

"You don't hook up a trailer unless you're gonna tow it somewhere." TSgt. Sid Atwood confirmed.

"Nice to know we're all thinking the same thing." Carr leaned over Atwood's shoulder and closer to the screen. He couldn't immediately see if Shake Davis and Mike Stokey were in the area watching his targets. If those two were still clowning around out there, he might have to delay the launch, and that was something he couldn't afford to do. For some reason his targets were about to move, and Joe Carr now considered the surveillance phase of his operation at an end.

"What's the story on those guys we spotted up on the hill?" The last thing he wanted was to get civilians involved when he sent in the arrest team. Anything could happen if people started shooting. He needed the prime targets alive for interrogation, and he was in no mood to explain how he let a couple of civilians get dinged in a high-priority operation like this one.

"One of them took off headed north about ten minutes ago." Atwood jiggled her mouse and the perspective on the screen shifted to include the high ground to the east of the site. "The other two are still up there." She adjusted the camera angle. "No—wait. Here you go, sir. The other two are backing off down the hill."

"Good." Carr slowly released the breath he'd been holding. Maybe Gunner Davis was ignoring his order to butt out and leave Mexico, but that was a concern for later. For now it was good enough to see that the potential turds in his punchbowl were moving away from the action. "OK. I'd like to know where those two are headed, but priority remains on the objective site. You'll be seeing some action shortly, and I want full coverage on that."

"Can you give us a little heads-up?" The pilot growled over his shoulder. "Or would that force you to have us all shot?"

"Full briefing when I get back," Carr said and headed for the door. When he was outside and away from interference, he hit a number on his speed-dial.

"They're about to move. Go!"

When they'd jogged a couple of hundred meters away from the site, Shake called a halt. They were at a point where the long cut they used to reach the site was interrupted by a rocky, meandering road. It wasn't much more than a trail through stands of cactus, but it would support a vehicle.

"They're not gonna take off on foot, right? They'll use that truck," he said pointing at the trail through the hard-scrabble terrain. "And this looks like the only route they can take."

Mike Stokey stood looking east and west. "Yeah. You don't go four-wheeling across this stuff in a piece-of-shit truck pulling a trailer. They'll take the easy route cross-country."

"And that means they'll have to come right by here…" Shake was trying to do the navigation in his head. "This thing has got to lead to some kind of main road—and they'd be headed for that." He flipped open his phone and stabbed at the number for Manny Chavez.

"You back at Uncle Manuel's?"

"Yeah. Just got here. We're loading the truck now."

"You know that little trail we've been crossing on the way to the site? Ask Uncle Manuel where it goes in the northerly direction."

There was a pause and Shake could hear Manny shouting in Spanish. "He says it runs for four or five clicks and comes out on Route 97. From there you go left for Reynosa or right for Matamoros."

"Got it, Manny." Shake began to improvise rapidly. "Here's what we do. You, Joaquin, and Carlotta take the truck and park it somewhere near where that trail intersects Route 97. Get Manuel to show you where that is on the map if he can. Just hang around there like you've got trouble with the truck or something."

"OK—then what?"

"Find out which way they turn on 97. You know what their truck and trailer looks like."

"You sure they're gonna be heading north, Shake? They could go south."

"Yeah, damn—ask Manuel what's to the south." There was more Spanish conversation and Manny was back on the call.

"He says a whole lot of nothing for a long way until San Fernando and that's way the hell south of here."

"So we figure they head north, either toward Reynosa or Matamoros to be closer to the border. You'll see them when they turn onto 97. When you know which way they're headed, you can drive back and pick us up at Manuel's place."

"Don't you think we ought to follow them?"

Shake thought about that for a few seconds and decided it was too risky. If the Mexican goons spotted a tail—and that wouldn't be hard to do with the sparse traffic on the desert highways—they might be inclined to lose it by ambush. "No, don't try to follow them, Manny. Just find out which way they're headed and give me a call."

"OK, got it. Anything else?"

"Yeah. Let me talk to Joaquin."

"Howdy, Shake. We're about ready to roll. You headed in this direction?"

"Mike and I are gonna stay out here and watch the trail to make sure our targets go where we think they're going."

"Where's that?"

"It's gotta be either Reynosa or Matamoros, which puts them across the border from McAllen or Brownsville. You still tied in to Rangers or Border Patrol in those areas?"

"I've got some numbers for both."

"OK. You've seen the pictures of their truck, and we made a note of the license. We've got pictures of the guys in training out here and the Mexicans including Ortega. Carlotta should have them all in her computer. Get hold of somebody you trust, and send them the photos. They should be on the lookout for any or all of them trying to cross the border."

"I can do that. Anything else?"

"Not right now, Joaquin. I'll talk to you soonest."

Two National Police UH-60 Blackhawk helicopters supporting the CT Task Force in northern Mexico chopped through the dry desert air in trail formation on a northwesterly heading. There was an American FBI Special Agent along with a team of four *Grupo de Operaciones Especial* Mexican SWAT cops in each bird. They represented some solid experience and serious firepower. Each highly trained *Federale*, wearing ninja-black nomex and body armor marked POLICIA in fluorescent letters, carried either an M-4 carbine or an H&K MP-5 sub-gun along with a sidearm. Most of those were the standard Beretta M-9, but a few of the cowboys in FBI Special Agent Bob Neely's lead helicopter were sporting Smith & Wesson 686 wheel-guns in .357 caliber.

And there was even a sniper armed with an M-40A3 militarized version of the Remington 700 bolt-gun. When these Mexican special operators went, they went strapped.

Special Agent Neely left the basic armament up to his GOPES counterpart. A display of significant firepower when they swooped down on their suspects might preclude a firefight. On the other hand, he thought as the pilot signaled they were five minutes from the objective, if the bastards want a fight, they'll get it. His orders were to do all in his power to take the Middle Eastern suspects alive. As senior man, Agent Neely briefed the mission with an emphasis on that.

As is the case with any potentially deadly raid operation, the FBI agents were authorized to shoot in self-defense, but Agent Neely and his partner Agent Sally Pritchett restricted their personal gear to issue Glock 19 pistols and raid jackets over SAPI plates. Their major concern was to locate the three men they'd been watching for the past week and take them into FBI custody. That shouldn't be too tough, but you never knew in a thing like this. The *Federales* were supposed to focus on this guy Ortega and the other two goons working as hired guns or border-crossing guides. If they thought it was necessary to blow those assholes away—well, you had to go with the host-country flow in a multinational operation.

Leaning out the right-hand door of the Blackhawk, Neely saw the objective looming on the horizon. From his airborne perspective, it looked just like the aerials from the Global Hawk they used to plan the operation. Afternoon sun glinted on the aluminum roof of the trailer, and he focused his binoculars on that. It looked like they were trying to move it. There was a cloud of dust and debris being churned up by the truck and some people pushing for traction. The only way out of the clearing was a little track that led away from the high ground in a westerly direction toward a faint trail that ran north-south.

Neely keyed his radio and spoke to the pilot. "We need to cut them off before they get rolling. Put us down right across that access trail leading out of the site."

"What the hell is this?" Mike Stokey stood pointing at the approaching helicopters. They could see black figures with weapons crowded in the aircraft doors. "Those are police helicopters."

"Damn sure are." Shake watched one bird descend in a cloud of dust and sand on the west side of the clearing and the other glide down onto the high ground they'd used as an observation point. Black-clad cops swarmed out of the helos and through the dust-cloud with their weapons at the high-ready. Then the helicopters lifted away and began to orbit over the clearing. That's when the shooting started.

Shake and Mike ducked instinctively. "That's a raid if I've ever seen one." Stokey listened to what sounded like a short, sharp firefight in the distance. "Looks like we got some action on this thing after all."

"Yeah, well…" Shake was fighting an urge to head for the site and watch the action, but it didn't seem like a good move for a couple of unauthorized gringos packing illegal pistols. The Mexican cops would frown on that, and they'd likely wind up in jail. "Give Manny a call and shut them down. Tell them to stay put for now, and let's get out of here."

They were crossing the trail at a trot headed north when they ran into Miguel Sandoval-Ortega and one of his fellow goons sprinting away from the clash in the clearing. Neither of the fleeing Mexicans paused longer than it took to level their weapons and open fire. The shotgun blast loosed by Ortega didn't do much more than make a lot of noise at a range of about 50 meters, but he had two barrels on the scatter-gun and he was closing fast. His buddy was the one with the mini-Uzi. The burst from that was badly aimed but more effective. Mike Stokey caught a round, dropped the phone he'd been using, and tumbled into the ditch on the other side of the trail.

Shake jumped down beside him and reached for the .45 at the small of his back. A second shotgun blast went over his head, but a spray of rounds from the Uzi chewed ground very close to Shake and stung him with flying shards. He shot a quick glance at Stokey who was trying to determine how badly he'd been hit and then peeked over the rim of the ditch. The two Mexicans were pounding toward him. If they reached the ditch it would mean a close-quarter fight that Shake and Mike would likely lose.

Shake propped his pistol on the edge of the cut and brought the front sight to bear on the guy with the sub-gun who represented the most pressing threat. He triggered two rounds and saw the man tumble. He shifted aim toward Ortega who had tossed the empty shotgun and drawn his pistol. He was rapidly trying to empty the Beretta magazine in Shake's direction, and rounds were flying close overhead. Shake was about to squeeze the trigger again when Ortega suddenly crumpled and went down hard. For a second Shake thought he'd fired reflexively without realizing it. It wouldn't be the first time he'd done something like that in a crisis. And then he saw two Mexican cops sprinting toward them with rifles in their shoulders. That explained their deliverance from a very close call.

"You OK, Mike?" Shake glanced down where Stokey was pressing a handkerchief to the left hip of his blood-soaked khakis. They could hear the Mexican cops shouting for them to come out of the ditch with their hands in the air. One shouted in Spanish and the other repeated the commands in English. "No serious damage. Those cops doing all the yelling?"

"Yep—we are busted."

"Might be time to ditch the guns."

Shake grabbed Mike's pistol and looked around for a place to hide the guns. He rolled over a good-sized rock at the bottom of the ditch, tossed both guns in the hole, and rolled the rock back in place. It wouldn't survive much searching, but it was all he could do for now. He glanced up at the approaching cops who were now splitting to flank them and put his hands in the air. *"Tomalo con calma, Senores. Nos rendimos…"*

The cops commanded them to slowly climb out of the ditch and get on their knees with hands behind their heads. Shake translated it for Mike and then helped him to his feet. Keeping their hands in clear view, they crawled up onto the road surface and complied. One man kept them covered from a distance while the other one moved in to strip their backpacks and the camera case. He was in the process of patting them down when the other Feds arrived.

Two U.S. agents were walking toward them with drawn pistols, a tall man and a shorter woman, both in black windbreakers that proclaimed they were FBI. The woman said something in rapid-fire Spanish and one of the cops responded, pulling their upraised hands to the small of their backs and strapping them with zip-ties. The male agent walked forward, holstered his pistol, and pointed a finger at Shake.

"Let's start with who you are and what you're doing out here."

"We're both Americans—my name's Shake Davis. The bleeding guy next to me is Mike Stokey." The female agent pulled Stokey to his feet and examined his wound. "Just tore a chunk out of his butt," she said to her partner and pulled a first-aid kit out of her pocket. "He'll survive."

"OK, so let's get to what you're doing out here."

"We were watching those guys training. The idea was to get some solid evidence that terrorists were training down here so we could get you guys to take some action." Shake nodded toward the Mexican cop who was picking through their camera gear. "You'll see the photos if you take a look at that camera."

"We don't need that crap." The FBI man's attitude was shifting from suspicion to anger. "We've been watching it all for a week." He pointed a finger at the sky. "We have methods that don't require back-up from a couple of vigilantes. Jesus Christ, you people are…" His phone buzzed and Agent Neely walked away to take the call while his partner unceremoniously dropped Stokey's trousers and began to apply quick-clot to the wound.

"If I'd known it was going to get intimate, I'd have worn clean skivvies," Stokey mumbled. Special Agent Sally Pritchett missed the humor. She told him to shut up and began to apply a battle dressing. Shake was still on his knees with his hands bound as the helicopters returned and swooped over the site looking for a landing zone. He heard a radio transmission indicating all clear from the radio clipped to the female agent's gear. Apparently the fight was over for now.

Special Agent Bob Neely walked toward them with his phone in hand. "You said your name is Shake Davis?" Shake just nodded. "You a retired Marine?" Shake nodded again and the FBI man pointed at Stokey who was standing nearby, newly bandaged with his trousers still down around his ankles. "And this guy is Mike Stokey—used to work for CIA?"

"Guilty as charged," Mike said.

"I don't believe this crap." Neely snipped Shake's restraints with a pair of wire-cutters and handed over his phone. "He wants to talk to you." With no idea who it was that wanted to talk to him, Shake stood and pressed the FBI phone to his ear.

"Hello?"

"Gunner Shake Davis, USMC Retired…" The voice said. "You just damn near compromised a very important operation—not to mention breaking a bunch of laws, both American and Mexican."

"Who is this?"

"My name is Joe Carr, and I'm the Supervisory Special Agent in Charge of a Joint Counter-Terrorism Task Force. Those would be the people pointing weapons at you right now. I'm watching it all as we speak." Shake looked at the sky but he could see no sign of the drone he knew must be overhead. "I'm also the guy who sent the message for you to get the hell out of Mexico, an order you apparently chose to ignore."

"I never got any message."

"You never heard from the man who calls himself Bayer?"

"My phone got damaged…"

"You're very lucky that's all that got damaged. Does my name ring any bells with you? Think back to when you were Senior Instructor for the Recon Training Course at Camp Pendleton."

"I seem to remember we had somebody named Carr in the course. Was that you?"

"It was, Gunner Davis. You taught me a lot and I've got a great deal of respect for you—which is the reason I'm not going to have my agents haul the two of you back across the border to face charges. Call it a little Semper Fi."

"Well, I certainly appreciate that."

"Here's what you're going to do in order to show your appreciation. You and Mike Stokey are going to immediately head back across the border. I'm going to give you a number to call when you are safely and legally back in the U.S. I have a strong suspicion you'll be hearing from some serious players who will want to talk to you about the error of your ways. That piece of advice comes in the form of an order, Gunner Davis. And how do good Marines respond to direct orders?"

"Aye, aye, Sir." Shake said and handed the phone back to Agent Neely.

There was some further conversation before Neely stuffed the phone in a pocket. Then he scribbled a number on a business card and handed it to Shake. "Here's the drill," he said. "You guys clear out of here right now and you keep your mouths shut about all this until further notice. And you proceed immediately across the border and back into the U.S. You call the number on that card as soon as you're on American soil. If you don't do exactly as directed, we will be on you like a plague with warrants and indictments in hand." He dismissed them with a motion like he was shooing flies. Shake just nodded and reached for the camera case.

"And we keep the camera."

Shake nodded again and reached for his backpack. There was no complaint about that, so he shrugged into it and glanced at the two dead Mexican thugs. The bloody bodies were already drawing clouds of big black horseflies. The Mexican *Federales* would likely be happy to claim credit for nailing the one he'd killed, but Shake was anxious to get moving before they started questioning who shot who.

Now that Mike had his hands free of shackles he was cautiously pulling his trousers back over his bandaged hindquarters. "Did you get the guys you were after?" Mike shrugged into his backpack and stood next to Shake.

"Not that it's any of your business," Agent Sally Pritchett said, "but we got all three plus one of the Mexicans. Now hit the road."

Shake led off heading north with Mike Stokey limping at his side. Mexican SWAT cops were recovering bodies and stuffing them into rubberized bags. They could hear the roar of helicopter engines spooling up and the whine of blades starting to turn. The familiar sounds grew muted as they covered ground. They paused to watch when the police helicopters lifted into a clear blue sky, wheeled smartly, and headed south.

"So much for that," Shake mumbled and then started walking again at a pace that wouldn't cause his friend too much discomfort. By the time they'd covered most of the distance to Uncle Manuel's house, the Mexican desert was once again pristine and silent except for the crunch of their boots on the rocky soil. Mike Stokey began to chuckle.

"Well, here's another fine mess you've gotten us into."

"Yep—pissing into the wind—sorry I got you involved in it."

"It's never boring with you, Shake. That's the bright side. Anyway, the border Texans will be happy to hear about it."

"Yeah. Now they can go back to just worrying about dopers and gang-bangers coming across the Rio Grande."

Shake was feeling like an idiot, a foolish old warhorse who jumped at any chance to get back in harness regardless of circumstances—or the dictates of good sense. He shook his head and draped an arm over his old friend's shoulder. "Think we'll ever learn?"

"Not a chance. You want to go back and pick up the guns?"

"Nope. May they rest in peace."

They got to Uncle Manuel's place a half hour before Joaquin, Carlotta, and Manny Chavez arrived in the truck. While Aunt Carmelita re-bandaged Stokey's wound, made a lot of clucking noises, and applied some of her own home-made aloe salve, Shake told the story of what happened out in the desert. Apparently, the FBI was all over the situation with jihadis training in northern Mexico for cross border ops, he told them. Hence a joint task force with the Mexican National Police. "Your South Texas militia in Hidalgo County and elsewhere near the border can relax," he said. "The Feds are on the case."

"They might have at least told us they were lookin' into it or somethin'," Carlotta grumbled. "Ain't we got a right to know? It don't make a lick of sense to me."

"Sure it does," Joaquin said. "They were blowing us off because they already knew about what was goin' on down here and they didn't want us muddying the waters—like we just did."

"Or it could be left hand-right hand," Stokey added. "Sometimes an outfit like the FBI gets on a secret-squirrel kick, and they won't talk to anybody much less concerned citizens, not even Homeland Security or ICE or the Border

Patrol or any other outfit that needs to know. Maybe the people you were talking to really didn't have a clue."

"What's got me wondering is how many they missed before this." Manny Chavez was hauling the last of their gear out toward the truck. "What about the first bunch we spotted down here? Did they get them too? Or are those guys still running loose north of the border?"

"Don't suppose they'd tell us if they caught them, would they?" Carlotta, stuffed a wad of bills in an envelope, walked over and handed it to Aunt Carmelita with a hug.

"We'll find out—sooner or later," Shake said. "At least we know they aren't ignoring the situation."

When they were loading into Carmelita's truck for the trip back across the border and saying their polite goodbyes to the Chavez family, Mike fished in his shirt pocket and produced one of the thumb drives they'd used to record sound at the site. "They missed this. Think we ought to turn it over?"

"I'll ask the FBI when I call. Let's head for home."

The sun was low in the western sky when they stopped for something to eat before driving on to the border crossing. There was a lot of discussion over burritos and beer in a cantina full of tourists or border shoppers who were at the end of a big day chasing cheap goods or native groceries in Reynosa. Shake mostly listened as his South Texas friends argued about the pros and cons of a new President's avowed commitment to build a wall across the U.S. southern border with Mexico.

"I'm all in for it," Carlotta Valdez declared. "It's way past time for us to get serious about this illegal immigrant thing. I'll vote for anybody who stops talking and starts acting."

"Well, your man is in the White House," Joaquin Sutler grinned over his beer bottle. "And he says he's gonna put a stop to it once and for all."

"And I believe it." She nodded and looked around the table for concurrence. "We finally get serious for once and you'll see things get better in Hidalgo County—and a whole hell of a lot of other places in the southwest."

"Not all the illegals come in from Mexico, Carlotta." Manny Chavez doused his plate with hot sauce.

"Well, a great number of them do," Joaquin Sutler said. "And I guess we know ain't all of them are wetback Mexicans."

"I hope he does what he says he's gonna do." Mike shifted in his chair to ease the pressure on his wounded buttcheek. "I want to see how we manage a border wall that's, what—two thousand miles long?"

"One thousand nine hundred and thirty-three to be exact," Joaquin said. "Of which one thousand two hundred forty-one miles are in Texas. That's a hell of a lot of wall."

"If them heathen Chinese can build a great wall, then Americans can damn sure build a better one," Carlotta decided. "The authorities got a pretty fair handle on the airports and seaports and the President says he's gonna put a halt to them pecker-heads from the Middle East comin' into the country that way. He ain't buyin' all that crybaby refugee bullshit. We gotta focus on this damn leaky sieve we call a border with Mexico."

They were still discussing it when Shake borrowed Joaquin's phone and stepped outside away from the noise to call Chan. She was just walking in the door from her U-T commute, and he could hear Bear barking in the background.

"I've been worried, Shake. I left you a couple of messages. Bayer called three or four times. He couldn't get hold of you either. He told me you were supposed to forget about Mexico and come home."

"Yeah, Chan. I found out about that a little late. My phone got soaked and I've been out of touch. I'm really sorry about that."

"Are you OK? Where are you?"

"I'm in Reynosa—just across the border from McAllen. We're gonna cross back in a little while."

"Then you're coming home?"

"Well, there may be little delay…"

Shake was tired and dejected about the whole thing, but he owed it to his wife to explain what went on in Mexico, so he leaned against a street-side railing and talked. He was focused on the story which made him lose a little of his usual keen situational awareness. He completely missed the wiry little Mexican in a soccer sweatshirt over tattered jeans who kept snapping pictures of him with a cell phone camera. After the man had five or six good shots of Shake, he tapped the phone screen to send the pictures as an email attachment. Then he turned the green mesh baseball cap backwards the way he usually wore it and walked up the street in the direction of the border checkpoint.

It was silent in the small room off the main worship area of the *Noori Masjid* mosque after Friday services. There was an aura of reverence still hanging in the air after the local community of worshippers departed. It felt to a True Believer as if God was still here, still smiling on the faithful in the land of the Infidels. It was just the right time and the right place for Hasim to enlist a martyr in service to the worldwide caliphate. He sat cross-legged on a cushion across from the chosen one, so close that their knees were touching, so intimately close that whispers were all that was required to communicate. And those whispers were in Arabic, the language of God, the language of grace, and the only language that could adequately communicate the importance of what was being said.

In the silence of the mosque, staring intently into wide green eyes, Hasim could sense the conflicts raging in Ibrahim's mind. Ibrahim slumped grasping an ornate copy of the Holy Quran that Hasim had just handed him. He was trying desperately to muster some fervor in a suddenly cold heart. He knew when he swore allegiance to the Islamic State that he might be called on to fight and maybe to die in helping further the inevitable triumph of Islam. But the news he'd just heard—what amounted to his death knell—stunned him nearly speechless. He wanted to say something fierce and inspirational but nothing came. He willed the man sitting across from him in this holy place to understand that his reaction was not fear or a lack of faith. His eyes fell to the book in his lap and he prayed for inspiration in the teachings of Allah.

"So, Ibrahim, like your namesake, you are chosen to be God's messenger. You will carry a message to the Infidels that tells them nothing they do will alter or deter His will. You will strike fear in their hearts. You will demonstrate that soldiers of Islam will fight until all the world is one in His name and in His service. Surely you see the importance of this mission. Surely you understand the glory that awaits you."

Ibrahim merely nodded and clutched the holy book to his chest. He was thinking about his mother. She was devout, a good woman of the true God, but she mourned the loss of his father and doted on her only son. Would she understand this? It wasn't just his death. He knew that was always a matter of Allah's will and so did his mother. He was to be a martyr? So be it—but so many others would die—and the survivors would make her life a hell on earth.

"I can see you are worried, brother." Hasim slipped an arm around Ibrahim's shoulders and hugged him. "It's because you have lived for so long among the *kafirs*. You have come to think of them as simple people and merely innocents in our great struggle. Do not be fooled. You see in the news of their desecrations in our sacred home lands. You hear them blaspheme and insult us. You have seen how they discriminate—how they treat us as animals. You know that they refuse to bow to Allah's demand for a worldwide Caliphate in his Holy Name. Your own revered father died in the struggle, Ibrahim. Think how proud he will be that you follow in his footsteps. These Infidels insult us, they spit on our honor, they defy the one true God and his Messenger. They are an abomination and they must be punished. This is your holy task."

"I…I'm just worried about my mother."

"She will be among the holiest of holies, brother, the blessed mother of a martyr of God. She is the mother of a hero in the eyes of true believers and she will be loved, cherished and protected by all good Muslims."

"I am a soldier of Allah," Ibrahim chanted in a monotone. The words sounded hollow and strange. There was none of the joyful ring that so inspired him when he'd joined the secret group of Islamic warriors in the heart of this very mosque. Why was he selected to die on this mission? Why not one of the others? Was he blessed or cursed?

"As we all are," Hasim whispered, "…now and in the future. You are the chosen one, brother." Hasim gripped Ibrahim's elbow tightly. "We must know now, Ibrahim. Can we rely on you?"

"I will do my duty," Ibrahim said with what he hoped was a little more conviction. "I am a servant of the one true God."

"Good—that's very good, my brother." Ibrahim sat back with a smile. "Do you know a place in Fort Worth called the Will Rogers Coliseum? Have you ever been there?"

Ibrahim nodded. In the past year, he'd worked for a man who delivered hay and animal feed to a big rodeo event called the Southwest Exposition. He'd been able to see some of the performers in action struggling to stay on top of wild bulls and bucking horses. It was fun, a big, exciting deal for the audience of thousands—maybe hundreds of thousands—packed into the grandstands around the arena.

McAllen

The border crossing at Reynosa was easier and a lot dryer for Shake and Mike than the last one headed in the opposite direction. They drew barely a glance from the Mexicans but had to endure a thorough shake down of the camper on the American side. Carlotta dropped them off at Joaquin's house where she took the opportunity during their goodbyes to give Shake's butt a last little squeeze.

"If your lady tosses you out one of these days," she whispered in his ear, "you got a place with me." She refused a nightcap and drove off to take Manny Chavez home. Shake and Mike had a little of the good bourbon and branch in front of a mesquite fire, but there was only cursory conversation over the whiskey. Everyone felt a little foolish. Even Joaquin Sutler, the retired Texas Ranger who had been on plenty of time-wasting stakeouts, agreed it was essentially a wild goose chase. "We were tryin' to do the right thing," he said. "But I guess we screwed the pooch."

"Maybe," Stokey said around a yawn. "Be that as it may, I had a hell of a time."

"Ain't even a very good sea story," Shake grumbled. "The next time I do something like this, you need to kick me directly in my tired old ass."

"Tried that, many times," Mike said. "Never does any good."

"I really don't want y'all headin' for home and feelin' bad," Joaquin said. "Would it help if I was to send you off with a bottle or two of this bourbon?"

"Early flight tomorrow," Mike said. "I've just got a carry-on and I can't stand the thought of some TSA asshole confiscating the bottle. You can mail me some." Mike polished off his drink and made his way toward a bed in Joaquin's loft.

"I might be persuaded to carry a bottle home in the truck," Shake said and refilled his glass. "This is some tasty stuff."

"Listen, Shake…" Joaquin settled in an easy-chair and propped his boots on the hearth. "I know we asked you to take a risk. You gave us your time and best effort. It turned out kinda dumb-ass in the end, I guess, but I don't want you thinkin' too badly of us. Hell, I guess we're just a bunch of Texas rednecks, but we meant well. I sincerely mean that."

"I know you do, Joaquin. And I know the people down here are solid Americans. I appreciate that. Guys like you and me and some of the others—well, we're Marines, and we've just got a penchant to take action. So we did. Nobody got hurt too bad and we learned a little something in the bargain." He stood and reached for Joaquin's hand. "I'll take Mike to the airport tomorrow morning. Thanks for the hospitality. Let's don't be strangers."

Nice sentiments, Shake thought as he crawled into bed and pulled a quilt up to his chin, but they sounded as phony as he felt. He stared at the ceiling fan for hours, wondering if he could ever learn to just stay home and let the weird world revolve around him.

* * *

At a stoplight on the drive back from the airport, Shake pulled the card he was given by the FBI agent out of his shirt pocket. The area code indicated it was a Washington, D.C.

number, which probably meant he was due for an ass-chewing lecture from some FBI bureaucrat. He wasn't anxious to make the call, but he was even less anxious to face a fleet of lawyers and wind up with a subpoena or something worse. The Feds could be cranky when crossed.

He glanced at the passenger seat where his defunct iPhone sat in sunlight slanting through the windshield still sweating Rio Grande River water. He needed a new phone, so when the light changed he accelerated toward downtown McAllen looking for an Apple outlet.

After cruising through a couple of downtown strip malls without any luck, he finally spotted the familiar logo and wheeled into a parking slot. The woman at the Genius Bar was cheerful, chirpy, and sympathetic when Shake told her a lie about being pushed into a swimming pool at a local bash. She'd seen or heard it all before and was truly sorry that the Apple warranty didn't cover death by drowning. He needed to buy a new phone, and she'd be right happy to sell him an upgrade to some combination of numbers and letters that represented top of the line. Shake pulled his plastic and asked if there was a way he could keep his old number. There was. The nice lady said the new phone would copy that and all the other data from his account via something she reverently called The Cloud. All she needed was Shake's password. Naturally, he didn't remember that, but Chan would, so he borrowed a phone and called her.

Armed with the password and his new phone, the chirpy guru disappeared into the back of the store leaving Shake to wander aimlessly among a stupefying array of gear and gadgets for half an hour. They did a test run when she returned, and it looked like Shake was back in the cell-phone business. All the icons looked right and the learning curve for users of this particular model—sleek gun-metal grey chosen over a variety of gaudy options—was not too steep. When they powered up the new instrument it went into an iPhone version of a hissy-fit protesting all the calls, texts and other electronic missives Shake missed while he was in Mexico. He got that under control and messed around with the touch-screen to determine if all the familiar numbers showed up in his contact list. They did, so Shake signed the credit card receipt, thanked the genius lady, and headed back to his truck.

There was a bunch of routine texts and some chatty messages on his voice mail service. He listened to the one from Chan, but there was no need to return it as he'd just talked to her. And there was the clipped and direct semi-shout from the man who calls himself Bayer telling him to get the hell out of Mexico in a hurry and call for details. That one was clearly overcome by events, but Shake decided to return the call anyway. The FBI could wait a few minutes more. Maybe he could enlist Bayer to run interference if the Feds decided to press issues about what happened south of the border. The man who calls himself Bayer sounded like he was in a manic mood when he answered after the first ring.

"Where the hell have you been? Didn't you get my message?"

"I got it—about three minutes ago. My phone was on the fritz—had to buy a new one."

"Where are you now?"

"Shopping mall in McAllen, Texas. Just back from Mexico."

"I know all about that, Shake. The FBI gave you a number to call, right?"

"Yeah. How did you know?"

"I'm back in the biz. Monday I got a call from the Office of the Director of National Intelligence. The new administration is draining all the bad blood from the previous gaggle of assholes, so I'm back in good-guy status. I'm on with ODNI as a staff consultant."

"And the first thing you hear is about this thing in Mexico?"

"Not the first thing, but it was up near the top of a long briefing list. The new Director knows we have a history. He asked for my opinion on what to do about you."

"And you said what? Court-martial, firing squad, exile?"

"In fact, I told him you are a valuable asset, often handy for stuff that requires official discretion."

"You may be back in the biz, but I'm not. I gotta make one call under duress from the FBI, and then I'm on my way home—assuming they don't send somebody down to arrest me."

"Shake, don't make that call. You don't need to anymore. That's all history. We pulled rank and doused most of their fire. You're off that hook. Maybe you'll have to submit a statement or something, but that's it."

"Wait a minute. Who pulled rank with the FBI? You?"

"Not me personally, Shake. I talked the Director of National Intelligence into doing it. He's a former Marine and he wants to meet you in person."

"Not interested."

"I think you owe the guy a little time. He's running interference between you and Stokey and a very pissed off FBI."

"Where would a meeting like that happen? I'm really not anxious to see Washington again."

"That's the sweet part, Shake. You don't have to travel very far. The Director is flying to Dallas tomorrow for a three-day conference. I've got a room for you at the Fair-mont."

"I guess I owe you—and him—that much for calling off the dogs." Shake was trying to decide what he needed to tell Chan who was expecting him home today or tomorrow at the latest. "It's probably ten hours from here to Dallas. When does he want to see me?"

"Any time in the three days he'll be in Dallas. Just call my number when you get in, Shake. I'll set it up."

"You're gonna be there?"

"The conference is about terrorism, Shake. That's my wheelhouse."

"Let me give Chan a call. Assuming she doesn't file for divorce, I'll hit the road headed for Dallas."

Reynosa

As one of the most influential and reliable links in the lucrative Mexican drug-smuggling chain, Eduardo *El Escorpion* Lopez didn't have to leave his heavily-guarded *gran finca* in Ciudad Rio Grande very often. He tolerated the long ride to Reynosa in his up-armored Mercedes GLS because he was confronted with a situation that demanded his personal attention.

Eduardo Lopez ran a network of cross-border couriers and contracted his services to the heavy-hitters in the cartels. He was an important middleman between the drug suppliers in the south and distributors in the north. *El Escorpion* was a kingpin in that aspect of the transportation business, managing a string of reliable mules that stretched along the border from El Paso to Brownsville. It was a lucrative business that he'd built through years of difficult, often brutal struggle.

But the business climate was changing. There was increased pressure from law enforcement authorities in Mexico City who were themselves under newly applied pressure from the *Norte Americanos*. They had a tough-talking cowboy in office that was demanding increased U.S. law enforcement presence on the border—including building some kind of stupid fucking wall. All this was vexing and eating steadily into profits everywhere. The powerful cartel bosses were complaining and pointing fingers—lately at Eduardo Lopez. His reliable mules were being busted at an increasing rate.

Every arrest meant lost product and lost money. Tempers were flaring, including his own. *El Escorpion* understood—as did everyone in his trade—that some losses must be tolerated as the cost of doing dangerous business. Now he had *gringo* civilians meddling in an already difficult endeavor. Just this past week, a trio of them ripped off one of his couriers and that cost him $250,000 to cover an indemnified shipment from Sinaloa suppliers that they felt cost them at least two million in profits. That sort of loss was not routine. It was a painful bite that they would not forgive or forget. It was also an embarrassment, an affront to his reputation that could not be ignored. He needed to demonstrate that he could—and would—take corrective measures.

Lopez glanced at his watch and nodded at one of his security men who was escorting his first appointment into the private room of the cantina just off the main drag in downtown Reynosa. A wiry man in sweatshirt and jeans stood before him with a green mesh baseball cap held at his side in a respectful manner. *Pequeno Zorro*—the little fox—didn't look very smart or cunning but he was one of the best smugglers in Tamaulipas State. He was a fighter, a veteran who had shot his way out of a few border confrontations in the past.

"So…" Lopez lit a cigarette and stared at his mule. "You lost your gun and your cargo."

"I got away from the *patrullas,* and I had the drugs safely back on this side. I would have carried them over later at another crossing, but the gringos ambushed me."

"You don't know who they were?"

"They said they were not cops, *Jeffe*. But they were hard men."

Lopez picked up his phone and found the photos. "And this is the man who took the shipment?" He turned the phone so his smuggler could see it.

"He is one of three—the one who was giving the orders. I spotted him outside a cantina down near the checkpoint, so I took the pictures and sent them to you."

Lopez stared unblinking for a long minute. The story of the busted border crossing resulting in the loss of such a valuable shipment lost to gringos who were not even cops was all over his network. It had even reached some of his regular suppliers. Such a thing eroded trust in his delivery system. He could live with the loss of cash but more was at stake. A thing like this might cause his customers to look for alternative courier services.

Blood needed to be spilled. He could easily have one of his *brutos* kill this fidgeting and sweating man before him, but that seemed counterproductive. Experienced mules weren't easy to maintain as they regularly wound up dead or in prison, and the little man's knowledge of safe border crossings was valuable. He sighed a cloud of cigarette smoke into the muggy air and reached into a jacket pocket.

"I'm very sorry, Jeffe." The smuggler flinched, expecting to see a gun emerge and his life ended. "Please believe me, it wasn't my fault."

Lopez handed over an envelope containing some cash and dismissed the little man with a wave. "Buy another gun," he said. "And wait for instructions. I may have a job for you soon. This time maybe you deliver some cash for me. Can you do that without fucking it up?"

"No more mistakes, Jeffe. I swear it."

When the mule disappeared, Lopez re-examined the photos in his phone. This gringo looked like an old dog and a tough one. Even slouched and talking on a phone, the man had the aspect of a cop or maybe a soldier. He studied the open and honest face below a shock of white hair. Unlikely that such a man would steal drugs to sell them. What was his angle? The next man due to arrive would fill in some blanks. Much would depend on that.

Eduardo Lopez crossed his arms and leaned back in his chair to review his options. The dirty work of disciplining or eliminating one of the hundreds of mules he employed was easily handled by his squad of enforcers. They were maintained and highly paid for that purpose. If some upstart courier should steal a load to go into business for himself, turn informant, or otherwise cross *El Escorpion*, he was dead in a matter of days, on either side of the border. Simple enough, but this situation was different.

His second appointment walked into the room a few minutes later carrying two bottles of cold beer. The man wore rich man's casual clothes and had a watch on his wrist that was even more expensive than the gold Rolex Lopez wore. He merely nodded, sat down at the table, and nipped at his beer bottle.

"No trouble at the border?"

"Why would there be? They know me on both sides. I import car parts for my shops in the Rio Grande Valley. Most of the cops are customers."

"And how is business?"

"It's pretty good—in both markets." The man rolled his beer bottle around the table. His face was fashionably tan, the kind of tan you get on golf courses, and his dark hair was well-tended. He looked like the successful businessman he was. He drove expensive cars and lived in a big house on the other side of the border, but Lopez knew a few auto parts stores did not provide the kind of cash this man had. For that he needed a lucrative sideline, and in this case it was distributing drugs to street dealers throughout the Southwestern U. S. Lopez knew that because his mules delivered most of those drugs.

"You got the photos I sent?"

"I got them—and I showed them to some people I know."

"You know who he is?"

"I do. My sources turned up his driver's license."

"Are you going to tell me?"

"I'm running short of product lately. The people on this end say it's your fault. Too many of your people are getting busted."

"There have been some problems."

"You know it will just get worse if this new loudmouth in Washington does what he says he's going to do on the border."

Lopez banged his beer bottle on the table and leaned toward his visitor. "And you know you have priority. Anyone else may get shorted by a lost shipment, but your stuff always gets delivered."

"And you always get your cut. We'll see how it goes in the future." The visitor toyed with a cigar and offered a light for the fresh cigarette Lopez pulled from a pack on the table. "What do you want to know about this gringo?"

"Who is he?"

"His name is Sheldon Davis, but he's known as Shake— strange name. He's supposedly a retired military officer— U.S. Marines—but he's a lot more than that. Some people I know tell me he's a tough hombre. Used to do a lot of special operations stuff. He still does occasionally."

"Any idea what he was doing swimming across the river into Mexico?"

"That I don't know. Maybe he's working undercover. Maybe he was down here off the books to screw with your business."

"Maybe. What else?"

The visitor pulled a manila envelope out of his jacket and laid it on the table. "It's all in there," he said, standing to leave. "If you're planning on going after this guy, I recommend you hire some top-notch people."

El Escorpion smoked and read for a time, learning what he could about the man identified as Shake Davis, the man who cost him a quarter of a million and a great deal of embarrassment. Apparently, he lived in Lockhart, Texas, just south of Austin. So the lesson would be costly, but it had to be taught. People on both sides of the border must see that you cannot fuck with *El Escorpion* or his couriers. He reached for his phone and found the number he wanted. There was a *Zeta* gangbanger, a former Mexican Army commando turned outlaw, who had been one of *El Escorpion's brutos* before he had to flee the police. He was holed up somewhere in San Antonio. For a job like this, he was top-notch.

Wafic Aziz and Ibrahim were in the warehouse sealing newly painted barrels full of ANFO slurry. It was delicate work as many of the old repurposed containers were off-round and their tops did not fit as tightly as they should. Wafic had to stop his assistant from using a hammer to force the lids into place. That was more than a little dangerous with an explosive as sensitive as ANFO, but Ibrahim just shrugged it off. As they worked on the barrels, now painted in red, white, and blue bands, Wafic worried about bumps or sharp turns on the drive to Fort Worth.

"You will have to be careful with your driving, Ibrahim."

"Hasim went over the route with me. Don't sweat it. I'm not."

That was glib—and also unconvincing. Wafic looked closely at the young martyr-to-be working with a pry-bar to seal a lid. His efforts were perfunctory and listless as if he really didn't care about the task. There had been a change in Ibrahim's demeanor since Hasim told him of his role in the attack. This lack of fervor might signal a lack of commitment. That had him worried more than jarring the six barrels that would be strapped in the back of the truck. Wafic could encourage him up until they stopped to arm the bomb. After that it would be just Ibrahim in the truck—Ibrahim and 300 gallons of volatile, extremely sensitive high explosive.

Wafic decided then that he would take the time to manufacture a back-up detonator for his bomb. A timer device would work. It would take him just a day, maybe two, to obtain the materials, make the secondary trigger and test it. He moved to the last barrel and examined the rim. It was round and undamaged. "Don't seal this one," he said. "We will leave the top loose so I can remove it to insert the trigger."

They were checking the work when Hasim arrived in a shiny new panel truck. He steered the vehicle into the warehouse through one of the big loading doors and jumped down from the cab. He waved at Wafic and then stripped some decals which he applied to the driver and passenger doors. To any observers on the street, the truck would now proclaim ownership by Livengood Feed & Seed, Fort Worth, Texas. He examined his work critically for a while and then tossed the ignition key to Ibrahim.

"Time to practice, my brother. Jump in and drive it around the parking lot."

Ibrahim wordlessly crawled into the cab and cranked the engine. He fiddled around a bit, getting used to the control layout and then he caught a gear and drove out of the warehouse. Wafic and Hasim stood near a window watching Ibrahim slowly steer the truck through a series of easy turns that had been laid out using traffic cones. "I specified an automatic transmission," Hasim said. "We don't want him fumbling with the detonator while he's shifting gears."

"Are you worried about his commitment? Do you think he will go through with it to the end?"

"Are you worried about that?"

"He seems changed since you told him. It's as if he's just not, I don't know—like he's not ready for what we are asking of him."

"No man is entirely ready when he's facing death, Wafic. He worries about his mother and many other things right now. He frets about the enormity of the attack. He worries that he will be considered a criminal rather than a holy martyr. It's natural."

"But will he do what must be done?"

"He is a soldier of Allah." Hasim pulled Wafic around to face him and stared hard into the bomb-maker's dark eyes.

"As are we all…" Wafic parroted the ISIL response as was expected but he still felt unsure. "Still—I am thinking we should construct a secondary trigger. I will prepare a list of the things I need for that."

"How long will that take?" Hasim asked as he pulled a folded sheet of paper out of a pocket.

"A day, perhaps two. Depends on how quickly you can get the items I need."

"That won't be possible." Hasim unfolded the paper and handed it to Wafic. "Look at this."

It was a computer printout of an article in the Dallas Morning News. The report said a capacity crowd of 6,000 was expected to jam the Will Rogers Coliseum for the opening day of the Fort Worth Stock Show & Rodeo. It listed the opening date as two days from now.

"So we have three days left to prepare," Wafic said refolding the paper.

"No, we will attack on opening day."

"We planned on the second day when security would be more lax."

"And I have advanced the schedule, brother. We go the day after tomorrow."

"Why?"

Hasim pointed at another paragraph in the article. "See here? It says the American Director of National Intelligence is scheduled to attend on opening day."

"There is no guarantee that we could kill him, Hasim. I don't like changes in long-standing plans. And I need time for the secondary trigger."

"There is another reason for the change, brother. I am informed that the follow-on team was arrested in Mexico. We go before anything else happens to disrupt our mission."

"I understand," Wafic nodded. "But you must understand something like this puts the mission in jeopardy. We should be prepared for any eventuality. It is the professional way to operate in these matters."

"The risk is worth the reward, brother. Nothing will go wrong. And if it does we must believe it is the will of God."

Dallas

Shake felt significantly underdressed in faded khaki and a t-shirt as he approached the hotel's front desk and shrugged out of his backpack. He was weary after the long drive up from McAllen with only the new Willy Nelson-Merle Haggard CD for distraction, and he needed a quiet place to take a nap. The Fairmont Hotel looked like it could provide that and a hell of a lot more.

Located in the heart of Dallas, one of the state's biggest and busiest cities, the Fairmont was the sort of venue that coddled high-rollers and catered to wealthy organizations in town for conferences or parties. He saw the occasional Stetson and some exotic boots, but most of the people wandering in or out of the nearby glitzy bars, shops, and restaurants were in business suits or dresses that were what the cool people called bespoke. And most of them had the pasty office pallor of lawyers or technology savants. Typical Texas endeavors like oil and cattle may have dropped a notch or two on the list of lucrative pursuits, but cash was still king in Big D.

As he waited for an available customer service rep to go through the inevitable welcome speech and find his reservation, Shake glanced at an electronic notice board behind the desk. In glowing LEDs it advised any patrons in town for the big Southwest Exposition to inquire with the maître d'. A second notice indicated the National Security Seminars would begin tomorrow in and around the Venetian Room. That explained the pair of obvious g-man types he saw standing near the elevator banks wearing ear-buds. Typical. Both tall and triangular with neat, short haircuts, wearing conservative suits cut just a little loose and kept buttoned to conceal their weapons. At least they weren't wearing shades. Someday someone ought to tell the leadership that the look was a classic tell. People up to no good would need to be blind or a special kind of stupid not to spot these guys and avoid them.

The desk lady handed over a key card plus a map of the hotel and directed Shake toward elevators that would carry him to the 18th floor. He headed in that direction and then changed his mind when he saw a men's clothing boutique on the other side of the lobby. They didn't carry any jeans that Shake could wear without constricting circulation, so he picked out some slacks and a nice collared shirt that he thought might not clash too badly. If they wanted him to wear a coat and tie, they could just piss up a picket-rope.

His room was sumptuous with a nice view of bustling downtown Dallas through a wide window. It smelled like a botanical hothouse, but it had an easy chair with a reading lamp next to it, a thing Shake always tried to find when he was staying in hotels—which wasn't very often these days. He unpacked his shaving kit, hung his new clothes on the bathroom door where he hoped steam would eliminate some wrinkles, and hopped into the shower. He let hot water from an adjustable shower head pound his neck and shoulders, trying to wash away some of the funk he was still feeling over the abortive mission in Mexico and wondering what kind of pitch was in store. There was no way he would sign on to a regular operative slot. Too old and tired for that grind—but consultant sounded relatively harmless. A consultant could probably do his thing from home via phone calls and email.

When his new clothes looked presentable, he shaved and called home to let Chan know he was safely ensconced in

Dallas. The big news from Lockhart was that their dog Bear had found and investigated his first skunk. Chan was anticipating a workout when she tried to wrestle the big boy into a wash-tub for fumigation. He set his watch alarm and collapsed for a three-hour nap.

When the alarm woke him late in the afternoon, he phoned the man who calls himself Bayer. Everything was locked on, but he was unable to break away from a meeting. He'd be in the lobby bar in two hours, drinks on him. Shake wandered around the Fairmont lobby in his new clothes, looking into windows and poking around a rack full of travel brochures. Outside the hotel restaurant, he saw an ornate menu that boasted "Finest Fusion Cuisine." Shake didn't know what that meant exactly, but the picture of a featured dish looked like a tiny, under-done pork chop perched on pine cones. The only other thing on the plate was a squiggle of some sort of dark liquid as if the chef meant to squirt it on the meat and missed. It was listed as a delightful bargain at 46 bucks. Shake passed, hit the street, and walked until he found a Whataburger.

Ninety minutes later, he was slumped in a leather chair near a table that had been engineered—probably in Taiwan—to look like it was made from an old wagon wheel. An attentive waiter in a red vest brought him a glass full of Bulleit bourbon on ice. The Fairmont's lobby bar was full of guests or locals seeking respite after a long day of dealing with whatever brought them to downtown Dallas. There were little clutches of well-dressed men with ties pulled down who were desperately chugging drinks. There were snuggling couples making dinner plans. And dotted throughout the intimate little lounge was some fine-looking ladies, advertising in short skirts and carelessly crossed legs, who were eyeing the action. Time with that caliber of woman didn't come cheap. Which, Shake reasoned, was exactly why they hung around a lucrative venue like the Fairmont Hotel.

The man who calls himself Bayer walked in right on time, waved when he spotted Shake, and began to weave through the crowd. He was smiling, obviously in a good mood, and much rejuvenated from the last time Shake saw him contemplating an end to his active career after the Cuba thing. The invitation to rejoin the weird world of professional spooks was clearly a tonic.

He slid into a chair on the opposite side of the table and ordered expensive scotch neat. Some things never change, Shake thought as he shook hands. The man who calls himself Bayer would starve before he gave up single-malt.

"Thanks for coming, Shake. Director Macintosh is really anxious to meet you."

"Yeah…" Shake tapped his new phone sitting on the table. "I googled him. He used to be an Intel officer—Seventh Marines guy in Task Force Ripper when Mattis had 1-7 in the first Gulf go-round. Figures. General Mattis probably recommended him for DNI when he became Secretary of Defense."

"You ought to know how it goes, Shake." The man who calls himself Bayer drained his drink and signaled for another. "Marines like to keep it all in the family."

"Uh-huh. And since you are a former Jarhead yourself…"

"No such thing as former, Shake. We are Marines from boot camp to the grave."

"That's what it says on the recruiting posters. So when do I meet Director Macintosh?"

"It's set for ten tomorrow morning in the Presidential suite. He's cleared an hour for you. I think he mainly just wants to take the measure of the man. You know, see how you might fit into the effort."

"What effort?"

"Use your head for something besides a hat-rack, Shake. We are at war with radical Islamists and their jihadis. Call it what you want: Asymmetrical, counter-insurgency, counter-terrorist—it all amounts to the same thing. It's a fight for survival, and it's not a war that can be won by touchy-feely diplomatic efforts."

"Well, it's refreshing to hear that the new guys in Washington are finally facing the truth. We've spent the past eight years trying to find a way to pick up a turd by the clean end."

"Those days are gone, my friend. And that's where a guy with your experience and insight can help."

"Shit." Shake chuckled and finished his bourbon. "Experience and insight like I demonstrated down in Mexico, I guess."

"Forget about that, Shake."

"I'm trying to, believe me. But I'm wondering if the Mexicans will ask me to make another little visit. You know—to face charges when they find out one of their finest citizens was shot at close range with a .45 by someone other than a cop."

"They know all about that. FBI and the Mexican National Police—no problem. Good riddance to bad rubbish. Don't worry about it."

"OK; if you say so. Let's have another one and then I want to hit the rack."

The man who calls himself Bayer signaled for fresh drinks and then pulled an envelope out of his pocket. He laid it on the table and gave it a little thump with his fingers. "That's the hottest ticket in town right now, Shake. The Director got us a couple of tickets to the Southwest Exposition

Rodeo in Fort Worth, and it's great seats in the VIP section. Tomorrow's opening day and you can't buy a seat anywhere in the Will Rogers Coliseum for less than the national debt." Shake opened the envelope and examined the ticket. Big show starting at 4 p.m. or about the time he wanted to be out of Dallas and on the road home.

"I don't know…"

"C'mon, Shake. Director Macintosh is going and I'll be there. We'll have a few beers and watch the animals stomp the shit out of the cowboys."

"Maybe. Let me think about it."

The next morning, Shake was intercepted by a security man as soon as he stepped off the elevator on the Fairmont's 24th floor where the Presidential Suite was located. It wasn't necessary to do much more than smile. The guy at the elevators was expecting him.

"Jack Barnett," he said offering a hand. "My Dad says he served with you in Beirut."

Shake thought about it for a minute trying to remember while eyeing another suit talking into his sleeve at the other end of a long hallway. "Hard to remember…"

"He was Gunnery Sergeant John Barnett at the time attached to 10th Marines."

"Now I've got it," Shake said. "Gunny Barnett—he was a good FO when we finally got permission to start firing back at the Druze up in the mountains around BIA. How's he doing?"

"Good shape, sir. I just talked to him. He sends his best."

"Give him my respects and regards."

Shake followed down the hall toward the other security man who was standing in front of a set of ornate double doors. There appeared to be only one room on this floor lit by muted bulbs in shiny silver sconces made to look like candle holders.

"You guys Secret Service?"

"That's right, sir. We're the Personal Security Detail for the DNI."

"You ever wear different clothes—let your hair grow out a little—stuff like that?"

Barnett looked at Shake like he was trying to determine if it was a serious question. "There are standards, sir. Why do you ask?"

"Just curious."

"Well—you know how it goes."

"I know," Shake admitted with a smile. I know, and so does everybody else who watches TV.

The man who calls himself Bayer opened the door and pointed Shake at a buffet table that held a coffee urn and platters of pastries. He was alone in the suite and it looked like he'd been there for a while. His laptop was open on a dining table and his coat was draped over a chair in front of it.

"Get yourself coffee, Shake. Director Macintosh is on the way."

Shake had just about settled into a chair with his cup when a tall man in an elegant suit bearing a small eagle, globe, and anchor lapel pin entered the suite. He was medium height with no excess weight showing. There were a couple of muted grey streaks in his neatly cut hair, but he moved like a young athlete. Director of National Intelligence Laird Macintosh shook hands and told Shake how pleased he was that they had this chance to meet. He got his own coffee and settled in across from his visitor wearing a muted smile. Shake returned the smile noticing that Macintosh had another small pin below the Marine Corps emblem in his lapel. The Purple Heart. Shake had one just like it that he usually wore with a sports coat.

"We probably know a bunch of the same folks," Macintosh said.

"Probably so, sir. I knew General Mattis a bit when he was a company grade. And there's probably a bunch of others we could name." They both thought about that for a while. Macintosh seemed content to simply cross his legs and stare at Shake as if he was distracted or making some kind of silent evaluation. It made Shake squirm so he tried to fill the conversational void.

"Couldn't help noticing your Purple Heart."

"The enemy marksmanship badge…" Macintosh chuckled and patted his lapel. "Nothing too serious. Caught a little piece of a one-twenty-two rocket on the march up to Baghdad. Your service record indicates we've got that in common."

"Shake is a well-known shrapnel magnet, Director." The man who calls himself Bayer said from across the room where he was working his laptop. "He's got three Purples. Likely rates more, but who's counting?"

They both laughed and sipped at their coffee. Macintosh jerked his head in the direction of the dining table. "He tells me you two have a long and lurid history."

"Yes, sir. I've known him—for good or ill—more years than I like to admit."

"Well, I'm really lucky to have him on the team. We've got a long, hard road ahead of us."

"It's not gonna be easy, Director. That's for sure."

"We're trying to figure out what to do and where to start, Shake."

"I'd say you've got a good start with that Task Force down in Mexico."

"Important stuff, that's for sure—but it's just one aspect of a huge problem. Can you stand a little lecture?"

Shake held up his coffee cup and the DNI nodded so he got a refill and sat down to hear what this likeable man had to say. Macintosh set his coffee cup down on a table and began to pace. It didn't seem like a lecturing posture, more like a Marine officer giving a briefing.

"Shake, I'm going to give you facts, not just speculation. I want you to understand that. What we're facing right now in America and in the rest of the western world is a war. Jihadist-inspired violence has occurred on every continent in the world at this point." Macintosh paused and smiled at his guest. "The only exception is the continent of Antarctica. Even the most committed jihadis aren't much interested in freezing their balls off to convert the penguins."

He got the laughs he expected and then began to pace again, tracing a pattern near the coffee table with his hands clasped at the small of his back. It was a familiar posture Shake had seen in good briefers who knew how to think on their feet as they spoke.

"There are probably around fifty to one hundred thousand active jihadists in the world right now. And of those, figure about ten to twenty thousand are the core leadership. Add to that some one or two hundred thousand militants that have had some military training but aren't regularly active. Those folks are committed and on-call, most of them with battlefield experience somewhere in the Middle East. They'd be what we'd call the enemy reserve force that guns up and goes to work for whichever jihadist outfit is willing to pay them. You can do the math and get an idea about the scope of the problem."

"That's a sizeable chunk," Shake said. "I didn't realize they could muster those kinds of numbers."

"They can," Macintosh said and resumed pacing. "We aren't facing some little shit-heel insurgency that we can defeat by playing whack-a-mole in Muslim countries around the world. And these people are religious fanatics, True Believers—capital T and capital B. It's their way or the highway. And their way is devout Muslim faith with no room or tolerance for anything else.

"Jihadists identify as Muslims, they use Islamic speech, writings, and symbols as their touchstones. They wrap themselves up in Muslim traditions and sacred scriptures to justify what they do, which eliminates the standard human conscience problems about right and wrong. These people see their enemies and primary opponents as Western culture and civilization. And that means they hate—and consider an abomination—anything Christian or secular in any form. That's what they preach, and it gets them sympathy and various degrees of active or passive support from millions of Muslims around the globe." Macintosh paused for a sip of coffee and apologized for his passion.

"No apologies needed, sir." Shake just nodded and motioned for his host to continue. "It's scary as hell, but we all need to hear about things like this."

"So what are these guys after? Simple. They want nothing short of the total destruction of Western culture—which they would replace with an explicit Islamic version of societies everywhere. That's straight out of the ISIS playbook. They want to establish and run a Fourth Caliphate under Sharia Law, and they believe that's a destiny decreed by God. Now, the kumbaya bunch that think we can all just join hands and dance around the maypole in worldwide peace will point to the depredations of Christian missionaries in South America and Africa during the last century, but that's unmitigated horseshit. Those missionaries tried to preach and persuade. They didn't kill or torture natives who refused to convert.

"The bottom line is this, Shake. Like it or not, we are fighting what I think of as World War III right now in the twenty-first century. It's not a conventional deal like World Wars I and II, but it certainly requires deploying military forces overseas and active law enforcement efforts here at home. What the U.S. and our western allies are facing right now is a worldwide insurgency in multiple independent theaters around the world. The fight has elements of the conventional battlefield and an insurgency. Just look at things like Paris, Berlin, Boston, San Bernardino, and Fort Lauderdale, Shake. In this fight, targets of opportunity could just as easily be the shopping mall across the street as it could a legitimate military target somewhere."

"That's a heavy concept, sir." Shake got himself more coffee and tried to wrestle with what he was hearing. "I've had some experience with it, but I'm pretty sure the run-of-the-mill civilian can't see the scope of the threat."

"No, and it makes what we need to do in combating the militants a tough sell. Part of what we're doing here in Dallas is trying to spread the word through various agencies about the extent of the threat. We need the American people behind our efforts because it could get draconian soon. I'm not talking about martial law or anything like that but it's going to take the combined will of the American people to tolerate what's necessary for our continued survival. I know that sounds like exaggerating but listen to this..." He walked over to the laptop on the dining table and read for a few moments. "This is a paper we've been putting together for the conference."

The man who calls himself Bayer began to read from the computer screen. "Both Al Qaida and the Islamic State have imported their philosophies and their operations around the world today. Collectively they have created and we have identified more than seventy-five so-called franchises in various countries in the Muslim world. They have set up and are operating cells throughout Europe, North America, and Australasia. In doing that, they have demonstrated the capacity to radicalize what are popularly known as lone-wolf jihadists. These are the people who often commit attacks and atrocities throughout Europe and North America.

"Since 9-11, there have been forty-eight separate jihadist attacks or violent episodes in the United States that have claimed the lives of a hundred and thirty-nine Americans. There have been scores of planned terrorist attacks, some of them so absurd as to be comical like shoe bombs or underwear bombs. A good number of those attacks have been detected and stopped by American law enforcement agencies. Right now, our FBI has identified and is conducting active investigations on more than one thousand American jihadists in all fifty of the United States."

"Son of a bitch," Shake whispered.

"Yes. It's what we're facing," Macintosh said as he slid into a seat near Shake. "And it's why we need all hands on deck—especially old, experienced hands. I'm hoping I can include you in that effort, Shake."

"What is it you want me to do?"

"I don't know just yet—maybe nothing in particular other than to add your views and expertise—maybe a lot. I mainly want to know I can count on you if we need your skills or your judgment."

Shake looked at the hand Director of National Intelligence Laird Macintosh was extending and took it. "I don't know how in the hell anybody could say no, Director."

"There you go," Macintosh said and stood looking at his watch. "We've got to go." He turned to the man who calls himself Bayer. "You've got all his contacts, right?"

Shake stood as they headed for the door. He felt like he'd just committed to something, but he was unsure what that might be. "Thanks for seeing me," he said to their backs. "And thanks for the hotel and the thing with the FBI—and everything."

"Least we can do," Macintosh said as he opened the door and stepped into the hallway. "See you for dinner tonight."

Shake spent the rest of the morning answering texts and emails and making a few routine calls that he'd been ignoring. It was back to a local Whataburger for lunch where he watched the hustle and bustle of downtown Dallas and thought about the threat the DNI described. How many of the preoccupied folks rushing along the streets of this big, prosperous city had a clue about what was squaring off around them? It was a duel to the death between the way of life they took for granted and hordes of religion-fueled radicals who wanted them either converted, sublimated, or destroyed.

Given the numbers he'd heard, "hordes" was not too strong a word. And somewhere out there—if not right here in downtown Dallas then somewhere close by—there could be a little cell of radicals planning to fire a devastating shot to western civilization. Maybe that dark, bearded man strutting by the Whataburger window was a lone-wolf warrior, radicalized by flamethrower screeds on the internet or by some lunatic Imam in a local mosque. And maybe he had a bomb or a gun in that backpack. A lot of deadly damage could be done in a very short time. The press would be all over it, of course. Shocked Americans would be treated to dramatic TV reports featuring interviews with sobbing friends, relatives, and neighbors of the gunman or bomber who swore they had no idea.

Shake walked back to the hotel thinking he would do what he could to help. It was what he'd always done in or out of uniform. He was barely a teenager, marching as a Missouri Military Academy cadet in President John F. Kennedy's 1961 Inaugural Parade, when he heard the words that still resonated with him. "Ask not what your country can do for you—ask what you can do for your country." Trying to answer that question pushed him into the U.S. Marine Corps and kept him going down some tough roads in war and peace. And somewhere along that road, he'd read the sentiments of General Stonewall Jackson who wrote: "All that I am and all I have is at the service of my country." He never made it a practice to preach, speechify, or wave the flag in public, but that was the sentiment he carried in his heart.

Later, he had a very nice and extremely expensive dinner with Director Macintosh, the man who calls himself Bayer, and a few functionaries from the conference. The conversation was mainly light and off-topic. Everyone seemed anxious to relax and discuss something a little less frightening than terrorism. Shake didn't talk much but gave his opinion when asked directly. And that wasn't often. The dinner party broke up early, and Shake declined several invitations for a nightcap. He was thinking about a good night's sleep and a leisurely drive to Lockhart. On his way out of the restaurant, Shake saw the PSD man he'd met earlier on his visit to the Presidential Suite.

"Hey, Jack. How goes it?"

"Surprised you remembered, sir." Agent Barnett smiled and nodded.

"Talk to your Dad?"

"I did, Gunner. He was happy you remembered him."

"Gunner, huh? I get the feeling you are a Marine."

"Most affirm. Dark Horse 3rd Battalion, 5th Marines—couple of cycles through The Sandbox."

"That almost makes us homeys." Shake shook hands and batted the agent on the shoulder. "I'm an old 5th Marines guy myself."

"You going to the rodeo with us tomorrow?"

"I don't know, Jack. I need to get home pretty soon."

"It's supposed to be a great show. Hope we see you there."

His hotel bill was covered, so Shake didn't feel too guilty about the two overpriced little bottles of Jack Daniels he snatched from the mini-bar in his room. He was sitting in the easy chair sipping whiskey and about half-decided to call Chan, pack, and head home in the morning. Lockhart was only a couple of hundred miles due south. He could it in four hours or so. He was working on a second drink when his phone chirped. Mike Stokey was calling from Vegas.

"Looks like you got home OK."

"Right—and you're gonna have to back me up about the bullet in the butt thing. Linda ain't buying it. She thinks I got stabbed by a hooker."

"I'll submit a sworn statement."

"I talked to Chan today. She says you're in Dallas. What's that about?"

"Meeting with the Director of National Intelligence—Bayer set it up. I drove up from McAllen because he got us off the hook with the FBI."

"The DNI did?"

"Yeah, him and Bayer. It's a long story. Tell you all about it when I get home."

"Listen, Shake—you remember I kept that thumb-drive with some of the stuff that we recorded down there?"

"Just shit-can it, Mike. It's all O-B-E now."

"Well, I loaded it all into the computer and listened to it."

"Anything interesting?"

"It's about that phone call. You know, the one that had one of those guys screaming and dancing around the area?"

"Wasn't that all in Arabic?"

"Yeah, most of it was, but you know how some words just don't translate so they just use the English? Well, I caught something, and I thought maybe you'd want to let somebody know about it."

"What did you hear?"

"The guy used the word cowboys twice. It could mean anything, but I immediately thought about the Dallas Cowboys and a football game or something like that. I mean why else would some Arab be screaming about cowboys?"

"OK, Mike—thanks. I'll talk to you soon."

Shake picked up his bourbon and then fished the ticket to the Southwest Exposition out of his pocket. There would be lots of cowboys at a big rodeo like that.

"Move to the right-hand lane," Wafic said checking his GPS. "We will connect with Highway 30 West in five miles."

Ibrahim flipped on a signal and gently eased the truck over to the right of the highway. He'd been silent for 40 miles or so, nodding or mumbling as his passenger extolled the glory of their mission. Ibrahim understood it would be a spectacular event, leading to his reward in Heaven, an event that would exact some appropriate revenge on the Infidels who blasphemed his religion and insulted his God. It was in the holy book. Such things must not be tolerated by those of the one true faith. He didn't need an outsider like Wafic to remind him of that. He needed silence, especially now at the hour of destiny. He needed to think and to pray undisturbed. Wafic could talk forever but he was not the one willing to die in this mission. Ibrahim tried to ignore the whispered platitudes and prayed silently for the strength he would need at the end of this journey.

Wafic looked into the rearview mirror on his side of the cab and saw that Hasim was following closely in the borrowed car they'd been using since his arrival. And then he glanced across the cab of the truck and noticed the sweat that was starting to show around the young martyr's hairline. Perhaps it was just a natural human reaction. Wafic badly wanted a cigarette, but smoking around a volatile mixture with a kerosene base was stupid. He could already sense fumes from the cargo behind him when the wind shifted behind their vehicle. The pungent odor would get worse when he pulled the lid off the center barrel to insert the trigger, but it could not be helped.

He fumbled in the bright orange backpack on the seat between them and re-checked the trigger for his bomb. One stick of industrial dynamite with an electrical blasting cap inserted and wires securely soldered into the little battery-powered switch. All was in order and intact, but Wafic found himself second-guessing the planned attack as Ibrahim steered them onto Highway 30 West headed for downtown Fort Worth. Perhaps Allah would provide, but so many things could go wrong. As an experienced professional, Wafic hated incomplete preparation. He didn't like to be rushed, and he rarely constructed a bomb that didn't include an anti-tamper device or a back-up detonator.

Perhaps he should have rigged a dead-man's switch. He'd done it before, and it guaranteed that the trigger would work even if the trigger-man was killed or lost his nerve. But the long drive to Fort Worth and the necessary stops at security checkpoints around the target area meant Ibrahim would need the use of both hands. For this mission, it was impractical to use a device that was safe when the ignition switch was depressed and fired when it was released. He would have to trust that Ibrahim would depress the switch as instructed when the truck was in the right position.

Fort Worth

Dithering until the last minute before heading west on I-30 was a bad idea. The Will Rogers Coliseum parking area was full, and Shake had to drive around for 20 minutes until he found a place to leave his truck. Some entrepreneur was gouging $20 for space in the rear of a strip mall, but it was all he could find within walking distance of the coliseum. The gates opened 30 minutes earlier, but the program he'd picked up at the hotel indicated that action in the arena wasn't due to start until 1700. He'd miss some of the gala opening ceremonies, but he'd heard enough pop singers butcher the National Anthem with annoying vocal frills not to mind. He keyed the truck lock and started walking.

Following a night of fitful sleep, Shake finally decided to delay his departure for home and head for Fort Worth. He was nagged by the reference to cowboys that Mike mentioned. It might mean nothing at all. Or it might be a vague reference to something like a planned attack on the crowd at a Dallas Cowboys game. Maybe it was just coincidence that a terrorist was talking about cowboys right around the time that some of the world's finest were gathered in Fort Worth to perform for a capacity crowd. On the other hand, it wasn't football season, and Shake didn't trust coincidences.

A happy, highly mobile crowd on the streets leading to the coliseum kept him moving in the right direction as he began the three-block walk to his destination. There was some early tail-gating going on in the parking lot of some of the strip-malls he passed. It's a big day in Fort Worth when a word-class rodeo was in town.

Climbing into the back of the truck, Wafic Aziz took small shallow breaths to keep from gagging at the kerosene and chemical smell. The six barrels of ANFO remained firmly strapped, but some of the liquid had sloshed out of the one with the loose lid. It was too late to worry about that. He carefully lifted the lid to reveal the thick explosive slurry, and then stripped off his orange backpack. He was cursing the change in schedule, wishing for the 100th time that he demanded time for a back-up trigger. But it was too late for anything more than the primary ignition device. He gingerly removed the dynamite accelerant and the trigger device from his pack and examined it for damage. It was in perfect shape just like all the other times he'd checked it during the 50-mile ride to the target area.

Using the special clip he'd manufactured, Wafic attached the trigger explosive to the rim of the barrel and uncoiled the arming wire. There was a sliding window between the cargo area of the truck and the cab. As he slid it open to pass through the trigger, Wafic heard Ibrahim mumbling prayers. It's all the man had done for the past 20 minutes, but prayers were preferable to tears. The emotion was understandable, but Wafic needed Ibrahim to focus.

"Take the wire and pull it through," he said. The prayers stopped and Wafic heard snuffling but Ibrahim did as directed. "Think of your duty, think of our God and your reward," he hissed as he replaced the barrel lid and shouldered his pack. "You are a soldier of Allah."

"As are we all…" Ibrahim's response sounded a little more firm and steady. Wafic decided it was all he could do at this late stage. The rest was truly in the worthy hands of God. He jumped down from the truck and waved at Hasim waiting behind the wheel of a car nearby. When he had the cargo compartment closed, he inserted a thin metal sealing strip in the latching mechanism. Security forces would be reluctant to break a cargo seal. He walked around to the cab of the truck where Ibrahim sat staring straight ahead through the windshield like man in a trance.

Wafic reached up and gripped his shoulder. "Do your duty to God," he said. *"Allahu Akbar!"*

Ibrahim did not respond but he did pull the truck into gear and drove slowly out of the parking lot in the direction of the target.

On the walk to the coliseum, Shake tried to keep from jostling people by moving to the edge of the flow. Something he'd barely noticed was nagging at him, something he'd just caught in peripheral vision. There had been a man wearing a bright orange backpack working near the back of a white panel truck. He looked directly at the parking area on his right. The man with the orange backpack was crawling into a yellow PT Cruiser with a cracked windshield. The truck had moved, and the driver was waiting to merge with the flow of traffic onto Lancaster Avenue. Placards on the cab said the truck belonged to a local feed and seed outfit. There were a lot of orange backpacks in the world. What were the odds it was the same one worn by the same guy in the pictures from northern Mexico? That DNI briefing would make anyone paranoid.

Shake shifted mental gears and decided to trust the pros. He was embarrassed enough about the northern Mexico fiasco. At the coliseum, he waited patiently in the middle of a long line stretching for nearly half a block around the perimeter walls. There were some ticket scalpers moving through the crowd hawking premium seats and cautiously eyeing the Fort Worth PD officers who were either walking around in pairs or scanning the crowd from parked patrol cars. There was a heavy police presence on the coliseum perimeter, and likely a bunch more cops on the other side of the walls. There was always the chance that a lone-wolf attacker with big balls could run off the rails at an event like this. It could be something like what happened at the airport in Fort Lauderdale or the deal in San Bernardino. Some cheese-dick who thinks he's on a mission from God just pulls a piece and starts firing into the tightly packed crowd. But a gun would be hard to smuggle here.

Rodeo fans carrying purses or backpacks were being subjected to search, and everyone had to walk through a metal detector before they were passed inside to find their seats. Ahead of him, rodeo fans wearing big western belt-buckles were causing alarms and gumming up the process. Shake could see a few irate customers being wanded or patted down for tripping an alarm. Just before he was ready to enter the security checkpoint, a couple of coliseum employees began to circulate, loudly reminding everyone in line that they should empty their pockets, remove belts and have their personal bags ready for inspection. Just like a big city airport—minus the requirement to remove your shoes. Having these rodeo fans hop around trying to pull off their tall cowboy boots would be a comedy of errors.

Shake cleared security, showed his ticket, and entered the giant venue. The coliseum had a standard arena layout.

Stairways and aisles led from a huge open concession area up ramps to seating tiers. Shake checked his ticket and looked for Section C. A wall map told him it was off to his left. He walked in that direction idly listening to Florida Georgia Line doing a pre-show warmup set. He'd walked about a quarter of the way around the coliseum arcade area when he spotted a crowded beer outlet. He was contemplating a giant cup of cold Lone Star when he heard someone calling his name.

Jack Barnett, in standard suit with ear-bug, was waving at him from a nearby field access ramp. "We were starting to think you weren't coming," he said as Shake approached. "The Director is already here. You're in the VIP seats."

"I'll follow you."

"No can do, Gunner. I'm posted here for the duration. There are two other guys up topside. I'll let them know you're inbound." Barnett whispered into his cuff as Shake walked up the ramp. The capacity crowd was huge and noisy. Bright lights flashed everywhere, but the focus was on the country duo performing down on the rodeo floor with a back-up band. The place had a very effective sound system that cut through the crowd babble. The pre-rodeo show was flashy with strobe lights and colored smoke blanketing the arena floor. It didn't look like there were many unoccupied seats on any of the three tiers that surrounded the performance area. He shuffled down a level or two and then immediately spotted the two suits flanking a roped off section of seats. The VIPs were assembled at what would be called mid-field at a football game. The seats provided a great ground-level view of the action due to start shortly.

One of the PSD guys pulled the rope for him, and he shook hands with Director Macintosh, the man who calls

himself Bayer, and several others he met at last night's dinner. Shake picked up the event program and settled into his
seat. When the opening act finished and the roadies were re-
moving the stage for rodeo action, Shake looked around at
the crowded tiers. It was just a sea of flesh, indistinct faces
under cowboy hats, baseball caps or styled hair. Stage hands
fired up some big fans to clear the arena of the colored smoke
the band used to juice their act, and Shake caught an eye-
watering whiff of animal sweat and cow manure. A Texas-
twangy voice boomed to let everyone know they were in for
a rip-roaring show featuring some of the finest stock and
most colorful cowboys in the world.

According to an arena diagram on the back of Shake's
program, the riders and ropers would emerge from chutes on
his left. All the cattle and horses were penned in corrals behind the chutes and ridden or prodded up for their time in the
spotlights by teams of wranglers. The diagram indicated
loading docks to the rear of the animal pens, and that was
likely where the breeders and ranchers delivered the stock
for the rodeo.

Carrie Underwood sang the National Anthem. Not bad.
At least she sang it straight. Shake watched a couple of the
initial bareback bronc riders bite the dust and then decided
he needed a beer.

Ibrahim wheeled the truck into an access road that led directly to the cattle holding area. He could see men in big hats
climbing the corral rails or poking at various animals with
long poles to direct their movement. Ahead of him was a security checkpoint blocking the road that led to a warehouse
fronted by loading docks. Another small truck was backed

up to the docks, and some men in overalls were unloading hay bales. He slowed to a sedate speed and cruised past a big yard of parked stock trailers where a few off-duty drivers milled around smoking and drinking coffee. It was relatively cool in the late afternoon, but Ibrahim could feel the sweat dribbling down his ribcage. In the glare of the fading sunlight on the windshield he saw an image of his mother with her hands raised beseechingly to heaven. She was weeping in agony, and her image appeared each time he blinked at the sweat dripping from his eyebrows.

He had a moment of panic as he approached the security guard when he couldn't find the cargo manifest Hasim had prepared for him. He looked around the cab desperately until he spied the clipboard on the floor beneath the passenger seat. He snatched at it and began to apply the brakes as he rolled slowly past two policemen in a cruiser parked near the entrance gate.

"Whaddya got?"

The security man standing at the side of the truck was chewing on a wad of gum and reading the placards on the door of the cab.

"Delivery," Ibrahim said mopping at his sweaty forehead with the sleeve of his shirt.

"No shit." The security man shrugged. "Paperwork?"

Ibrahim handed over the clipboard.

"Feed supplement," the guard said reading from the manifest and sniffing at the air. "Smells like high-octane shit. You got a leak back there, buddy. Better have them check it"

Ibrahim could smell the kerosene funk as the guard walked around behind the truck. Hasim said that might happen. He would be looking to see if there was a seal in place.

The gate guard rounded to the driver's side again and handed Ibrahim the clipboard.

"OK; drive around and back it up to the docks. They're gonna want to check the seal, so take your paperwork to the office inside." He pointed into the gloomy interior of the loading area and waved Ibrahim through the gate.

Whispering prayers for strength, Ibrahim put the truck in gear and steered straight ahead toward the loading docks. The truck had no radio, but he was hearing music. It was an Arabic lullaby his mother sang for him when he was just a baby. He shook his head but the song would not mute. Ibrahim worried that at this crucial moment of his life he was slipping into insanity. He'd often wondered about the celebrated martyrs at the moment of their death. What were they thinking about at that last moment on earth? Did they hear the words of an Imam? Or did they hear the sweet voices of their mothers?

Ibrahim turned right toward an access road leading into the arena concession area. There was an open gate just ahead and he could see golf carts wheeling through it carrying supplies for the booths that sold food, drink, and souvenirs. It was just as Hasim had described on the diagram they studied. He was to look as if he was turning to back the truck into the loading docks and then accelerate through that gate. Ibrahim glanced down at the trigger device on the seat beside him. Tears mixed with the sweat streaming down his cheeks. I must drive to the ramp marked letter C before I press the switch.

And then I must die.

Shake was about three customers away from a cold beer when a commotion to his left scattered the concession stand crowds on the mezzanine near Section C. There was a big white truck bumping aside some golf carts and two security guards were chasing, shouting and trying to flag it down. The truck was grinding in low gear, unable to make much speed due to the crowds and impediments. Shake recognized the placards on the driver's door. It was the same truck he'd seen on the walk to the coliseum—the same truck being tended by the man in the bright orange backpack.

"Jack!" He shouted to get Agent Barnett's attention and pointed at the truck grinding in their direction. "Bomb!"

The word had a terrifying effect on the people nearby. There were screams and shouts and people running in all directions. That's what Shake wanted: Get as many people away from that truck as possible in a hurry. He spotted Barnett elbowing through the panicked crowd with his gun drawn. The Secret Service Agent was likely an excellent shot with the Sig-Sauer 9mm he was pointing at the truck, but Shake knew they might be facing a dead-man's switch. He'd seen it before in Beirut. Kill the driver who releases the trigger and the bomb detonates.

"Hold your fire, Jack!" Shake shouted and sprinted toward the truck. For some reason, the vehicle had not accelerated. It was just bulling along in a low gear as if the driver was reluctant to hit any of the fleeing pedestrians. That gave Shake a chance to hop up on the running board. The fumes were nearly overpowering. It was a familiar odor and a warning signal. Shake had once helped clear debris and bodies from a car bomb in Beirut. The lingering high-octane stench was the same. Fuel oil or kerosene—it was explosive stuff. At that instant, Shake knew he was right to shout the alarm that was causing turmoil all around him. He was hanging onto a truck bomb and it might detonate at any second.

The driver was staring straight ahead as if he was in some sort of trance or maybe drugged. He barely glanced at the man hanging on outside his door with an arm wrapped around the side-view mirror. At a glance Shake saw the wires extending through the access window. They led directly to the driver's lap and a small device that had to be the trigger. The man was mumbling something incoherent but Shake ignored that. He focused on the man's right hand. His thumb was poised over a button on the switch which likely meant it was a pressure trigger rather than pressure-release. The driver would have to mash that switch to detonate the bomb. It would barely take an instant, not much more than a muscle twitch, and Shake realized that was all the time he had to prevent a massacre.

He reached in with his right hand, got a grip on the driver's thumb and bent it back hard. The man screamed and started shouting, but it wasn't from pain.

"Please! Please! Please!" If the guy was begging Shake to let go of his hand, he was completely out of luck.

Somehow Shake had to separate the driver from that trigger switch before he started to struggle. The only leverage he had at the moment was the man's thumb, and if the guy decided to reach for the switch with his other hand, the lights would go out in a very violent fashion. Shake swung hard to his right and pulled open the door of the cab with his left hand. Still gripping the driver's thumb, he let himself fall backward and pulled the man out of the truck.

They landed on the concrete floor in a tangle. Shake nearly lost his breath as the driver's weight hit him, but he was able to roll over and determine that the trigger switch had been dropped. It was behind him dangling from the cab, lost somewhere in the throng of people running for exits. The driver was not struggling other than to squirm around into a fetal position. Shake aimed a hard left at his temple for insurance and turned his attention back to the truck. It had stopped in contact with a concession stand with its engine idling sedately.

Agent Barnett and a couple of local cops stormed through the crowd pointing their weapons at Shake and the man on the ground. "I'm not the bad guy!" Shake shouted pointing at the unconscious driver beneath him. "He is—and there's a bomb in that truck!" Agent Barnett flashed his ID and the cops turned their muzzles on the driver. Both policemen looked quite happy that someone was giving definitive orders. "Take charge of this asshole," Shake said to Agent Barnett, "and get someone to call the EOD guys."

Elbowing through the crowd, he found the detonator and began to gather the wire. The last thing they needed now was for some panicked civilian to accidentally step on the trigger device. There were still a lot people in the mezzanine, either milling around confused or heading for exits. Shake could hear a PA announcer telling the crowd not to panic and wait for instructions. That just made things worse. He needed to get this bomb out of the coliseum and away from the crowds.

He jumped into the cab and slammed the door. With a glance at the outrigger mirror, he pulled the gear selector into reverse and leaned on the horn. As the truck started to roll in reverse, Shake spotted a gold badge and pointed at the officer. "I've got to get this thing out of here. Tell your cops not to shoot!" The senior policeman looked at Agent Barnett and got a nod before he grabbed his radio mike off a lapel and began to issue orders.

There was barely room to maneuver the truck, but it was mostly a straight line back to the access gate. Shake kept his eyes on the side mirror and ignored the flash of bodies dodging out of his path. The cops and stadium security people were cooperating and pushing frozen bystanders out of the way. Shake made minor steering corrections but kept his speed low as he aimed carefully to fit the truck through the gate in the chain-link fence. It looked like a tight squeeze which would be much easier to negotiate in a forward gear, but there was no time or space for a turn. Shake kept it at a slow, steady speed and hoped he wouldn't run into anything that would jostle whatever was in the cargo bed.

As he eased through the gate, flinching as the side of the truck scraped on the fencing, Shake saw he was backing into the livestock holding area. There were several Fort Worth PD cars parked across the access road with their lights flashing. He might steer past them, but a nervous cop could take a shot at him. Even if he made it, the truck bomb would wind up somewhere on a busy downtown street. He was concerned that it might have a back-up trigger, maybe a timer or something, and that meant he needed to take a look at what was back in the cargo bed. He shifted gears and steered toward a lot full of empty stock trailers. It looked like the best bet for minimal loss of life if the bomb at his back suddenly exploded.

When he had the truck parked, it was immediately surrounded by cop cars that roared into a perimeter. The police officers jumped out of their cars with weapons drawn. Shake hoped the senior officer inside had passed the word. He wouldn't last long in a hail-storm of rounds if one of those cops got nervous. He spotted Agent Barnett, a couple of other suits, and the senior Forth Worth cop running toward him. Shake jumped down from the cab still holding the detonating device gingerly. He thought about cutting the wire, but his experience with battlefield explosives made him think that might be a bad idea. It might trigger an anti-tamper device.

"Bomb Squad's on the way," a senior policeman wearing captain's insignia said. "We're gonna start an evacuation immediately."

"Let me take a look before you do," Shake said. "Might be there's no need for a panic."

"That's a job for my EOD team," the senior officer said. "They estimate fifteen minutes."

"And that might be too late, Captain. If this thing is what I think it is, it might be rigged with a timer. Lots of times these people use a back-up trigger device."

"Who the hell are you anyway?"

"I'll vouch for him, Captain!" Agent Barnett shouted flashing his ID and badge now visible on a neck chain. "He knows what he's doing."

Shake didn't wait around for further jurisdictional discussions. He needed to see what was in the back of the truck and he needed to do it in a hurry if a clock was ticking. If the bomb-makers were amateurs, they were probably OK at this point. If they were pros it was a different and very dangerous story. "Hang onto this," he said handing the detonator device to Agent Barnett. "It's a pressure switch so keep your fingers away from the buttons."

There was a seal strip on the latch of the cargo bay, and he cursed the requirement to leave his trusty Kerhsaw pocketknife in his truck. "I need something to cut this seal," he shouted looking around at all the Fort Worth cops looking back at him over the sights of pistols and shotguns. "Anybody got a Leatherman or something like that?" One of the cops reached into his squad car and came trotting up with a multi-tool. "You gonna open that damn thing up?"

Shake grabbed the tool and cut through the security seal. "Gotta see what we're facing—we ought to wait for the experts, but I don't want to take a chance."

"You know what you're doing, Mister?"

"I've had some experience. Do us all a favor and just keep everyone back."

He could hear sirens screaming as he slowly, carefully rolled the door to the cargo compartment open. The fuel oil stench was overpowering. Shake saw the barrels held in place with cargo straps and realized what the explosive was. "ANFO," he whispered and moved carefully into the truck bed. He spotted the wires leading to a barrel in the center of the clutch and carefully reached over to lift the lid. There was a small wire clip that held a stick of dynamite to the rim. Given the wires, Shake realized the dynamite was rigged with an electrical blasting cap. And that cap had to be removed as far away from the fume-saturated interior of the truck as possible. Screwing around with fused dynamite in a small space saturated with ANFO was a very dangerous proposition. He checked quickly for something that might indicate a secondary trigger or timer, but didn't see anything suspicious. He moved to the rear of the cargo area and peeked out to spot Agent Barnett. He could trust a fellow Marine.

"Jack, we can't wait on this. Put that trigger down and get someone to guard it. Then climb up in the cab. I'm gonna hand the detonator out to you."

Shake gently twisted the dynamite out of its clip and maneuvered forward where he could see Barnett kneeling on the seat of the cab. "Go real easy with this thing, Jack." He handed the dripping explosive through the access window. "It's rigged with an electrical cap. Once you get it clear of the truck, just lay it down on the ground somewhere and keep everybody away from it. Then we'll wait for EOD."

"What's in the barrels? Cops are asking."

"I'm pretty sure it's ANFO—ammonium nitrate and fuel oil. At this point the fumes are almost as dangerous as the guts of this damn thing. So be careful—and tell the cops to establish a wide perimeter."

Ten minutes later, the Fort Worth SWAT EOD team arrived and confirmed his suspicions. The cops cleared the area and the experts in bulky protective suits went to work. The press, already in the area to cover the rodeo, was flooding the area, screaming into their microphones about breaking news. A half-hour later, a HazMat truck showed up to deal with the ANFO. Shake was talking to one of the EOD techs who was full of gory speculation about what might have happened if Shake hadn't saved the day. By this time, the parking lot in the rear of the coliseum was a zoo. There seemed to be more people milling around than there were cattle and horses in the nearby corrals.

At the center of it all was a clutch of city officials with the Mayor in attendance who had been at the show gladhanding. Now they were trying to decide whether it was better to evacuate the coliseum or call it a lucky break and go ahead with the rodeo. Shake overhead the Mayor's final decision. The EOD guys would do a sweep and then he'd make an announcement. The show would go on for anyone still left in the stands for opening day of the great Southwest Exposition. And then they started pointing in his direction. The Mayor walked over in company of another man who was introduced as a Public Affairs Officer for the city. They were joined shortly after handshakes by Agent Barnett, the man who calls himself Bayer, and the Director of National Intelligence. There were more introductions, more handshakes, and then the PAO starting jabbering about the press flooding the area and how someone needed to make a statement. He was looking in Shake's direction. Shake was looking for an opening to tell the man where he could stick his suggestion when the Mayor decided it was his job.

He caught the Police Chief's elbow and headed for a little security perimeter where FWPD cops held a growing throng of reporters at bay. Shake stood as far away from all that as possible in the background with the clutch of city officials making contingency plans. They were ignoring Shake which was fine. He was in a sort of mild trance, trying to shake off his usual bout of post-action adrenaline jitters and wondering if the beer concessions were still operating.

"I guess 'thank you' doesn't half cover it, Shake." Director Macintosh said, glancing at the truck which was now surrounded by yellow crime-scene tape and guarded by four cops. "Thank God you were here."

"I finally put two and two together." Shake shrugged trying to stretch some of the tension out of his shoulders. "This all ties in with some stuff we saw in northern Mexico." He pointed at Bayer. "He's got the pictures."

"We're gonna need you to do a full de-brief on that."

"Can do, Director—but not in Washington, please. I need to get home."

"No hurry. I'll take a couple of people from the shop after Shake gets settled in at home," the man who calls himself Bayer said. "We can debrief in Lockhart and eat some good barbecue."

"Fort Worth PD and the Tarrant County Sheriff's people want to interview him, sir." Agent Barnett pointed at a clutch of SWAT cops and detectives standing nearby. "We should do that and then maybe they'll cut Gunner Davis loose."

"You up for it, Shake?" Director Macintosh looked like he was willing to short-stop the effort if required.

"I guess we owe them that much. Soon as you can get your hands on him, you guys need to sweat that driver. He's just a kid. He didn't rig all this—someone else did and it probably means they've got a cell working locally."

If there was a modified rodeo staged for the remaining fans, Shake didn't get to see any of it. He was taken to police headquarters downtown for a detailed and carefully recorded exposition of events and his role in it all. The first thing he did was to let reps from the Texas Rangers and State Police know that they needed to issue an immediate BOLO for two men in a yellow PT Cruiser with a cracked windshield. He gave the location where he'd seen the vehicle on the walk to the coliseum, but he didn't have tag numbers or much description of the men beyond the fact that one of them would own a bright orange backpack. What he was sure of was that the people in that car had something to do with the truck bomb and would likely have some very valuable information once they were apprehended and interrogated.

The man who calls himself Bayer flashed his new credentials shortly after the testimony began and saved some trouble by indicating that Shake was on the staff of Director of National Intelligence. He threw in a colorful précis about Shake's background and military experience which deflected most of the early questions about who he was and what he was doing in Fort Worth. After an initial recitation of his basic timeline and activities, the session evolved into a long, tedious question and answer session with individuals from an alphabet soup of local, state, and Federal agencies.

The police PAO was next in company with the Tarrant County Sheriff and a representative from the Governor's office. Apparently, they were besieged by reporters who all wanted something beyond the official statements that had been issued.

"There's a press conference in half an hour," the Public Affairs guy said. "We'd really like to have you say a few words." Shake was about to decline, hoping the DNI or the man who calls himself Bayer would intercede and save him, when the Tarrant County Sheriff, a no-nonsense guy fondling an off-white Stetson, made his pitch. "Mr. Davis, you ought to understand like it or not you're a hero around here. Texas likes her heroes—and you being from just down the road in Lockhart and all…"

"Sheriff, first of all I'm nobody's hero. I was just in the right place at the right time. I've got some experience with this kind of thing and I…well, you know…"

"Shake, there's a lot of anxiety these days about home-grown terrorism," the Governor's man said, "and that's clearly what this is. We ID'ed the driver. He's a part-time student from Dallas. Member of a mosque over there so there's gonna be some knee-jerk against Muslims."

"He was driving, but a kid like that didn't rig that ANFO bomb. That was the work of outsiders, likely pros in the terrorism game. I told you all about that just a little while ago."

"And we're following up on it," the Sheriff said. "But right now we need to deal with the press, and they're focused on this incident and what kept it from being a disaster. That's you."

There was the usual thank you, thank him, thank all the agencies involved, and thank God speeches before Shake had to face the local and national press mobs. The PAO man gave a little of his background, saying that Shake was visiting in Dallas for the National Security conference, and then the questions flew hot and heavy.

"Mr. Davis! Mr. Davis!" He could barely see who was shouting at him for the TV lights. It was nearly impossible to sound locate amid the babble of male and female voices bellowing for attention and the click-whirr of motor-driven still cameras. Shake just nodded and pointed at the first spring-butt smart enough to stand.

"How did you know there was a bomb in the truck, Mr. Davis?"

"I didn't know. I just strongly suspected it based on my past military experience with that kind of thing. Once I got close enough to smell the ANFO, I knew I was right."

"And for the record, sir…" A petite female holding a microphone flagged for a network affiliate said, "Please explain what ANFO is."

"Well, it's a volatile mixture of ammonium nitrate—the kind of stuff farmer's use for fertilizer—and fuel oil. A-N-F-O. You get the mixture right and add an accelerant—such as dynamite in this case—and you've got a bomb. This deal was a lot like what that whack-job McVey used in Oklahoma City…when was it? Back in ninety-five, I think. The local EOD guys can give you more details."

"And how did you come to be in Fort Worth?"

"I was actually in Dallas for a conference. I got invited to go to the rodeo, so I drove over here and you know the rest. Shame I didn't get to see much of the rodeo by the way."

"What was your role in the Dallas National Security Conference?"

"I didn't have a role. I just got invited by the Director of National Intelligence."

"Do you work for him?"

"I don't work for anybody. I'm retired."

"What can you tell us about the driver of the truck?"

"Nothing much. He was just a young guy—didn't look too much like he wanted to be where he was—didn't put up much of a struggle. Anything else, you'll have to ask the police."

"Are you confident from your past military experience that this was an act of terrorism?"

"Well, I'm confident that driving a truckload of high-explosive into a big public gathering with the intent of detonating it is something a terrorist would do. If you're asking about motivation, I think it's pretty obvious what was intended. If you're asking about radical Muslim sponsorship or something like that, I can't tell you because I don't know. Ask the cops."

"Can you tell us something about your background, Mr. Davis?"

"Don't know what you want. I'm a Marine, retired from active duty. I live in Lockhart, Texas…" He was saved by the police PAO who ducked in toward the bank of microphones. "We are preparing a hand-out with Chief Warrant Officer Davis' bio. You should have it shortly." Shake just nodded his thanks at the man and wondered where they'd get all that information. Likely something the man who calls himself Bayer would provide.

"Mr. Davis…" The woman with the flagged-microphone and about a ton of blonde hair surrounding her face was back at it. "How did you *feel* when you defused that bomb?"

"How did I feel?" Shake just shook his head. How would any rational human being feel fucking around with several hundred gallons of high explosive? And what the hell did what he was feeling have to do with what happened? "Listen, ma'am. I don't know how to answer that question and—with all due respect—I don't know why it's relevant. You get in a situation where you've gotta do something like that; you don't feel, you think—and then you act. Feelings have got nothing to do with it."

"But were you frightened?"

"I was seriously concerned that I might get my butt blown all over the area, if that's what you want me to say."

It went on that way for most of an hour. The questions began to deteriorate toward the end as reporters tried to elicit speculation or things Shake didn't want to say. Mostly he just stood in the glare of the TV lights, trying to control his temper and telling them to ask the cops or the FBI. One of the PAO's assistants finally arrived with a stack of paper and began to pass out a basic sketch of Shake's career, and the press mob began to filter out of the room.

"We really appreciate this, Mr. Davis." The Governor's man shook his hand.

"Well, I'm not very good at it, but if it helps…"

"Oh, it helps, Mr. Davis, believe me. The Governor asks me to convey his personal thanks. He's working on a DPS Medal of Valor for you."

"Well, tell the Governor thanks, but something like that isn't necessary."

"I think every Texan would beg to differ. We've got a hotel room for you tonight. Is there anything else we can do?"

"I need a ride to pick up my truck."

They finished their prayers at a roadside turn-out off I-20 and then got back in the car hoping God would send them some better news. The news continued to be bad. Every station they could find on the radio dial carried reports about what happened in Fort Worth, and it was not what the two ISIS operatives expected. The mission failed.

Most of the radio reports featured comments from some cursed Infidel who apparently interfered and wrecked their plan. Perhaps it was the will of Allah, Hasim speculated as he snapped off the radio chatter. Or perhaps it was poor planning and shoddy preparation, Wafic responded, lighting another of the cigarettes he'd been chain-smoking since they left Fort Worth.

Wafic cursed long and loud in florid Arabic about the damage to his professional esteem. Hasim waved a hand at the smoke billowing inside the car and tried to remain calm. He was also angry, but one failure should not be allowed to bleed their courage and motivation. There was another mission ahead of them in California, another bomb to be built, for the planned attack on something the *kafirs* in that state called the Hollywood Bowl. That one might go better—if God wills it. This was no time to let their spirit to falter.

"Don't lose heart, Wafic. We don't know what happened."

"We know the mission failed, Hasim. We know the bomb was detected somehow and disarmed. You rushed me in preparation. I could have made a backup detonator given sufficient time. And we wouldn't be facing this failure, this humiliation."

"The plan and the preparation were…"

"They were shoddy, Hasim. Rushed and shoddy! And the man you picked to carry it out was weak."

"We do not know Ibrahim was at fault."

"I tried to tell you that man was unreliable." Wafic lit the last of the cigarettes and tossed the crumpled pack out the car window. "I could see that he was losing his nerve. And the idiot survived! Now he is in police custody. Do you suppose he will have the courage to keep his mouth shut?"

"It is a problem, but only a temporary one." There were brothers—facilitators or ISIS sympathizers more than operatives—that would likely be arrested in Dallas. If nothing else, the police would quickly discover the mosque where Ibrahim worshipped and they would start probing. Some pieces of the long-range plan for subverting The Great Satan would fall, and those involved in America would have to suspend activities or go into temporary seclusion. "I will make some calls," Hasim said. "We will scatter the flock."

Wafic Aziz pointed at a tall neon sign next to an I-20 off-ramp. "Stop there so I can buy some cigarettes."

Texas State Trooper Marcus Casburn was nearing the end of his shift as he sat watching traffic heading west on I-20 about 15 miles from his home station in Abilene. It had been a relatively peaceful patrol with only a couple of minor wrecks and a handful of tickets, but that was all routine stuff. Like every other cop in Texas, Trooper Casburn was giving a great deal of his attention to news reports about the terrorist incident in Fort Worth. And like every other cop in every agency of the Texas Department of Public Safety, he had received the BOLO to be on the lookout for a yellow PT Cruiser with a cracked windshield.

It wasn't much of a description, not as detailed as usual and not including any tag numbers that could be traced, but it fit the vehicle he saw heading west at a legal speed right past his position. He waited for a few cars to pass—just one or two to keep the driver of the PT Cruiser from thinking he was being tailed—and pulled out onto the highway matching traffic speeds. Then he reached for his radio.

"Dispatch…Unit 53…be advised I'm rolling behind a vehicle that looks a lot like the one in the BOLO out of Fort Worth."

"Fifty-three…Dispatch…is that the yellow PT Cruiser with a cracked windshield?"

"10-4, Dispatch. He's headed west on I-20 about fifteen miles out of town. I'll be 10-38 on him shortly."

"Fifty-three…10-12."

While he was standing by, Trooper Casburn jabbed at his computer and glanced at the BOLO alert. It said probably two persons, no description available. That fit. As vehicles shifted lanes, he could see two people in the vehicle's front seat. The BOLO also indicated he should be looking for a bright orange backpack. He'd find out about that shortly.

"Fifty-three…Dispatch. Consider all after as 10-30…"

Danger or Emergency. Casburn reached down to his right hip and unsnapped the retainer strap locking his Sig Sauer P226 in the holster. He'd never had to fire one of the .357 rounds at anything but paper but he was a cautious man.

"Unit 53, do not approach subject vehicle. Texas Ranger SRT out of Region Four is now the responding agency. Stand by." In seconds, there was a loud squelch break from Trooper Casburn's radio and a new voice came on the air.

"Unit 53, this is the Ranger SRT commander. Do you copy?"

"10-2, Rangers…go ahead."

"Be advised we are putting in a roadblock at the intersection of I-20 and Texas 84. How far are you from there?"

"I'm guessing about three of four miles, give or take."

"Is there much other traffic in your area right now?"

"About usual, I guess. Not too heavy."

"Copy. Here's what we need you to do. Drop back out of sight of the suspect vehicle and then conduct a traffic break. Stop everything headed west until further notice. We are dispatching additional THP units and a helicopter to assist with further surveillance."

"10-4, Rangers." Trooper Casburn slowed to let the yellow PT Cruiser disappear over the western horizon. Then he flipped on his light bar and began swerving from lane to lane across Interstate 20.

"Roadblock!" Wafic Aziz screamed, pointing through the cracked windshield at a line of four police cars blocking the road ahead. There were policemen in cowboy hats and others in all black jumpsuits standing around the vehicles with weapons in hand. He reached between his legs for the pistol he carried in his orange backpack. It was not much up against police rifles and shotguns, but Wafic had long ago sworn a solemn oath that he would never be captured and condemned to die in some cage at Guantanamo Bay.

"I can't get around them," Wafic shouted, glancing at a police helicopter which was now orbiting over the highway. "We are trapped."

"Then we fight our way out of it." Wafic jacked the slide on his pistol. He glanced at the flat open ground on either side of the road and understood he would very soon be in the crosshairs of some *kafir's* rifle sight. *Insh'allah.*

"Stop your vehicle immediately." A voice roared and echoed across the prairies. "Exit the vehicle with your hands raised and get down on your knees."

"There is nothing we can do." Hasim looked over at Wafic squeezing the pistol with one hand and gripping the door handle with the other. He let the car roll a few feet and then applied the brakes.

"Run!" Wafic bolted from the car and sprinted toward the side of the road. There was more amplified shouting for him to halt. Wafic responded by snapping a few running shots at the police. There was an immediate, blinding response. Gunfire roared in a dazzle of muzzle flashes from the roadblock. Wafic collapsed on the pavement like a limp rag and then the guns turned on Hasim, still sitting frozen behind the steering wheel.

"Get out of the car immediately with your hands raised." The loudspeaker voice was even louder and more intense at this point. "If you do not comply, we will open fire!"

Hasim glanced quickly from all the guns trained on him to Wafic Aziz lying dead in a puddle of blood. And then he cranked the steering wheel to turn the car around and hit the accelerator. Bullets immediately shattered the rear window and splattered loudly through several body panels with a sound like someone beating on a cooking pot with a metal spoon. The wheel began to vibrate wildly as his rear tires were flattened. The police helicopter was diving lower and lower as it chased Hasim back east toward Abilene. Hasim just kept his foot jammed on the gas pedal with no real destination in mind. He was much too frightened to think about where he was going or about the very slim chance he had of staying alive much longer.

Trooper Marcus Casburn, standing outside his cruiser at an impromptu traffic block he'd managed to establish just a mile from the action, heard the crackle of gunfire in the distance off to the west. He took a look at several motorists standing outside their vehicles gawking at the police helicopter and shouted for them to get back in their cars. The radio indicated that a suspect or suspects were fleeing in his direction. The helicopter was cleared to open fire when the sniper Casburn could see hanging in the door had a clear and safe shot. And then he saw the yellow PT Cruiser headed his way.

The shot-shredded tires didn't allow much speed, and if the vehicle continued straight ahead it would pass within 15 feet of where Trooper Casburn stood in front of a line of idling cars waiting for clearance to continue westbound. If the lunatic at the wheel got that far, he'd be weaving right into the halted vehicles. And that would mean that the long-gun man in the helicopter probably couldn't make a safe shot without a chance of hitting civilians.

Keeping his eyes on the approaching car, Trooper Casburn drew his weapon, crouched behind the right front fender of his cruiser, and steadied the Sig. Alignment was good, position supported and steady. He placed his finger on the trigger and stayed focused on the front sight just like a qualification day on the range. When the protesting vehicle drew abreast, he saw the wide-eyed fear on the face of the driver. Trooper Casburn squeezed the trigger when the yellow PT Cruiser was just 10 feet from him passing right to left. He swiveled and kept squeezing the trigger until the slide locked to the rear.

Fort Worth

When Shake finally managed to retrieve his truck and get to a hotel room, paid for by the Governor's office as indicated by a note on a sumptuous basket of cheese, sausage, wine, and crackers, it was getting on toward nightly news time. He stuffed himself with snacks, raided the mini-bar for whiskey, and watched excerpts from the press conference on TV. Didn't matter which channel he tried, local or network, they were all carrying coverage of the foiled bomb plot wall-to-wall. Shortly after he heard himself hailed as a national hero for the fifth or sixth time, Chan called.

"I guess I don't need to ask why you didn't call."

"Guess not. You've seen the news I take it."

"You take it correctly. I've seen it—three or four times—and so has everyone else you and I ever knew. I'd have called sooner, but the phone has been going nuts."

"It wasn't all that big a deal, Chan."

"The hell it wasn't. You're talking to your wife, remember—a woman who knows a thing or two about this stuff?"

"Like I said. Right place at the right time."

"More like the right *man* in the right place at the right time. I'm very proud of you, Shake. I'm also a little pissed that you were messing around with high explosives. They don't have EOD in Fort Worth?"

"I was worried they might not get there on time. You know how some of these dudes play the IED game. They usually include a Plan B in case Plan A fails."

"Was there a Plan B?"

"No. I got lucky."

"So when can you come home?"

"Soon as I can duck out of here, Chan. The front desk is flooded with requests to talk to me, but I'm dodging that. An hour with the press is about all I can take. I'll probably hit the road tomorrow morning."

"Well, we'll have to erect barriers. I've got a bunch of messages from the press on the answering machine already."

"Ignore all that. If we have to we'll go into hiding."

"Just get home as soon as you can. We moved down here for some peace and quiet, you'll recall."

"It'll all blow over, Chan. See you as soon as I can. I'll call with updates."

Shake was still wet from a long shower when his phone rang again. It was the man who calls himself Bayer.

"Nice work today, Shake."

"Thanks, but I'm over it. Gonna head for home tomorrow morning or as soon as I can sneak past the press."

"Give Chan my best. I'm guessing she knows all about this, right?"

"Yeah, she just called a little while ago. The press is hounding her, too."

"It'll blow over, Shake."

"That's what I told her, but I'm probably due an ass-chewing for messing around with high explosives when I'm supposed to be officially retired from that kind of nonsense."

"Listen, I'm at the airport and they're calling my flight, but I wanted you to know they got the guys in the PT Cruiser. Unfortunately, that's no help to us intel-wise. Texas Rangers killed one of them at a roadblock. The other one tried to run, but a State Trooper blew him full of holes."

"That's good news, I guess, but it's a shame we won't be able to squeeze them."

"Yeah, it is. I got a quick look at the morgue shots. It turns out they were two of the guys in the original photos you sent me from South Texas. So we know they came in across the border. We'll find out more about all that shortly."

"Maybe so—but these fucking guys are like a blob of mercury, you know. You smack them and they just scatter and spread. Shut down the Mexican border and you better start watching Canada."

"One thing at a time, Shake. I gotta go."

"Where you headed?"

"Mexico City. We're interrogating the second batch of assholes we busted down there, and the Director wants me to sit in on it. I'll fill you in later."

One thing at a time—Shake finished his drink, set an alarm and dropped into bed.

San Antonio

Emilio Contreras had just finished inventory for the new job that would take him on the road and finally get him the hell out of shadows where he was forced to live. Sitting on his sister's kitchen table, cleaned, oiled, and ready for loading, were the tools of his trade. He had a very nice Glock 19 with an extended magazine and 100 rounds of 9mm Speer Gold Dot ammo, a Benelli M2 12-gauge semi-auto shotgun with two boxes of deer slugs, and a Ruger Mini-14 Tactical Rifle with 50 rounds of ball ammo. It had been difficult, risky, and very expensive to amass all the firepower, but he wasn't paying the bills.

Chico, a trusted *compadre* from the local MS-13 organization, was due around midnight at the wheel of a Jeep Wrangler Unlimited that featured a hidden compartment under the floorboards where the guns would be stored. When the call Emilio was waiting for came through, they could hit the road to make some money. Emilio ran his practiced hands over the arsenal and recounted the ammunition. It was probably a lot more than required to deal with one troublesome gringo, but Contreras learned when he was running with the *Zetas* that you never had too little firepower. You got in trouble doing wet work only when you lacked enough guns—or enough balls.

He got a beer from his sister's fridge and counted out the money she would need while he was on the road. Emilio would be glad—and so would his sister—when he could afford to get out of Texas and out of the country. And that wouldn't be too much longer. For now he was flush—minus a sizeable chunk for the guns and ammo—from the down-payment sent by his old employer in Mexico. The $25,000 in cash delivered by an Eduardo Lopez courier earlier in the week got the job started and provided some front money for Chico. When the target was dead, there would be $25,000 more—all his and more than enough to buy his way around the cops and down into Guatemala where he knew some people, more of the old *Zeta* gang that would set him up in business.

Emilio snapped on his sister's little TV set and sat down to watch. The news about the thing in Fort Worth was all over Spanish-language channels. There were some good shots of *Senor* Davis and he leaned forward in his chair to study the images. Why would a pasty-faced, salute-the-flag gringo like this rip-off a load of *El Escorpion's* dope? Maybe it was all a sham. Maybe this dude was dirty on the side. None of Emilio's or Chico's extensive contacts in the drug underworld had ever heard of Shake Davis, but you never knew. He was tough man from the looks of him and a brave one according to the news reports. But Emilio had killed tough hombres in the past, and brave men sometimes made easy targets. They often believed their own press and got cocky.

He stared at the TV screen with the sound muted and watched his target escorted into a building surrounded by cops. Would they provide the big hero with body armor in case of retaliation by some raghead fanatic? Maybe the rifle should be the choice.

Emilio shrugged and snapped off the TV. This would not be a simple hit and run unless he got extremely lucky. Concerns were different now that his target was a big hero. He had to have more information, some good intelligence. Emilio was a well-trained soldier when he left the army to run with the *Zetas*. When he did jobs like this one on either side of the border, he operated like a soldier. There were questions and the answers determined the tactics to be used. Did the target have police protection? Would he be at his home? Or would he remain in Fort Worth? Or would he be in Dallas? The location was important. Much easier to hit a target and escape in a little shit-heel burg like Lockhart. If he had to do the job in some big city, it was much more difficult and escape was a much tougher proposition. Was the big hero a gun-nut like most *Tejanos*? Was he likely to be strapped and fight back? This job would require reconnaissance.

His phone rang and Emilio saw his employer was calling from Rio Grande City.

"*Ola, Escorpion.* You got something for me?"

"You have seen the news?"

"About the thing in Fort Worth? Yeah, I saw it. He's the big hero."

"Does it change anything?"

"I'll get it done. Don't worry about that. Where is he now?"

"He left his hotel in Fort Worth this morning. You gotta figure he's headed home."

Emilio checked his watch and shrugged. "He should be there in a couple of hours. No problem—makes it easy."

"So you will do the job in Lockhart?"

"I'll do the job. That's all you need to know."

"He will be a hard man to kill."

"Stop worrying. I have a plan."

"It better be a good one. Don't fuck this up, *amigo*"

"Don't threaten me, man. Just get my money ready."

"I have it here. A courier will deliver it when you've done the job."

"Tell him to get his ass on the road. I should be back here in a week or so."

"I need to know the job is done before I send any more money."

"He's a fucking hero, right? You'll see it on the news."

Black Site—Mexico City

The man who calls himself Bayer sat at a rickety card table with Supervisory Special Agent Joe Carr and his Mexican National Police counterpart on the International Counter-Terrorism Task Force. Neither man seemed overly anxious to get started. Bayer accepted a paper cup of coffee brought into the room by a uniformed Mexican cop and explained his visit. The DNI wanted a full report on their most recent captures, and both governments had authorized an all-access detailed briefing. The FBI man and the senior *Federale* both nodded. They'd been told that much.

Bayer fiddled with the briefcase at his feet. The place was depressing. Despite the altitude on the outskirts of the capital, the air felt muggy and cloying. On his way in, he'd not seen much more than some small cells with a few prisoners barely discernible in the gloom. The black site had an imposing look with armed guards manning a barbed wire perimeter. It also had an ominous feel as if it was a place few people were allowed to enter and even fewer were allowed to leave. The Mexicans didn't screw around wasting money on frills when they built their little version of Guantanamo Bay.

He placed a small recorder on the table and tested it for function. "The following information is classified secret," he said for the record and gave the date and time plus the names of those present. Then he sat back and waited.

"Here's what we've got so far…" Supervisory Special Agent Carr checked his notes and sipped cold coffee. "The honcho is an Iranian, former Revolutionary Guard Quds

Force, according to the CIA. He's dummied up and playing the hard-ass. We've been ordered to send him to Gitmo for further interrogation. The other two are a little different story. There's no known record of them in the data base. Both are Syrians and both have military backgrounds."

"Are they talking?"

"We've got them isolated from each other and we have been able to get some basic intelligence…" He nodded at the Mexican cop. "And that's thanks to our partners who don't have to play by so many rules and restrictions."

"So, you're gonna keep the two Syrians and continue working—sorry, poor choice of words—continue interrogating them?"

"That's right. We're particularly concerned, as is the Mexican Government, about how they got into Mexico undetected and who they've been hiring to smuggle them across the American border. That and anything they might know about plans by ISIS or any other radical groups targeting North America is the primary emphasis in questioning."

"Got any early ideas about that?"

The Mexican *Federale* spoke excellent English and didn't mince words. "Like you in America, we have a long coastline on both sides of our country. So far, our information leads me to believe these people mostly come in by boat somewhere along our west coast. Either that or they illegally cross our southern borders from other countries in Central America. The two we are currently holding indicate that's the way they got here. They hired guides in Belize who took them to the Mexican border."

"And then what?"

"And then they contracted with criminal elements to take them north to remote training sites such as the one we raided."

"And both of these men are confirmed as ISIS operatives?"

"That's what they claim. Both indicate they were sent here by ISIS command in Syria. The mission was to train and prepare in my country for follow-on strikes in yours. If you let them do their religious rant, they often reveal what we want to know in the process."

"Now that we've got photos and names, assuming the names are legit and not aliases," Agent Carr added, "we're running them against refugee records and international immigration data bases. I don't know how much good it will do, but we want to see if we can trace their route. We know both guys started in Raqqa. I'm hoping we can find out about the ISIS pipeline from there to here."

"Let's try to drill down a little if we can." Bayer refilled his cup from a carafe on the table. "I'm sure we'll get a handle on some of the nuts and bolts but there's got to be more to all this on the Mexico end of that pipeline. What I mean is, how do they manage to hire these guides and security people? How do they contact the smugglers that can get them across the U.S. border?"

"You never want to underestimate outfits like ISIS," Carr replied. "It's a bad mistake to assume these people are amateurs or don't have worldwide tentacles. Believe me, they do. One of the Syrians admitted that he was part of a cell that sent people to Western Europe as well as to the States. That takes some long reach and…"

"And plenty of money," the Mexican cop interrupted. "It's what we say in law enforcement investigations: Follow the money. These people have plenty of that, mostly oil revenues or cash grants from the Muslim supporters around the world."

"OK, but how do they get hooked up down here? Do they just make a phone call or what?"

"There are businessmen from Muslim countries here just as there are north of our border. Some of those people are co-religionists or sympathizers who put outfits like ISIS in contact with our criminal elements."

"You mean like the drug cartels?"

"No one knows more about smuggling things across the U.S. border than they do. Drugs or people it makes no difference to them if they are paid enough for the expertise."

"That's why we've formed this international Task Force," Agent Carr added. "We know there is a connection between Mexican criminals and these terrorists. We need to find the people involved and put a stop to it. Raids like the one we conducted just put a band aid on the problem. We need to keep digging. We've gotta stop this thing before it gets any worse than it already is."

"Are you getting any help with that from the Mexican national you arrested?"

"He's a little fish—a small-time player—gun for hire. We know he has been employed as a smuggler for a man named Eduardo Lopez. We are looking into that."

"OK, thanks. Anything else?" Both men shook their heads and the man who calls himself Bayer stopped the recorder. "I'll be in touch regularly, and the DNI will appreciate reports on your progress."

The Mexican cop got his cap and left the room. Agent Joe Carr remained, smiling at the visitor with his arms folded across his chest. "Saw the reports from Fort Worth on local TV. I'm told you know Gunner Shake Davis personally."

"Yes. Shake and I are old acquaintances in some dicey business over the years. I like to think he's a friend."

"Me, too. I trained under him when I was in the Marine Corps. That's one of the reasons we didn't make too big a stink about what happened with him and Mike Stokey down here."

"The other reason being that my boss called of your dogs."

"Guess that's right," Carr said with a shrug. "Anyway, you might tell him to leave this business to the pros."

"He'd likely be glad to do just that. But I think things like what he did in Fort Worth indicate he's a valuable man to have involved in the CT business."

"Fine—but have Shake let me know beforehand if he plans another visit south of the border."

A dark green Jeep Wrangler Unlimited made one slow circuit of the town square and then turned onto North Commerce Street. It was a balmy hour in the late afternoon, so the two men in the vehicle had the windows rolled down. They could smell the hickory smoke from Black's barbecue just a half block to their left.

"Dude, we gotta get us some *barbecoa* tonight." The stocky man behind the wheel braked for a stop sign at the Market St. intersection and sniffed at the fragrant air. Despite the weather, he was wearing a windbreaker. The man next to him insisted that he hide what he could of the telltale MS-13 ink covering most of Chico Sandoval's upper body. Many of the tats were applied while Chico was doing a nickel in Huntsville and they were on file with state cops.

"After we get to your *compadre's* place. Did you make the call?"

"Damn, dude—you saw me do it a half hour ago."

"And he lives just up there?" Emilio Contreras pointed south along Commerce Street toward a bridge that spanned Plum Creek, an ancient watercourse that meandered around the town.

"It's marked right there, dude." Chico tapped the map spread in Emilio Contreras' lap. "It's a little shack on Live Oak—see, right there."

"Run by the house and then go around the block." Emilio was also wearing a light jacket, as much to cover the Glock 19 in his waistband as to cover the slightly less lurid ink on his own arms. He wanted to remain low-profile and off the police radar while he scouted the job. "When you come back around, park over there." He pointed at the lot of a local funeral home directly across the street from the big house which Chico's cousin indicated was owned and occupied by Shake Davis.

The big ornate house had once been owned by a *Chicana* fine artist who painted and decorated the place in colorful Tex-Mex salmon and turquoise pastels. It was a two-story affair set on about five acres, much of which was dotted with tall old pecans that grew in a big patch of low ground south of the residence. It featured a circular gravel driveway that wrapped around two ancient live oaks that spread long branches over a little barbecue patio. As they rolled slowly past, Emilio noticed a new Ford F-250 pick-up parked between the main residence and a little adjacent bungalow that looked like a guest house. The truck had a U.S. Marines sticker on the cab window. That would be the gringo's ride.

Chico motored across the Plum Creek Bridge and pointed ahead to where a smaller street crossed Commerce. It looked like the Lockhart slums began on this side of the bridge. "Over there is where *Juanito* lives. It ain't much, but it's cool for watching the house."

The cross street was called Live Oak for obvious reasons. It was lined with the native trees. It was also lined with shanties, most of which had tin roofs over cracked and faded clapboard. Many of them had a distinct lean. It looked like any good size wind would blow them over the rest of the way.

"And your cousin's cool with us crashing there?"

"Dude, *Juanito* is cool with anything that turns a buck, you know? He's got a habit he needs to support. He told me he sometimes does yard work for this gringo, OK? He knew right away who I was talking about."

They parked in the funeral home lot and sat watching the big house across the street. A few lights upstairs and then downstairs flicked on and off, but there wasn't much to see. At one point Emilio got out of the vehicle and strolled along the sidewalk heading south. He stopped at the bridge and looked in both directions. Running through the pecan stand on the lower part of the target's property was a little watercourse, fed by an artesian well that flowed into Plum Creek. Tall elephant ear-type plants and succulents grew in profusion near the water. A man watching from one of the houses over on Live Oak, on the other end of the big pecan patch, would have a clear view of the property. Maybe there was even a good shooting spot down in all that green. It was ground that needed to be explored.

How quickly would the local cops respond to shots fired at a place like this? Chico's cousin would know something about that. Emilio was walking back to the Jeep when he saw a blue Ford Expedition wheel off Commerce Street and into the driveway. He sat down on a low stone wall surrounding the funeral home parking lot and watched.

A woman carrying a briefcase climbed out and headed for the house. He could hear a dog barking inside, a big dog from the throaty sound of its bark. Emilio made a mental note about that. Dogs could be trouble. He lit a cigarette and watched the woman turn to aim a key fob at the SUV to lock the doors. She was a good-looking number. Short and a little thin for Emilio's taste, but she was well built with a nice ass that churned under her skirt as she climbed the steps to the front porch. The woman looked Asian or something—short black hair and almond-shaped eyes.

Emilio had fucked a ton of white chicks in his time but never an Asian. He wondered idly what that would be like and then flipped his smoke into the street. This was just the initial recon. There were plenty of questions still to be answered.

Chan Davis begged off her class commitments on Shake's first full day home. She was hanging some new curtains in the living room and he was just recovering from a morning PT run when the phone rang. Shake ignored it. He was funny about phones. He used them as required but never got chatty or spent too much time on a call. Probably a result of too many years of clipped conversations on tactical radios. Chan climbed down off her little stepladder and picked up the call.

Shake was nearly naked and headed for the shower, but he paused at the bottom of the stairs. The look on his wife's face had him guessing it might be bad news. She listened for a moment and then brought the handset over to him. "I think you better take this."

"Who is it?"

"Just take the phone."

"Davis—send your traffic."

"I don't really have any traffic, Shake—but I did want to talk to you. Got a minute?"

It was the President of the United States.

Shake looked at his wife and mirrored her shocked expression. Then muscle memory kicked in and he assumed the position of attention.

"Yes, sir. Sorry, I was just a little shocked."

"Well, I was shocked too, Shake, when I heard about that thing in Fort Worth—and then I was very happy that you were there to stop it."

"Uh…thanks, Mr. President. I don't know what to say."

"Fine, then let me do the talking. This country owes you a debt of gratitude. I've read your service record, Shake, and I know this isn't the first time you stepped up and put your life on the line. I just wanted you to know that I'm grateful, and I'm saying thank you—for me personally and for every other good American."

"Uh…thank you, sir. It means a lot to me that you'd take the time to call."

"It's my honor to speak to a real American hero, Shake. And I expect you'll be getting a few more calls. Spoke to Governor Abbott this morning and he says they're ginning up a special decoration for you."

"That's not necessary, sir."

"Oh, yes it is." The President chuckled. "You're a Marine and I'm the Commander-in-Chief, right?"

"Yes, sir."

"OK, then. I'm ordering you to stand still and get that medal you so richly deserve."

"Aye, aye, sir."

"I'd come down there and pin it on myself, but I'm headed overseas. One of these days we'll get to meet face-to-face, Shake. I'd be privileged to shake your hand."

The connection ended abruptly but Shake just stood, frozen and naked with the handset still pressed to his ear. "That was the President," he mumbled.

"Yeah, I know. I answered the call." She took the phone back and hugged her husband. "You are a piece of work, Gunner Shake Davis."

It took some talking to convince Chan she should continue with her regular daily commute to Austin. Over dinner in front of the TV, she announced that she planned to enlist a substitute lecturer or cancel her scheduled classes. She wanted to spend a week or two at home. That was nice for

Shake to hear, but he knew how much the work meant to his wife. Her International Relations classes and seminars were increasingly popular at U-T, and Shake didn't want to let an incident like this tamp the passion she had for teaching and discourse on campus. At a liberal school like the University of Texas at Austin, Chan's conservative ideas and background in intelligence work was becoming a big draw. The mainly left-leaning faculty and administration tolerated her because it was good for the school. There was a lot of knee-jerk among tuition-paying parents in Texas about liberal indoctrination of sons and daughters on college campuses, so it was handy for the administration to point to Dr. Chan Dwyer Davis when Texas conservatives started complaining.

Chan called herself a lonely little petunia in an onion patch, but Shake couldn't remember a time when she was happier. She got a kick out of playing the gadfly. Shake managed to change her mind finally and she trotted off to her home office to prepare notes for tomorrow's classes. He finished washing dishes, fed Bear some table scraps to supplement his kibble, and wandered in to see if there was anything on TV he could tolerate. Local papers and TV stations were still carrying stupid backgrounders and sidebars on Shake and the incident in Fort Worth, but it was petering out and the stories were shifting focus to what might be done to prevent another attack. The news shows were featuring the usual gaggle of talking heads, some of whom were whining about peaceful coexistence and others blustering about retaliatory military actions.

Shake decided that few if any of them could differentiate between shit and shoe polish and laid out the gear he used to clean his weapons. He had a pair of custom Kimber .45s that needed care and an appointment in the morning with the Caldwell County Sheriff.

From a north-facing window in a shack to the south of the target's residence, Emilio watched the Asian woman drive off in her SUV. He knew she was headed for Austin and would probably be gone all day. There was a U-T sticker on her car, and Emilio assumed she spent the day at school. Maybe she was a teacher or maybe a student. It didn't matter, and it helped to have her out of the way. Then the gringo target emerged with the big golden dog on a leash. They milled around a bit near the big live oak trees in the yard and then headed north on Commerce Street. A pattern was developing.

It was just past eight in the morning and Chico was moaning about driving somewhere to get a breakfast burrito. There was no food in the house, and last night Emilio refused to give Cousin Juan money to buy groceries. That would likely disappear into the hands of a local dope dealer. He would just have to send Chico to the local H.E.B. store to get provisions for the next few days, but that could wait. He wanted to see if the target stayed home during the day or went somewhere for work.

Ten minutes later, the gringo and his dog returned from their walk. The man unsnapped the dog's leash and Emilio saw what looked like a streak of gold roaring around the property, first up near the outbuildings on the high ground and then peeing on all the pecans down on the low section. It was a big damn dog—and it looked powerful with a long, lean muscle rippling under its fur. He heard the throaty barking as the dog roared across the property investigating with his nose. He might have to deal with that animal, especially if the gringo took him along wherever he went. Some gringos did that—and some of their dogs were trained to attack.

He heard a voice shouting from the house. Apparently, the dog's name was Bear. The big animal made one last circuit among the pecan trees and galloped back into the house. The target emerged a while later carrying a small satchel and heading for his truck. The dog was nowhere in sight.

"Get the Jeep," he said to Chico. "I'm gonna see where he's going."

The surveillance trip was relatively short. The Ford truck Chico was following at a discreet distance turned off Texas Highway 130 just west of town and pulled into a parking lot. It was the headquarters of the Caldwell Country Sheriff.

"Damn, dude—it's a cop-shop. What's he doin' there?"

"Who the fuck knows? He ain't a cop, maybe he's just seein' somebody or he's gotta do some paperwork." Emilio didn't like this turn of events. If the target is tied in with local law, the cops might keep a close eye on him or do extra patrols by his property. It was a complication—just like the fucking dog. "Drive on. We'll get the groceries and then swing back by here."

Shake gave his name at the front desk and waited for instructions. A uniformed deputy arrived after a few minutes and escorted him to an office in the rear of the building. The Caldwell County Sheriff was John Law, a big, meaty man with a perfectly appropriate name, who rose from his desk with a wide grin and offered his hand across the desk. The county's top cop was in western style civilian clothes with what looked like a well-kept 1911-style pistol on his hip opposite a spare magazine holder. Shake liked the guy immediately.

"Have a seat, Mr. Davis." The Sheriff pointed at a coffee service on a sideboard and raised his eyebrows.

"Coffee would be great, Sheriff—and please call me Shake."

"You know, I've been wondering about that ever since you moved down here to Lockhart." The Sheriff handed over a cup and sat back down behind his desk. "Never met anybody named Shake before, I don't believe."

"It's actually Sheldon. My folks lacked a little taste in the name game."

The Sheriff had a big infectious laugh. "Lord knows I get that. By the time I was ten, there was no doubt about my career. What else is a guy named John Law gonna do?"

"I appreciate your seeing me this morning, Sheriff."

"If I can call you Shake, you can call me John."

"OK, thanks. Anyway, I appreciate a little of your time."

"No problem. I should have come by your place long ago to say hello and introduce myself. Now that you're our big celebrity, I feel double bad about that."

"I usually try to keep a low-profile, John. We moved down here because we love the place—and because both my wife and I were looking for a little peace."

"Well, I'm in the peace business. I'll help any way I can."

"It's about this thing that happened in Fort Worth…"

"Hell of a thing, Shake. I've got some good buddies on that team in Fort Worth, and they're telling me we'd have had a massacre if it hadn't been for you."

"John, here's what I'm thinking. The people who built that bomb and sent that stupid kid into the coliseum as a suicide, are jihadis—Muslim terrorists. Now a lot of what I know about that is classified, so what I'm gonna tell you here has to remain confidential."

The Sheriff just nodded and motioned for Shake to continue.

"The Feds are fairly sure it was an ISIS inspired and funded mission. There's solid evidence that the players got into the U.S. guided by expert infiltrators, mostly Mexican nationals who cross the border all the time smuggling drugs."

"Makes perfect sense to me," the Sheriff agreed. "The dopers know the ropes and the routes."

"Check. That's the thinking at the FBI and Homeland Security. So now they're all focused on the border looking for jihadis as well as dope smugglers and your run-of-the-mill illegal crossing to look for work or whatever. Bottom line is that we know ISIS or Al Qaeda or any of their offshoots are hooking up with the cartels south of the border. And those people have long tentacles that extend into the U.S. It's like the terrorists and the smugglers have formed an alliance and that makes for serious trouble."

"I've seen some mention of that kind of thing. There was a backgrounder this morning." Sheriff Law pointed at the computer screen on one corner of his desk. "We're on the Police Intelligence Net and I try to stay up to speed. You think we might see some of these jihadis around these parts?"

"Ordinarily, I'd say no, John. These guys like to make a splash when they strike and there's not too many targets around here they'd consider worthy."

"But…."

"But I screwed up one of their big operations and with all this publicity lately, they know who to blame. They just have to watch the TV news to know who I am and where I live. These people do a lot of crazy stuff that's basically emotion-driven. They like to send messages that say anyone who screws with them gets hurt, you know? They might just decide to find me and exact a little revenge."

"Are you asking for police protection, Shake? I can talk to the local PD."

"That's probably not necessary, John. I know you guys and the Lockhart PD are strapped just trying to keep track of the local issues. And I'm a pretty fair hand at defending my-self anyway."

"I believe that, my friend." Sheriff Law kicked back in his chair and pointed at a plaque behind his desk: 75th Ranger Regiment. "I knew some good Marines during my time in harness. All of them were good troops, harder than billy-goat balls. From what I read in the papers, you're one of those."

"Coming from a Ranger, that's an honor. And it brings me to why I wanted to see you." Shake reached down into his gym bag next to his chair. "I'm gonna show you a couple of my guns, John. OK if I do that?"

"Glad you asked before you moved, Shake. I get a mite nervous when folks produce firearms in my office. Let's see what you've got."

Shake racked the slides and laid his two favorite pistols on the Sheriff's desk. "I noticed your weapon when I came in," he said, "and I figured you were a .45 guy."

"Kimbers…" The Sheriff looked at the weapons with a grin but made no move to inspect them any closer.

"Yeah, these two are custom made for me. I'm a lefty, so they both have ambidextrous controls, tuned triggers, com-bat sights, and a few other modifications. What I'd like is a license from you to carry one of them concealed. I'm willing to go through the process, training, or whatever is required."

Sheriff John Law picked up the smaller of the two pistols, a Kimber Ultra Carry II with Marine Corps emblems etched in the coco-bolo stocks, and examined it carefully, working the slide and testing the trigger. Then he put it back on the desk and smiled at his visitor.

"I'm guessing you're a pretty fair hand with these—and likely an expert with anything else that goes boom and throws lead."

"Pretty much, John. I'd say that's accurate."

"Here's what I think, Shake. Running you through a CC drill would be a waste of time and probably a little insulting. What we're gonna do is just issue you that CC permit this morning soon as we can get your prints and a picture. And the $90 fee is hereby waived."

Shake shook hands, recovered his pistols and followed a deputy to a little alcove where they got his fingerprints and a photo. He was wiping ink off his fingers when Sheriff Law stuck his head in the door.

"What are you doing tomorrow, Shake?"

"Nothing I know of. Why?"

"Don't plan on anything. I just got a call from the Governor's office. He's gonna be here at 10 a.m. to present you the Lone Star Medal of Valor."

"That's all we need."

"World's gotta have heroes, Shake—and that world includes Caldwell County, Texas." The Sheriff was laughing loudly as he walked back down the hallway to his office. Shake had to chat about the medal with two more deputies before he could reach the front door. Apparently, the Lone Star Medal of Valor was a big deal and word was spreading fast.

He was walking to his truck when one of the deputies flagged him down. This one was carrying a flat-topped box which he handed over with a grin. "Sheriff Law wanted you to have this," he said. "Brand new—there ain't many of them around."

"What is it?"

"It's called Dragon Skin—body armor. We got a few of them when the Army decided they didn't like it. Hell of a lot better than the bulky old plate-carriers we wear."

"Well, many thanks. And tell the Sheriff I said thanks."

"I'll do that," the deputy said. "Here's hoping you don't need that thing."

On a very dark night with just a sliver of moon and low clouds hanging over Lockhart, Emilio Contreras waded across Plum Creek and up onto the Davis property. Crouching low and moving carefully through the tall weeds, he found a good spot near a pecan stump and aimed over his finger at the big house on the high ground. This was a drill, not a shooting run. Emilio was looking for the most favorable position, the best angle, and estimating range. From the stump where he crouched on the soggy ground to the front porch was about 80 to 85 meters. It was an easy shot with the Mini-14 for a trained marksman. And there was no reason to expect the gringo would do anything different than he'd done for the past two days Emilio had been observing him from the house on Live Oak Street.

The woman would leave in her car around 7 a.m. An hour later, the man would emerge to walk the dog. And Emilio would fire two quick but well-aimed shots with the rifle. One for the dog and one for the gringo. No—the gringo first, then the dog. A tough guy like *Senor* Shake Davis would have time to run or take cover if his first shot took the dog. Be accurate and be quick. Too early for much traffic and Chico would have the Jeep standing by on the other side of the bridge. Four minutes—maybe five at the outside, and they'd be on the road to San Antonio. And then wait for his money—and then *adios* Texas, *ola* Guatemala.

Emilio checked his watch. It was nearly time for the big dog's nightly piss call, and he didn't need a confrontation with that monster. He slid slowly backward until he was lost among the tall elephant ears and then waded back across Plum Creek. He would be back in the morning, same route in and out, but this time it would be a shooting run.

Chico was working over the road maps when he got back to the shack. Cousin Juan was sleeping off a buzz on a cot in the corner. "You got a route figured, Chico?"

"No big deal, dude. Highway 130 out of here and then pick up the ten near Seguin and it's a straight shot home. Be there in maybe a little over an hour."

Emilio picked up the Ruger Mini-14 and tested the spring on the magazine. The ammo was in a box nearby, all bright shiny and new. The shotgun was leaning against a wall in the corner. It was just like he figured. More firepower than needed. "Take the shotgun and shells somewhere and lose them. We ain't gonna need that."

"Probably sell that fucker for a lot of money back home, dude."

"You got plenty of money comin' when we get paid. Get rid of the shotgun."

Chico wrapped the Beneli in some old denim, picked up the boxes of deer slugs, and headed for the door. "You gonna ding that fucker with the rifle, dude?"

"Him and his fucking dog—tomorrow morning around eight. You're gonna have the Jeep standing by and pointed in the right direction."

"What you gonna do with the rifle, dude? We don't want that fucker in the car with us in case we get stopped and they search the Jeep."

"Deep water under the bridge. I'll lose it there on my way back."

Emilio was fiddling with the rear sight on the Ruger rifle, aiming at Cousin Juan's prostrate form for practice, when his phone rang. It wasn't his sister and she was one of only two people who had his number. It would be *El Escorpion* wanting a progress report.

"Where are you?"

"Where I'm supposed to be—doing reconnaissance."

"Why haven't you done the job? Is there a problem?"

"There's no problem. I'm a professional, man. I do things right—takes time."

"I expected it to be done by now. All the money I'm paying you."

"Watch the fucking news. Tomorrow, man."

"I'm sending the courier to San Antonio. If you don't call me that the job is done, he turns around and comes back with my money. I'm tired of fucking around with this."

"Relax. I'll call you tomorrow."

"Call me tomorrow and tell me the job is done. That's all I want to hear."

Emilio disassembled the rifle and cleaned it meticulously. It would be nice to test it, maybe establish a zero, but it was too late for that now. No big deal. At 85 meters, the shot was easy. If he was off a bit, he had enough ammo for insurance. He reassembled the rifle carefully, checking each part, pin, and spring.

El Escorpion was paying a lot of money for revenge—and the Mexican dopers he was trying to impress with his long reach might not even know about it in the end. Fucking guy had too much ego and not enough brains.

Governor Greg Abbott's office called shortly after Shake got home from his visit with the Sheriff. Normally, a medal presentation like this one would be done in the Governor's office in Austin, but he was heading out on a swing through the state and thought it might be nice to do the presentation in the hero's home town. Would that be fine?

He didn't want to put the Governor's office on hold to check with Chan, so Shake agreed it would be fine. The Governor's guy said that was just fine and he'd make all the press and security arrangements. So everything was fine—until Chan got home.

"My God, Shake! The Governor's gonna be here to pin a medal on you at ten tomorrow morning?"

"Actually, I think he's gonna hang one around my neck. I looked it up."

"I'd like to hang something else around your neck! I've got to find something to wear and we need something for people to eat and drink."

"We'll go over to Black's and ask them to bring over a brisket or two. They like us there, it's nearby and well, hell—they'll be feeding the Governor. I better go buy a bunch of beer and sodas and stuff."

He was saved from further abuse when Sheriff John Law called. He'd be over around eight—if that was OK—with local cops and a Texas Ranger or two to check the set up for security. Shake said it was OK since he didn't want to distract Chan from the closet trashing he could hear upstairs. He hung up the phone and found a beer in the fridge. That gave him time to wonder what he ought to wear and ponder the remote possibility that something like that might be hanging in his closet. Getting back in uniform with all his previous medals and decorations seemed like a bit of upstaging. He was about to go investigate his meager wardrobe, but the phone prevented that. It was turning into a busy day at *la casa* Davis.

It was Joaquin Sutler who let Shake knew he was inbound about halfway to Lockhart with Carlotta and Manny Chavez. They heard about the medal from an old Ranger buddy of Joaquin's who works in the Governor's office. Wouldn't miss it for the world and he wanted to know if Plum Creek had good water since he was bringing along some of the Duke of Paducah's finest bourbon.

Shake finished his beer and then got the truck keys to go get lots more.

Emilio Contreras crossed Plum Creek at 7 a.m. leaving Chico dozing behind the wheel of the Jeep, packed, parked, and pointed south toward Highway 130. The air was damp and muggy. He could smell the creek muck and slime as he slowly and quietly waded through knee-deep water. The sky through the pecan boughs looked clear, and there was no appreciable wind blowing. It would be a hot day when the sun got a little higher. Good visibility and nothing to alter his aim or ballistics.

Moving slowly along a familiar path through the long grass and elephant ears, he followed the watercourse and spotted the pecan stump he'd selected as his shooting position. He low-crawled to it and checked the rifle and magazine to be sure he hadn't picked up any mud and debris. It was OK—clean and ready—with five rounds in the magazine.

There were lights on in the house, upstairs and downstairs. That was unusual. Mostly he'd just seen one light upstairs and one downstairs. This morning it looked like every light in the house was burning. So what? It was probably just the woman getting ready for work or school or whatever. He saw her moving around quickly, window to window, but she was making no move for the door. Emilio cradled the rifle and sat still watching for the pattern of behavior he expected. He checked his watch and tried to keep himself focused. Emilio was feeling the familiar tightening in his guts as his breathing became shallow. It was a good feeling, a heady sense of power, just the way he used to feel on *Zeta* missions in the old days. *Los Zetas* were kings in old Mexico, a force to be feared by everyone. Now most of his old *compadres* were scattered all over Central America hiding from the law. Maybe he could rebuild in Guatemala and recapture some of that sweet power and the money it generated.

At 7:45, the woman was still in the house. Emilio caught glimpses of her rushing around from room to room. Something is different today. Maybe she took off work. Maybe she's sick. Emilio decided that didn't matter. She wasn't the target. He checked his watch again, expecting the gringo and his dog to appear. That was the important thing. Emilio edged the rifle forward on the pecan stump and squinted through the sights. He'd take the shot just as the gringo cleared the porch. If the woman was inside when it went down, even if she called the cops immediately, he'd be long gone before they could arrive.

And then the cops did arrive. Three cars: County Sheriff, local PD and the fucking Texas Rangers! They pulled into the driveway, nose to tail like a convoy. Emilio pulled the rifle back and edged lower behind the stump. The cops got out and started eyeballing the property. Were they looking for him? Was he busted? Emilio felt a cold clutch in his guts. What the fuck was happening?

The gringo emerged from the house, walked down the steps and started shaking hands with the cops. Emilio watched it all intently tensing his leg muscles to run. But there was no sense of panic or urgency, none of the cop had guns in hand. No police dogs sniffing around the area up there near the house. That's not how it would go if the cops were called in to look for a shooter on the grounds. He probably wasn't busted. They didn't know he was less than 100 yards away with a high-powered rifle. Maybe it was a social call. Maybe they'd all go away in a while and he could get back on the plan.

As he watched trying to decide what to do, Emilio saw a TV remote truck drive up and park along North Commerce Street right next to the house. Something strange was going on here. Maybe it had to do with that meeting at the Sheriff's Office yesterday. Or maybe it was something else. Emilio didn't know. He only knew he wouldn't be taking the shot this morning, not while the place was crawling with cops and reporters. He slowly and carefully edged back into the weeds and retreated across Plum Creek.

Joaquin Sutler, Carlotta Valdez, and Manny Chavez arrived in a road-dusted, insect- spattered silver Mercedes about 30 minutes before the Governor's party. They were all checked into a local motel and ready to party when they called his cell phone complaining that they couldn't get through to the house. Shake had to go down and see Sheriff Law personally before they were allowed through the cordon of cops that stretched around the block. There was a crowd starting to gather, and several of them waved at him. Back inside, with introductions made for the South Texans Chan didn't know, Shake turned his attention to the struggle he was having to make his one old and outdated grey suit look a little less like a circus tent hanging off his shoulders. Carlotta pitched in to help Chan set out a couple of huge barbecued briskets and a pan full of ribs that had been delivered from Black's. She passed through the hallway where he was staring into a mirror adjusting his one presentable tie.

"Pretty nice little gal, you got," she whispered. "Guess I shoulda figured what with you spendin' all that time overseas in Southeast Asia..."

"Jesus, Carlotta."

"My offer still stands." She cackled, patted his butt, and headed for the kitchen where Joaquin and Manny Chavez were testing the beer for proper temperature on what they predicted to be a chili-pepper Texas day. Bear was whining behind a locked door and more than a little miffed that he was excluded from the party—particularly the barbecue which was filling the whole house with delicious aromas.

By the time the press and TV crews were set up, fed, and watered, the Governor's motorcade was turning into the driveway that had been specially cleared with Shake's truck and Chan's SUV parked out of sight. The crowd of spectators had grown considerably. It was a big event in a sleepy little hill country town. There were a few local friends and neighbors and a lot of people they'd never met waiting patiently in a roped off section of the lawn. It wasn't so much about seeing the State's Chief Executive or its newest hero at a big ceremony. What drew many in the crowd was a chance for some free barbecue and beer. Word got around fast that there was a sort of impromptu open house happening on North Commerce Street. The good folks of Lockhart, Texas had their priorities in order.

When the official caravan arrived, Governor Abbott waved for the cameras, did some hand-shaking, and stood still for a brief TV interview. Then he barged into their kitchen, smiling and chatting about Lockhart being the undisputed barbecue capital of his state. Tagging along behind was the same assistant Shake had met in Fort Worth. As if they'd been rehearsed, Shake's wife and his rowdy South Texas friends formed up in a sort of impromptu receiving line to shake the chief executive's hand.

Governor Abbott was a good-looking man with the genial air of a politician trying to convince the good folks of small-town Texas that he was just one of them. He charmed Chan and Carlotta while the assistant cornered Shake and explained the drill. On the hour, they'd troop outside to a marked spot under the live oaks where the TV crews indicated they had the best shots. Shake and Chan would stand there side-by-side while the assistant read out the citation. Then the Governor would hang the medal around Shake's neck, shake hands, and socialize for a while before departing for his swing through other voting districts nearby.

One of the TV producers peeked in the kitchen door, caught the Governor's eye, and tapped his wristwatch. The assistant immediately swung into action and started shoving everyone toward the door. The Governor would remain inside until it was time for him to make his entrance. Shake and Chan marched out to the appointed spot underneath the live oaks.

There was some raucous applause from the crowd and Shake could hear the motor drives on the still cameras aimed in his direction. He just smiled, feeling like an awkward show-pony and self-conscious about his suit. "C'mon, Shake." Chan whispered as she wrapped an arm around his elbow. "This isn't the first time you've had to stand and get decorated." That much was true—a Silver Star and a couple of Bronze Stars and a bunch of other decorations he'd received on active duty required him to stand and be recognized in official ceremonies. He knew that protocol even if he didn't particularly care for it. It always seemed a little like tub-thumping mixed with cheerleading, and he rarely recognized any of the things the citations claimed he did. Mostly, he just stood still and thought about the men who died and couldn't be there. It was usually very solemn, featuring hackneyed terms like "traversing fire-swept terrain" and "selflessly ignoring painful wounds." And he'd never known quite what to do or say to the well-wishers when it was over. The Purple Heart presentations were different—and much easier. He'd mostly been just lying prostrate at attention in a hospital bed for those.

The Governor took his place in front of Shake and smiled at Chan while the citation was read by the assistant in stentorian tones. Shake heard his name and the date of the incident in Fort Worth and then he mostly tuned out, watching a pair of white-wing doves flitting around the branches above his head. He heard something about at the risk of his life, and disarming a terrorist truck bomb and an act of valor in keeping with the highest standards of the Marine Corps and of the military forces of Texas, but most of it was over-blown rhetoric and he could read the details from the citation later. As the assistant approached carrying a padded case embossed with an outline of the state of Texas, Shake glanced to his right, and saw Bear watching with his tongue hanging and his big paws perched on the sill of a bathroom window.

The Governor reached into the box and came out with the actual Lone Star Medal of Valor. It was a five-pointed star overlaid with the word VALOR suspended from a sky-blue ribbon and designed to be worn around the neck, and that's where Governor Abbott hung it. He passed the circle of ribbon over Shake's head, let he decoration drop and then tinkered a bit to get it just right for the cameras. Shake had to keep himself from staring down at it—a move that he knew would make him look like he had more chins than a Chinese phone book—and took the Governor's hand when it was offered. There was a loud burst of whistles and applause that seemed to go on way too long. Recognizing this moment was the dramatic heart of the ceremony, Governor Abbott kept a tight grip on Shake's right hand.

"Shake, this gives me a great deal of pride and satisfaction. Your action, at great personal risk to yourself and others, is an inspiration. You saved a lot of lives that day. I want you to know that what you did in Fort Worth was in keeping with the highest standards of the Marine Corps and the military forces of Texas. I speak for all the people of our state when I tell you how proud we are to have you as a Texan, as one of us."

Shake had to fight the giddy urge to say something like "Aw, shucks, it weren't nothin'." He just nodded, said thanks and posed for the pictures the press was loudly demanding. The Governor stood with Shake and Chan for about five minutes in the typical grip-and-grin tableau before he walked over with Shake in tow to address the crowd and the cops standing all around the house. It was more of the same stuff about how proud and honored all Texans should be to have a man like Shake call the state his home. And then it was over.

The Governor and entourage departed in a convoy of limousines taking most of the Texas Ranger contingent with them. Sheriff Law, a couple of his deputies, and some local police officers hung around to monitor the crowd and sample the brisket while Shake shook hands with neighbors and well-wishers. It took a couple of hours for everyone to get something to eat and a few beers or sodas, but by noon, the house was mostly empty except for the South Texans who were sprawled around the living room sampling Joaquin's whiskey.

"Where's this Plum Creek water, Shake?" Joaquin held up a glass half-full of amber liquid. "It ain't bourbon and branch without the branch."

"Let me put this gong back in the box and change clothes," Shake said stripping the medal from his neck and folding back into the presentation case. "Then we'll go down to the lower forty and get some."

While he was shucking out of his suit and reaching for jeans, Mike Stokey called from Las Vegas. Chan had taken some snaps with her phone and sent them along to Shake's best friend.

"Hail, the conquering hero!"

"That's what everybody's been telling me this morning."

"Wish I could have made it down for the ceremony."

"It wouldn't have been worth the airfare, brother. And the flight would have been rough on your wounded ass."

"I want you to know I'm proud of you, Shake. I'm always proud of you, but—you know."

"Yeah, I know. Thanks."

"OK. Well, I love you, brother. Talk soon."

Shake got into jeans and an old chambray shirt and clumped down the stairs. Bear was waiting with that look in his big brown eyes. "C'mon, Joaquin…" He got a mason jar from a kitchen cabinet and headed for the door. "Bear needs to pee, and we'll get some crick water."

They followed the big dog down through the pecans and toward the creek. Bear seemed obsessed with one particular tree stump about 80 meters from the house. They stopped for a while to watch him sniff all around and dig at the ground nearby.

"What's he after—coon or something?" Joaquin kept a pair of setters for bird shooting and thought Bear might make a good hunting dog.

"We had a pair of red foxes running around on the property. He's probably found one of their dens."

Joaquin ran a practiced eye along the watercourse and pointed. "Something bigger than a fox came through those weeds, Shake. See that path right there?"

"Maybe a deer," Shake said eyeing the line of bent vegetation that led up from the creek. "We get a lot of them roaming around down here in season."

They walked the rest of the way down to the water while Bear continued to explore with his sensitive nose. While Joaquin searched for a spot where the creek water ran clean and clear over some rocks, Shake followed the trail through the weeds with his eyes. Had to be a deer came through there, he thought, and then glanced at the shacks just beyond a little public park on the other side of the creek. Or maybe some of the poor folks snuck over to watch the festivities and get a look at the Governor.

"Get the gun, dude!" Chico pointed out the window of the shack. "He's right fucking there."

Emilio glanced over Chico's shoulder. The gringo target was just standing on the banks of the creek watching the big dog romp around the area. There was another gringo with him—big hat and big mustache—looked like a cop.

"No fucking way." Emilio had been watching the ceremony on the target's property most of the morning and trying to come up with an alternate plan. It was getting late, and *El Escorpion* would be expecting a call. That would be touchy. He needed to convince the sponsor that the shot was impossible today. All he had to do was watch the news on TV. The press was all over it and the story would be on the nightly news on both sides of the border. *El Escorpion* was a mean bastard, but he wasn't entirely stupid. He'd understand the situation. Emilio needed him to be patient for one more day. If things got back to normal pattern tomorrow, he'd get the job done. And this time, he'd have all the advantage he needed. No more delays. He had a scheme in mind that would cause the gringo to walk right into his sights. He picked up the phone and tapped a number in the memory.

"Tell me it's done."

"No way I could do it today."

"I told you what would happen if you failed. I'm bringing the money back. You fucked up a good thing. Don't ever come back to this side of the border."

"Hold on a fucking minute, man. Did you see the story on TV?"

"What story?"

"Watch the American TV, man! There was a big ceremony at the gringo's house, cops everywhere. He got some kind of medal. The fucking Governor of Texas was there. I was ready to drop his ass—all set and everything—then every fucking cop in the state showed up."

"That's your problem. You failed to do what I paid you to do."

"Listen, I've got a new plan—can't miss. I'll get him to-morrow."

"One more chance. Twenty-four hours. You fuck it up and it's over. Someone will be looking for you to collect the money I already paid you—for *nada*."

"I'll get him tomorrow, man. Guaranteed. Watch the news." Emilio tossed his phone on the rickety table and cursed.

"What's your big fucking plan, dude?" Chico was munching on a burrito he'd warmed over a coal-fired stove. "And when am I gonna get the money you promised?"

"You get your fucking money when I get mine, Chico." Emilio unfolded the map of the local area and studied it. "Get the Jeep. We gotta find a new place."

They drove out into the pasture lands and grassy plains north of Lockhart, exploring paths and country roads that kept Chico steering the Jeep in four-wheel drive most of the time. Emilio needed a desolate spot, preferably east or west of Highway 130 on the 30-mile stretch between Austin and Lockhart. They found the spot just before dark. It was an old cluster of abandoned farm buildings set in the middle of overgrown pasture land. There were no other structures in sight, and the map indicated nothing nearby in any direction. To be sure, they drove every country road they could find running through the area. Most of them either meandered back to the highway or just dead-ended.

They drove back to the selected area about five miles north of the Lockhart city limits and began to explore. There was an old grain silo crunched on one side and leaning precariously. There were a couple of old cowsheds that clearly hadn't seen man or beast for a couple of years. And there was a rickety barn with both big doors crashed down on the ground. A few of the stalls still stood and the place had a loft that looked like it would support some weight. Emilio looked around one last time.

"This is it. Let's go."

"Where we headed, dude?"

"Back to town. You're gonna buy a ladder and some other stuff."

News stories about Shake's medal were carried on every statewide TV station and it was in all the local papers, print editions, and on-line. Chan heard a couple of interviews on the car radio where her comments about Shake were featured. The one that frosted her was by a female reporter from some Austin blowtorch AM station. The woman had pressed her to tell what it was like to be married to a big hero and a macho Marine. She was disappointed with Chan's initial terse response. "Well, it's interesting—never boring." Chan thought that was pithy and might make a good sound-bite, but the reporter kept wheedling until she finally got the comment she wanted and that was the one that kept replaying on the radio newscasts.

Trying to please the reporter, Chan finally said, "He's a solid guy, good husband—very brave man in or out of uniform." That would have been fine and she should have shut up after that, but the woman had raised her eyebrows expecting more, so for some reason she currently regretted, Chan added "He's a hard man." And there was just enough levity in her voice to convince the reporter she was referring to Shake's bedroom prowess. That snippet was all they used and all anyone seemed to remember. She spent most of the day talking to female colleagues who wondered with smiles and raised eyebrows how hard a man Shake really was. There was even a round of applause from her students when she arrived for one of her lectures. She reluctantly stayed after hours to give an interview to a reporter from The Daily Texan university newspaper. She'd had about enough celebrity by association stuff by the time she finished her preparations for classes in the morning.

She called Shake at 5:30 when she finally got to her car and told him not to wait for supper. She'd grab something on the way home, and there were a bunch of leftovers from the ceremony in the fridge for him and Bear. It was late in the day when she wheeled onto Highway 130 heading south. The air was early summer sweet, so she killed the air-conditioning and powered the windows down to let it circulate in the vehicle. It was so nice that way. The sun was well down on the western horizon, a glowing semi-circle of bright orange, as she steered the blue Ford Expedition south. It was that beautiful time just between day and night, what the filmmakers call magic hour, and the pale-yellow light over the rolling prairies reminded Chan of why they moved to this area. It was beautiful, a vision of the prairies that spoke to her of the great sprawl that was America and of all the rugged pioneers who settled it. People like her husband were in that throng of hardy settlers and survivors.

When the news teased another interview with her upcoming, she snapped off the radio and punched up a CD for distraction. And then she thought about someplace along the road to get a sandwich for supper. There were plenty of left-overs at the house, but after yesterday she was up to here with barbecue and potato salad.

Chico spotted the blue Ford Explorer as it approached the little gas and groceries joint where they were parked waiting for the woman to return from Austin. She was later than they expected, but he could see it was definitely the gringo's wife behind the wheel. Emilio had called it. She was bound to pass this way on her way home. Chico cranked the engine and dropped the Jeep into gear.

"Get on her ass but not too close." Emilio pulled the Glock from under his jacket and held it down out of sight. "When I say so, you cut her off and force her to the side of the road—just the way we planned. You got it?"

Southbound traffic was sparse as Chico wheeled out onto the highway. Now it was a matter of finding the right time, just the right place along this stretch of ribbon-straight road to make their move. Chico accelerated and fell in about three car lengths behind the SUV. "We gotta be careful, dude. We wreck her car and some local cowboy might call the cops."

Emilio shot him an angry glance. They'd been all over this for most of the day. What they planned out here on an open stretch of Texas highway was risky at best, but he needed to get this damn job done. The scheme was to force her off the road where Emilio would hijack her car and drive the woman to the abandoned site they'd selected. Then he'd use her phone to call the gringo. He'd come get his wife or they'd kill her. Emilio would make some ransom demand to make it sound real—maybe 500 bucks—something the gringo could get in a hurry. It would look like a couple of cheap-ass amateurs or dopers were staging a kidnapping of the hero's lady. When *Senor* Shake Davis arrived way out in the country to rescue his wife, he'd find out he was facing a professional. Emilio planned to kill them both and hit the road. He'd be in Guatemala before the cops even found the bodies. The only hard part was forcing her off the road for the hijack without causing a wreck or any unwanted attention.

He was about to tell Chico to make his move when the woman saved them the trouble. A turn blinker flashed from the SUV tail light. She was pulling off into a little country store that offered gas, food, and drinks.

"She's pulling off, dude!"

"I see that. Follow her and park it somewhere."

Chico rolled into the parking lot and found a spot on the side of the building. The woman locked the SUV and walked toward the store carrying her purse. There was only one other vehicle in sight, a dusty pick-up with out of state plates parked near a propane tank. This was perfect. Finally something about this job was going right. Emilio shoved the pistol into his waistband and opened the door. "I'm gonna make my move when she comes out of the store," he said. "When you see I'm behind the wheel of her car, you pull out and drive directly out to the place. I'll follow you."

The woman was in the store for about 10 minutes and then she emerged carrying a greasy sack and balancing a large drink cup. Emilio waited for her to key the door locks and slide in behind the wheel where she was distracted dealing with the food and drink. He walked toward the front of the store and then made a quick turn to place himself near the driver-side door with his back to the store front. She glanced up at him and he opened his jacket to reveal the pistol. Her eyes went wide when he placed his hand on the grip of the gun.

"Do anything stupid, lady, and you're dead. Roll down the window."

The woman clicked the ignition key to cut in battery power and hit the switch to roll down her window. She kept her eyes on the pistol in Emilio's waistband, but she didn't seem as terrified as Emilio hoped she'd be. He eased a little more of the pistol into view and she glanced up at his face. She looked more angry than scared.

"I've got some money in my purse." She gestured at the seat beside her. "Just relax and I'll get it for you."

"I don't want your fucking money, bitch!" Emilio put a practiced growl of intimidation into his voice. "I'm taking you and your fucking wheels. Move that shit and slide over to the other side."

"You know that's a whole lot more trouble than a simple robbery, don't you?"

"I know you're gonna be dead in about ten fucking seconds if you don't move. I ain't playing around."

The woman reached for her purse and sandwich, placed both on the floorboards, and then worked her way over the center console. Emilio got an enticing flash of her thighs before he jerked open the door of the SUV and crawled behind the wheel. He pulled the pistol and aimed it at her across the console. She ignored the gun and kept her eyes on his. She seemed way too calm, as if she encountered this kind of thing every day. She held his gaze for a moment, then shrugged and snapped in her seatbelt. Emilio decided he was dealing with a tough *gringa* and took the planned precautions.

"Put both your hands right here." He pointed at the console with the pistol barrel. When she complied, he reached into a jacket pocket and retrieved one of the zip-ties Chico had included in his purchases at the hardware store.

"That's not necessary," she said. "I won't give you any trouble."

"Fucking right you won't," Emilio growled and manacled her hands tightly with a plastic strip. "Now all you got to do is sit there and keep your fucking mouth shut."

He cranked the engine and backed the SUV into the parking lot. Chico swung in front of him in the Jeep and they pulled out onto Highway 130.

Chan alternated glances from the man at her left to the passing scenery trying to figure where they were headed. They'd turned left onto the highway which meant they were rolling back toward Austin. Is that where they were headed? Why? Her situation seemed to be something more than a simple robbery. That could have been easily—and voluntarily—accomplished in the initial encounter. These people—she was sure the man in the Jeep ahead of them was involved—were apparently kidnapping her. Either that or they simply planned to take her somewhere, and what? Steal the car? They could have done that back at the country store and left her standing. Rape her? Kill her? The rape might be understandable if that's what they had in mind. But if they planned on shooting her—why would they do that? She was sure she'd never seen the driver before, anywhere or anytime.

Could it have something to do with school? Neither of these two men looked like they'd spent much time in any kind of school, much less the University of Texas. As the driver steered she caught glimpses of tattoos. Were they gang-bangers? Had she run afoul of some gang? The driver was clearly a Latino. Was she the target of one of the Tex-Mex gangs that deviled Texas cities? And then she thought of Shake's trip to Mexico. Could it have something to do with that? When the time was right, if she had any kind of opportunity before the situation got any worse, she intended to find out what she could about their motives. It might be the only advantage available to her.

Shake had always wanted her to carry a gun in the car, but she refused. That kind of thing was behind her, she said when they talked about it, and she wanted to keep it that way. Her phone was in the purse at her feet with Shake's number in the contact list, but it didn't look like she'd get much chance to call for help. Her best bet, she decided as the SUV followed the Jeep into a right turn off the highway and down a country lane, was to remain as calm as possible. The Jeep stopped and her driver braked behind it.

The Jeep driver got out and Chan noted he was also a Latino. So she was likely in hands of a couple of gangbangers. They hadn't blindfolded or gagged her. These were likely not professionals, and that was at least something positive. They might make stupid mistakes. Maybe they'd screw up and give her a chance to make an escape. The Jeep driver dug around in the back of his vehicle and produced an orange traffic cone. He walked to a spot where the country lane intersected the highway and placed in on the ground. Then he was back in the Jeep and they were following it deeper into the deserted countryside.

"Tie the bitch up over there," Emilio tossed the bundle of plastic rope at Chico and pointed at an upright next to one of the stalls in the barn, "and find something to gag her." That probably wasn't necessary. The woman could scream her head off out here and no one would hear it. But a bound and gagged hostage just looked more convincing.

"I'm gonna check the loft," he said watching over his shoulder as Chico got the woman seated on the dirt floor and bound securely. Then he whipped a red bandana out of a back pocket and tied it around the woman's jaws. Bound and gagged, she looked a little less calm and composed. She was starting to understand she was in a world of shit here. Good, Emilio nodded and retrieved the new aluminum ladder they'd bought with the other supplies in Lockhart. He dragged it across the dirt floor of the old barn and under the loft. He pulled it open, locked the braces, and settled the ladder beneath what looked like the sturdiest section of the crumbling overhead platform. The top of the ladder was about three feet short, but he could pull himself up easily from there. What he needed to know was whether the loft floor would hold his weight. He wanted a high shooting platform to nail the gringo when he arrived.

Emilio scaled the ladder to the top and swept a flashlight over the splintered surface of the loft. There was a rotting pile of hay bales in one corner and not much more. The surface was littered with rat shit, but the support beams looked OK and there were a couple of areas that appeared solid enough to support him. He pulled himself up and crawled around a bit on hands and knees until he found the vantage point he wanted. There was room enough to shoot from prone and it felt like the old floorboards would take the strain. He pulled two of the musty bales to the edge of the loft, leaving just enough space between them for the rifle. He bounced carefully to test the perch. The flooring creaked ominously, but it would hold. Emilio stepped back onto the ladder and climbed down to look at his captive. She was getting nervous at last, glancing around at him and the ladder trying to figure the play. She looked like a frightened victim, helpless and vulnerable, just the look Emilio wanted for the next move. It was getting late and the light was fading so it was time to make that move.

Emilio retrieved the woman's purse from the SUV, found her phone, and powered it up. He scrolled through her contact list until he spotted the number he wanted under S for Shake. As he figured—all going good and as planned. He felt the old gut-tightening and smiled. Just a couple more steps and it would be over. Emilio experimented with the phone to find the camera app and then took it back inside the barn. He handed the Glock to Chico and pointed at the woman.

"Stand over there with the gun pointed at her head." When Chico complied, Emilio aimed the phone camera and snapped the shot. Then he checked his work. It was just right, a helpless captive staring back at the camera with her dark Asian eyes wide and fearful and a hand holding a pistol pointed at her temple, finger on the trigger. He attached the photo to a number and tapped out a text message. CALL NOW—and then he hit send.

Shake was back from a nightly walk and feeding Bear when his phone chirped. He grabbed it out of his pocket, expecting a message from his wife explaining why she was so late getting home. He'd been worrying that she'd had car trouble or an accident. It was Chan's number on the caller ID, but the photo that appeared on screen when he opened the text shocked him. He stared at it for a few numb seconds before he read the two-word message. Someone was holding Chan somewhere bound and gagged. No further information or details, but he'd get some of that when he returned the call.

Shake took the phone into the living room where there was better light and studied the disturbing image. It was framed tightly. The gun was a Glock. He could see the hand holding it was tattooed, but the forearm above it was covered in what looked like a tan satin windbreaker or light jacket. He could see nothing else helpful there. Was this some sort of gang-related thing? And if so, why Chan? Obviously because she was his wife, but as far as he could determine in an instant he thought about it, Shake had never crossed swords with gang members, here or anywhere else. The background in the photo was no help. It looked as if Chan was strapped to some old wooden pole or upright, but there was not enough depth of field to provide any clue as to where it might be. Probably some older place from the weathered look of the upright Chan was leaning against, and likely somewhere relatively close to Lockhart given the time he knew she left the University. Kidnapping, he decided. The rest of the questions had to remain unanswered until he made the call demanded. Shake took a couple of deep breaths, tried to broom away his fears, and tapped the recall icon.

"We got your wife, Davis."

"I saw that. What do you want?"

"You're gonna bring us five hundred—you hear me, man?"

The voice was accented with a Latin flavor. If Chan was in hands of gangbangers, they were either Tex-Mex or Latinos of some kind. That confirmed what he thought when he saw the tattooed hand. Five hundred dollars was chump change in the kidnapping game. Maybe it was some low-rent locals who saw the news broadcasts and an opportunity to turn a quick buck. Five hundred dollars would be a lot to some people in this area. Had to be—unlikely anyone from too far away would know Chan was his wife or where to grab her on the way home from work.

"I hear you—and I'll get the money."

"Better do that and do it quick. You don't and she dies. Two hours before I start shooting. We ain't fucking around here, hero."

Yeah, they saw the news. Shake mentally cursed his mistake in allowing all the publicity. He could have refused that damn medal. He should have just walked away and kept his mouth shut. Maybe the guy on Chan's phone was someone from the crowd that watched the ceremony yesterday. Maybe some broke-dick petty criminal running a very dangerous game that he really doesn't know how to play. This guy is probably a doper looking to score quick cash. Anyone with more serious motives would be demanding a lot more and be willing to wait while Shake raised it.

"It's after hours. I might need a little more time."

"Better find a cash machine or borrow it if you ain't got it on you, hero. You got two hours and then your old lady is dead."

Shake fought hard to keep from exploding with threats. The key here was to keep these assholes calm, thinking they'd pulled it off on an easy mark. If he started describing what he wanted to do to them in all the colorful descriptive running through his mind, they might panic.

"I'll do exactly what you tell me to do. I'll get the cash. Just tell me where you want it delivered."

"Head north on 130, hero. About six miles outside of town you'll see a little farm road runs off to the right. There's a traffic cone down there. You turn and stay on the road until you see your old lady's car. I'll be waiting in the barn. I see any cops, any helicopters, anything besides you and five hundred dollars and I'm gonna bust a cap in her ass. You got all that, hero?"

"Got it. It'll take me about an hour to get the cash and then I'm on the way."

Shake stuffed the phone back in his pocket and began to pace. He rapidly shifted to tactical mode, scrambling mentally for a plan. With a willful effort, he submerged all the fear for his wife's safety and the anger that was boiling in his guts. A situation like this demanded cool tactical thinking and he was good at that. Just like the situation in Fort Worth, broom aside the emotions, see the situation for what it is—and act. Even if he was dealing with amateurs, they'd know enough not to let him or Chan survive, that much they could learn from TV. So he'd have to fight through this—likely a fight for his survival and more importantly a fight for hers.

And then a thought struck. Maybe it wasn't about the relatively paltry ransom demand. Maybe it was something else, some way to reach him through his wife. Could this have something to do with the radicals who planned the strike Shake spoiled in Fort Worth? They had long tentacles that ran everywhere, the FBI said. Could the people who had Chan be carrying out some kind of revenge strike against him?

In the end, it didn't matter. Chan had to be rescued. He had a lot more than five hundred in an emergency stash of twenties he kept handy in a dresser drawer, so he folded 25 twenties into a pocket and went to his gun safe. The smaller of his two Kimber .45s was nestled in a fine leather pancake holster at the small of his back where he'd been carrying it since he got the CC license from Sheriff Law. He thought briefly about giving the lawman a call, but quickly dismissed the notion. This was something he'd have to do alone—at least for the first part of the plan he was rapidly devising.

He got two eight-round magazines from his range box and loaded each to the max with 165-grain Federal Hydra-Shock rounds. It was a type of man-killer ammo he'd hoped he would never have to use again, but the rounds were brutal fight-stoppers and he didn't plan on doing too much shooting; none at all unless it was necessary. Then he dropped the loaded magazine from his carry pistol and loaded a new one brimming with Hydra-Shocks and jammed a second mag in a trouser pocket. He charged the chamber, snapped on the thumb safety, and re-holstered the pistol. He slipped on a long-sleeved shirt and left it untucked to help hide the gun. Then he reached into the safe and found one of his treasures: a Model 97 Winchester Trench Gun. The 12-gauge was a veteran with shrouded barrel and bayonet stud, the same weapon Shake had carried for a while in Vietnam. Loaded with six rounds of double-ought buckshot, five in the magazine tube and one in the chamber, it was a hard-hitting, highly maneuverable scatter-gun that could be slam-fired by simply holding back on the trigger and pumping the slide. It was a technique Shake had mastered long ago on the range and in combat.

It was 15 minutes into the first of his two allotted hours. Shake carried the shotgun and his second Kimber pistol into the kitchen and called for Bear. The big dog leaped up off the couch and trotted in to sit by the door expecting his nightly romp among the pecans. "We've got more important work tonight, big boy." Shake snapped on a leash and then called Joaquin's number. He'd made arrangements to meet the retired Texas Ranger for a farewell drink tonight, but that would have to wait.

"Joaquin, can you come by the house—right now and by yourself?"

"Here's the drill…" Emilio Contreras stood outside the barn in twilight and looked up at the star-studded sky. "He's gonna come right up the road—only way to get here. You're gonna be standing inside with the pistol aimed at the *chica*, right?"

Chico nodded and puffed hard on his smoke. He wasn't planning on this situation, but it seemed simple enough. What had him worried was the big hero. Dude like that might do something fucking crazy. And then what? He just nodded and didn't ask.

"You got to look *loco*, man. Maybe lose the jacket and show your ink. You got to make him think you are the type of man might be gonna shoot her in the fucking head any minute, right?" Chico fondled the Glock and nodded wordlessly again.

"You keep his dumb ass focused. You hold out your hand and make him bring the money to you. When he's in the light and I got a good spot, I'll pop his ass from up above. You got all that?" Chico nodded again and stuck the Glock in his back pocket. "OK. We got maybe a half-hour. Hide the Jeep behind the barn and then come back inside and bring the light—don't forget the fucking light, man."

Chico nodded again and walked toward the Jeep, jangling the keys and feeling gas rumbling in his stomach. He took one last look down the weed-covered access road, then crawled into the vehicle and started the engine. He really wanted this bullshit to be over so he could get his ass back to San Antonio. Easy money was morphing into some kind of fucking crime spree that made dope-dealing and gang-banging seem like playground stuff. Two fucking murders, dude? That was serious shit. Maybe he should tag along to Guatemala when it was done.

Emilio walked inside and stood looking down at the woman. He could see a nice pair of well-muscled legs where her skirt was hiked up under her butt. He squatted to take a closer look and squeezed one of her breasts. Her head snapped around but she couldn't speak, so he gave the breast a little jiggle. It was not big, but it was firm. He thought about opening her blouse to take a look but decided it could wait. Emilio saw no reason not to fuck her after he killed her gringo husband. Bust a cap in him—and then bust a nut in her. No need to kill her right away. He checked his watch. An hour and fifteen minutes until show-time. He picked up the rifle, jacked a round into the chamber and walked across the barn floor to the ladder.

Shake spotted the orange traffic pylon on the right side of the road and flashed his lights at Joaquin following in his silver Mercedes rental car. They wheeled off the highway and traveled a little ways along the bumpy farm road before they stopped and cut the lights. Shake gave Bear a tussle on his ruff and hustled back to the Mercedes and leaned in the window.

"It looks like there's a bend to the right up ahead. Park this thing across the road just this side of it. If it doesn't work out, I don't want that bastard to get away."

"I still think I should go on up there with you, Shake. It ain't my first rodeo and you oughta have back-up. Ain't no tellin' if it's just one or a bunch of them bastards."

"Can't chance it, Joaquin." Shake glanced at his watch and noted he had 45 minutes left until the kidnapper's deadline. I figure these guys must be getting nervous in the service about now. They see anyone besides me, they might just start shooting."

"Well, it's your call."

"You got the gun?"

"I got your shooter and mine." Joaquin held up a big nickel-plated Ruger Redhawk .44 Magnum. "Plus I got flexties if we wind up catching one or two without having to kill them."

"Good. If it goes down the way I want, I'll call you to come running. Otherwise, it's on you to stop them right here."

Shake motored slowly up the road until he saw the silhouette of dilapidated structures off to his right. He was too far away to spot Chan's car, but this had to be the place. There was nothing else in sight anywhere on the horizon. He slowly braked to a stop and cut the engine. He reached up to kill the dome light and then quietly stepped out of the vehicle. It looked to be about 200 yards across mostly flat ground to the buildings. The weeds were high and irregular which would help mask his approach. Shake ordered Bear to lay down on the seat and slid the shotgun out through the window. "Stay, Bear—and be quiet." He took a look at the quarter moon showing high in the western sky, and headed into the weeds off the side of the road.

Shake moved with the skill and stealth he had learned over years of doing reconnaissance work close to any number of enemy targets on battlefields around the world. He moved slowly as a ticking clock in his head would allow in a meandering path so that his direction would be unclear to any observer who noticed a disturbance in the vegetation. There were several patches that he had to traverse in a crawl, but he'd long ago learned how to do that quickly and quietly.

The quarter moon and some scudding clouds made for a dark night and that prompted him to move a little faster than he normally would on an approach to a hostile target, but he was afraid to lose too much time. He ignored the night insects flying and crawling everywhere in the field and kept his eyes on the objective. About 30 meters from the largest of the rundown structures, he saw Chan's SUV. There was a spill of yellow light coming from the building that must have been a big barn at one time. There were no doors that he could see, but there was an old shattered window on the side facing him.

Shake glanced at his watch. The approach took 20 minutes. He'd have to hurry. He made his way cautiously to the wall of the barn and peeked through the window. Chan was there, lying bound and gagged on the ground. Standing over her in the glow of an electric camping light was a chubby man showing serious gang ink on his bare arms. He saw the tan jacket nearby hanging from a nail on one of the uprights. So, this was the guy in the photo. Did he shoot the photo as a selfie? Or was there another man somewhere? He couldn't see anyone else, but there might be one of more tucked back somewhere in the dark shadows. Maybe there were no booby-traps, maybe it was just the one asshole trying to pull this off.

If that was the case, maybe he could end it right here and right now. Shake thought about taking the guy out with a shot from the window—25 meters max. It would be a relatively easy shot with either the shotgun or his pistol. But what if there was another one of them—or two—waiting somewhere out of sight? Too risky, and he wasn't about to try something that might get Chan killed based on this one brief observation.

He decided to stick with his original plan and crawled around the corner of the building. When he was just outside the big open barn door, he carefully leaned the trench gun upright against the wood. It was good to go with a shell in the chamber. All he would need to do in an emergency is reach around, grab it, pull back on the trigger, and keep pumping the slide. Shake backed away until he thought it was safe to stand and then began a low, crouching run back through the weeds toward his truck.

When he reached the vehicle, Bear was whining with his muzzle perched on the console. The dog immediately sat up and looked hopefully for the next action. Bear was well trained, but a dog was a dog and dogs responded to instincts. Shake said a prayer that his pet would behave tonight and not become distracted by new scents or some night crawler.

Shake peeled off his shirt and checked his watch. Time was getting tight. He grabbed at the gift from Sheriff Law and shrugged into the Dragon Skin body armor. It was relatively thin and flexible as body armor went, composed of overlapping two-inch circular silicon-carbide discs that made the vest look like it was covered in reptile scales. The publicity he read on line claimed the stuff could stop an AK round, so Shake felt fairly certain it could handle a 9mm from the Glock if a shoot-out started. He'd do everything he could to avoid that with Chan anywhere in the line of fire. He put his shirt back on, buttoned it over the vest, and slid behind the wheel.

Chico checked his watch again and looked up to the loft where Emilio was lying behind the hay bales. He could barely see the barrel of the rifle. He couldn't see anything in the gloom outside the barn door, and the only thing he heard besides the woman's loud breathing through her nose was a chorus of bugs and night things in the fields near the barn. Fifteen minutes left and there was no sign of the gringo.

"Dude, maybe he ain't coming."

"He's coming. Just keep your eyes open."

After another five minutes, Chico heard engine noises and walked to the barn door. There were headlights bouncing up the road toward the barn. "Here he comes, man. Looks like his truck."

"Get over by the woman. You know what to do."

Shake parked his vehicle next to Chan's and slowly got out to look around. There was nothing to see but gloom and shadows but that didn't mean there wasn't someone out there pointing a gun at him. He glanced to the side of the big gaping door frame and saw his shotgun was still where he'd left it. If there was someone patrolling the exterior they'd have spotted that. He patted his thigh and Bear jumped nimbly down to the ground.

"Sit, Bear—and stay," he whispered to the dog and when he felt fairly certain that the animal was focused and obeying commands, he raised his voice.

"I'm here," he shouted. "How do we do this?"

"Come on inside, dude."

Shake walked slowly to the barn and stopped just outside the spill of light from the lantern hanging over his wife's seated form. He was in semi-gloom here and fairly close to the shotgun leaning against a wall just outside the door. Chan looked OK. He saw her glance at him and it looked like she was trying to say something through the gag but he forced himself to ignore that.

"You got the money, dude?"

"I've got it."

"Show me."

Shake carefully reached into his trouser pocket and pulled out the wad of bills.

"Bring it over to me, dude—real slow and careful."

Chan shuffled her legs to attract her husband's attention. He cut a brief glance her way and then locked his eyes on the man with the gun standing over her. She tried again to attract his attention and jerked her head up toward the ceiling, desperately trying to signal presence of a sniper up in the loft. It was no use. Shake was a man on a mission, totally focused on the immediate threat. She'd seen him in action.

Please, Shake! Look at me! Look up!

She did everything she could to send some sort of signal that the man she loved was slowly walking into an ambush. And there was nothing she could do about it. She blinked away the tears that were starting to spill down her cheeks.

Shake paced slowly forward until he was on the edge of the pool of light from the lantern. He was holding the wad of cash out in front of him. And the guy with the Glock was staring at it, not at him. There you go, he thought, and made the little kissy-clicking sound to cue Bear. It was the sound that Shake and Chan used when they wanted to know where the dog was. Bear was trained to start barking and he did, long and loud.

As expected, the man with the Glock startled and began looking for the dog who sounded like it was about to attack. Shake reached for the gun in the small of his back and drew it, falling automatically into a shooting crouch. He thumbed the safety off and brought the front sight blade up to center mass for a double-tap but he only managed to squeeze off one round. He was suddenly tossed violently backward and he slammed to the ground like a wet sandbag dropped from height. He didn't hear the shot until he was on the way down, but it had hit him squarely in the chest. It felt like he'd been hit with the broad side of an axe and poked with a cattle prod at the same time. His legs went numb and he was gasping for breath. He fought to stay conscious against the agony that was spreading in all directions from his sternum. At that instant, Shake realized what Chan had been trying to communicate. The ladder—he should have noticed that. There was a sniper up in the loft above him. He tried to move but it was all he could do to fight a descending fog and stay conscious. Squinting through the pain, he lay still, hoping the high shooter wouldn't decide to fire an insurance round. He could see the first man was down and crawling backward away from the action. Likely his single round of Hydra-Shock did significant damage. The low shooter was still alive but he was out of the game.

Shake still had the Kimber in hand, and he was hoping for a chance to use it in a snap shot at the hay bales he could see up in the loft. That had to be where the high man was hiding. Suddenly he heard a loud canine howl and he was vaulted by a streak of gold fur. Bear's basic canine instincts had taken over and the dog was streaking through the barn, growling ominously and heading directly for the man on the ground.

The high shooter screamed something in Spanish and stood up from behind the bales to take aim at Bear. Shake rolled onto his right side and blasted three quick rounds in the shooter's direction. They were inaccurate shots from an unsteady hand, but it was enough to distract the high shooter and drive him scrambling into the shadows at the rear of the loft.

Shake's eyes were watering, but he could see Bear with his two huge front paws planted on the low man's chest. The big dog had his powerful jaws clamped on one of the wounded man's ears and was avidly attempting to tear it off. He was an easy target for the high shooter.

"Bear—leave it! Run home!" When the dog galloped out of the barn and into the dark, Shake mustered what strength he could and got himself up on hands and knees. He needed to follow the dog out of the barn and regroup. The sniper pumped two more rounds down from his new position but he didn't have the angle this time. Both bullets smacked into the dirt behind Shake. It was enough motivation for him to rise and stagger into the dark headed for the door.

He was nearly within reach of the hidden shotgun when the sniper reappeared out of the dark and braced his rifle against one of the support beams. Shake saw the move and winged a shot in the man's direction, but it was not accurate and simply blew some wood chips off the ledge of the loft. He turned and tried to steady himself but it was too late. This time he saw the muzzle flash and felt another agonizing impact on the vest near his right ribcage. Shake crumpled to his knees willing his torso to remain upright. He launched himself backward into the gloom and reached around the doorframe feeling for the shotgun. The rifle fired again, but the shot was high and sizzled off somewhere in the dark above Shake's head.

Gasping for air, he craned around the barn doorframe and triggered three pistol rounds up at the shooter. These were better aimed and sufficiently close to drive the rifleman scrambling for concealment in the shadows at the back of the loft. There was a momentary pause and Shake ran a quick check for serious signals from his body. He'd been hit hard by two high-power rounds in the torso, but the vest apparently did its protective job as advertised. He was badly bruised and likely suffering two or more broken ribs, but he was still in the fight. He took a shallow breath smelling the reek of cordite in the night air. He needed to get the sonofabitch with the rifle before he decided to just shoot Chan—or maybe threaten to shoot her and get Shake to step out in the open.

Naturally, that's exactly what he did.

"I got her in my sights, hero. Throw your gun inside where I can see it and get back in here with your hands showing."

"I'm doing it…" Shake's voice was barely a croak. He got to his feet and leaned against the wall wiling the necessary strength to return. He made an underhand toss and sent the Kimber skittering across the floor of the barn. He saw the shooter standing with the rifle aimed at Chan. And then he picked up the shotgun and pulled the exposed hammer to the rear.

"OK. Now you walk inside—very slowly."

Shake swiveled around out of the dark with the trench gun shouldered and slam-fired two rounds on the move. The buckshot blew the shooter backward, but Shake couldn't tell if he was hit or just startled. Either way, it was not likely that the man was out of it just yet. He grunted away the pain in his chest and shuffled into a position under the loft where he was in defilade. If the rifleman wanted to shoot at him now he'd have to expose himself—or maybe just shoot down through the loft floorboards.

He glanced over at his wife. Smart move—she had managed to scoot around to the opposite side of the upright. It wasn't much cover, but it was better than her previous exposure. "Sit tight, Chan! I've got this." His voice sounded like a hoarse bullfrog but he heard her mumble through the gag. She was OK—for now.

He heard scraping above his head as if the shooter was crawling around looking for a position. Shake fired two more shotgun rounds up at the loft and was rewarded with a shower of wood splinters. A gaping hole appeared over his head and he immediately scrambled out from underneath it. As expected the rifleman fired down through the hole. Shake caught a glimpse of the sniper as he stared wide-eyed down over his rifle sights, but he scrambled away too quickly for an accurate shot. Shake made a guess and fired another load of buckshot upward.

He heard the shooter creeping around up there. The loft floorboards creaked ominously and Shake tried to follow the sound with the muzzle of his shotgun. And then he caught a critical break. He heard a loud crack and a couple of the rotting floorboards suddenly gave way. The sniper's left leg plunged into sight dangling over Shake's head. The leg was kicking wildly and the sniper was screaming in Spanish. Shake didn't hesitate. He shouldered the trench gun and fired his last buckshot round into the leg, splattering shot from the man's thigh to ankle and hoping one or more of the pellets would sever the femoral artery.

The sniper was moaning and cursing, but Shake ignored that. The bastard threatened his wife, could have killed her. That was a death sentence. He set the shotgun aside, staggered across the barn floor and retrieved his Kimber. He walked back under the loft as he loaded a fresh magazine into the grip. Then he stood directly under the dangling leg, aimed slightly right of it where he computed the man's body would rest, and pumped eight rounds up into the loft. The leg stopped twitching.

As he stood there with the burning pain coursing through his upper body barely held at bay by a huge adrenaline surge, Shake looked down at his pistol with the slide locked back over an empty magazine. He glanced at the shotgun nearby. It was empty. He was basically unarmed on the battlefield. That came to him almost as a jolt of fear. He felt naked and a little stupid, like he'd done something dumb—like crawling into your car and realizing you left your car keys inside the house. He was in a bad place. Unarmed is a bad thing to be whether you think the fight is over or not. He walked across the barn floor and found the Glock dropped by the first kidnapper who now lay unconscious and bleeding not far away. He press checked it for ready rounds and then slowly swept the sights around the barn interior looking for more threats. It's what you do after a firefight. You consolidate your position and stand ready to repel a counterattack.

"Shake! My God! Are you OK?" Chan had managed to chew her way through the gag and when he heard her voice, he realized the fight was really over. She was alive and so was he. Shake jammed the pistol into a pocket and staggered over to her. He managed to get his pocketknife deployed and sawed her free of the ropes, but that was about all he could manage. He fumbled his phone out of a pocket and handed it to his wife. "Call Joaquin—he's just down the road."

And then he passed out sprawled across her legs.

Gunner Shake Davis woke up staring at a white tile ceiling. It was 1015 wherever he was according to a clock on an adjacent wall. And that was likely 1015 in one morning or another since he could see daylight streaming in through a nearby window. He took a couple of experimental breaths— shallow was OK—anything deeper, anything that expanded his chest hurt like hell. It was a lot less pain than he remembered after the gunfight, but that was likely thanks to the tube plugged into his right arm. The tube led to a hanging bag about half-full of liquid and he supposed there was morphine or some other pain-killer mixed in with whatever else the bag held.

So I'm in a hospital, he thought calmly—not the first time and probably not the last. A clipboard near his head was filled with little penciled entries recording his vital signs and he read the heading: Seton Edgar D. Davis Hospital, Luling, Texas. He wasn't too far from home, which is where he really wanted to be as opposed to prostrate on a slab at the Seton Edgar B Davis Hospital in Luling, Texas. And who the hell was Seton Edgar B. Davis anyway?

A rotund ward nurse stuck her head in the door and smiled at him. "Well, good morning glory!"

"Who the hell is Seton Edgar B. Davis?"

"He was a philanthropist who built a lot of Texas Hospitals. You're in the one in Luling."

"Yeah. So how am I doing?"

The nurse picked up the chart and his hand to take his pulse rate. "I think you're doing just fine for a man who got shot twice."

"Thank you, Dragon Skin."

"Who?"

"I was wearing a ballistic vest. They call it Dragon Skin."

"I think that must be what they've got down in the lab. The doctors were very impressed."

"Not half as impressed as I was—believe me. How much damage?"

"Not too bad at all given the circumstances. Two broken ribs, a badly bruised sternum. Nothing torn up inside that we could find." She patted the winding of tape and gauze compressing his chest. "You might want to wait a while before you peek under there. The bruises are ugly."

"I can live with bruises."

"Uh-huh—and you look like a good healer, Shake Davis. I'm gonna see the doctor when he makes rounds. We might just let you out of here today or tomorrow."

"Can I call my wife?"

"You can, but you probably don't need to. I think she's already here. There's a bunch of folks waiting downstairs to see you."

Chan trooped in ten minutes later by the wall clock. She was leading a party that included Joaquin Sutler, Carlotta Valdez, and Manny Chavez. They all stood around the foot of his bed except for Chan who propped herself up beside him and wrapped an arm around his neck.

"Well, now that we see you're gonna live," Joaquin grinned, "I guess we can head back to the Valley."

"I appreciate your help, Joaquin."

"Shit, son. I was damn little help sitting on that road-block. Didn't need that did we? I come runnin' as soon as Chan called and found you passed out."

"What else did you find?"

"One dead asshole and another one damn near it. He's alive, but it's touch and go whether or not he stays that way. Chan tells me that mangled ear was Bear's doing."

"Oh, shit—I forgot. Is Bear OK?"

"He's fine." Chan gave him a little kiss on the forehead. "He came whimpering out of the dark a little while after Joaquin arrived. Just stood there barking until he was sure we were OK. He's home guarding the spread."

The South Texans all wanted him to come visit—and bring Chan and Bear—when he was able. Then they left passing Sheriff John Law who was arriving with his Stetson in hand.

"Well, you had you an interesting night, Shake."

"I guess interesting fits as well as anything, John."

"You know, we're gonna need you to come by and make a statement as soon as you're able."

"Glad to. Did you find out who those guys are—were—whatever?"

"Well the dead one—and he was plenty dead, believe me—was a guy name of Emilio Contreras. Mexican national and former member of the *Zeta* organization according to the *Federales* who had several active warrants out on him." The Sheriff saw the look of confusion on Shake's face. "The *Zetas* are a gang of former Mexican soldiers who ran from their army several years ago and went into the crime business big time—very bad hombres. The other guy down in intensive care with a couple of my deputies guarding him is Carlos Sandoval, known as Chico. He's a small-time gangbanger. MS-13 out of San Antonio, we think."

"What were they doing in Texas and why were they after me?"

"Well, we're looking into all that, Shake. Likely Contreras was up here hiding from Mexican law. Why he was after you is something we don't know just yet. We do know he used to work as an enforcer for a guy name of Eduardo Lopez, aka The Scorpion, out of Rio Grande City. He runs a string of smugglers all over the border area. Contacts tell me the FBI and the *Federales* are all over that dude. Maybe we'll find some kind of connection to tie it all together. I hope so. I don't like mysteries that involve people getting killed on my patch."

"Any inkling that all this had something to do with the thing in Fort Worth?"

"Nothing obvious so far—but it's hard tellin' not knowin'." The Sheriff checked his watch. "Lots of times these things tie together once you start digging around. I gotta get on the road, Shake. Come see me as soon as you can."

"I'll do that, John—and many thanks for the Dragon Skin. I owe you big-time for that."

"Not a bit of it, Shake. Just glad you were wearing it. I'm thinking my budget could stand to buy a bunch more of those."

When they were alone, Chan scooted down onto the bed and hugged her husband. "Mike called, and there were two messages from the man who calls himself Bayer."

"I'll call him back when I can. So, how are you?"

"I'm just fine, thanks to you."

"It's what I do—take care of the old lady, guard the homeland, crush the evil-doers—you know the drill."

"If it's all the same to you, your old lady can do without another incident like the last one."

"It scared me half to death, Chan. I don't ever want to lose you."

"You won't. Not if I have anything to do with it."

"What's that mean?"

"Well, I'm probably gonna have to fight Carlotta one of these days."

Shake tried to laugh but it hurt too bad.

Two weeks later, Shake was in his shop working on an intricate free-form table that Chan wanted for the house. It was supposed to look like a long oval slab supported by a tree branch. He had the parts all finished and prepared, but assembly was making him crazy. Bear was happily watching in his sphinx pose near the table saw and covered in sawdust.

The session with the Sheriff to make his official statement had morphed into a two-day grilling with questions from several State and Federal law enforcement agencies. By the end of it, after curious lines of questioning from the Feds, Shake decided that he had been the target of a contract hitter. Why was still an open question, but he was beginning to think it had something to do with their encounter during the Rio Grande crossing. Nothing else seemed to fit, and he'd likely never know the exact details. If terrorism or the incident in Fort Worth had anything to do with the shooters chasing him, no one seemed able to make that connection. Sheriff John Law replaced the Dragon Skin vest and even deputized Shake so he could continue to carry a weapon, concealed or otherwise. He said it seemed like a prudent thing to do.

He was in the kitchen about to make a sandwich and open a cold beer when the phone rang. It was the man who calls himself Bayer.

"Shake, the DNI wants to talk to you."

"Well, give him my number."

"I think this is gonna involve a face-to-face."

"I am not coming to Washington."

"You might change your mind when you hear what the subject is."

"I'm not changing my mind. What's the subject?"

"Ever hear of a place called Koh Tang island?"

"Yeah, little speck in the Gulf of Thailand off the coast of Cambodia. We sent in some Marines to rescue a civilian ship's crew back in 75. Major cock-up…"

"That's the subject."

About the Author

Dale Dye is a Marine officer who rose through the ranks to retire as a Captain after 21 years of service in war and peace. He is a distinguished graduate of Missouri Military Academy who enlisted in the United States Marine Corps shortly after graduation. Sent to war in Southeast Asia, he served in Vietnam in 1965 and 1967 through 1970 surviving 31 major combat operations.

Appointed a Warrant Officer in 1976, he later converted his commission and was a Captain when he deployed to Beirut, Lebanon with the Multinational Force in 1982-83. He served in a variety of assignments around the world and along the way attained a degree in English Literature from the University of Maryland. Following retirement from active duty in 1984, he spent time in Central America, reporting and training troops for guerrilla warfare in El Salvador, Honduras and Costa Rica.

Upset with Hollywood's treatment of the American military, he went to Hollywood and established Warriors Inc., the preeminent military training and advisory service to the entertainment industry. He has worked on more than 50 movies and TV shows including several Academy Award and Emmy winning productions. He is a novelist, actor, director and show business innovator, who wanders between Los Angeles and Lockhart, Texas.

Gunner Shake Davis, U.S. Marine Corps, might be out of the active ranks, but he's anything but retired. Catch all his adventures by bestselling author Dale Dye in the Shake Davis series of scintillating novels.

Laos File: Searching for American POWs listed as Missing In Action in Southeast Asia, Shake Davis uncovers a conspiracy and some very painful memories from his days as a combat infantryman in Vietnam.

Peleliu File: When anti-Western power-players plan to unleash biological warfare, Shake uses his contacts, historical acumen, and military skills to help in a breathtaking chase through infamous World War II battle sites.

Chosin File: While attempting to rescue his buddy lost on a covert mission to North Korea, Shake revisits the infamous Chosin Reservoir and discovers a plan to hit the worldwide power grid with a devastating EMP generator.

Beirut File: When his wife disappears on an intelligence mission, Shake is desperate to find her. His quest leads him through the tragic Boston Marathon bombing and back to Beirut where Shake had served on active duty.

Contra File: As they investigate gang-bangers running drugs by land and sea, Shake and Mike slog through the jungle, operate at sea against dopers, and discover human-trafficking running rampant in Central America.

Havana File: Shake investigates Guantanamo Bay during normalization talks in Havana, revealing that an American is being held hostage. Shake, Mike and a team of Marine Raiders stage a daring rescue from the sea.

For these and other quality military fiction and nonfiction, visit
www.warriorspublishing.com

www.ingramcontent.com/pod-product-compliance
Lightning Source LLC
Chambersburg PA
CBHW071744190726
48292CB00003B/862